know how much I want you, Casey. How much longer are you going to hold out?" Ross demanded.

With the mere touch of his lips, Casey surrendered beyond reservation. Her hands came up to stroke his dark hair almost desperately when Ross's bold tongue mingled with her own, darting and exploring with artful precision.

"Do you have any idea how many times I've wanted to do this these last few days?" Ross questioned hoarsely. He opened the bodice of her dress, and Casey surged upward urgently, wanting the loving caress of his mouth on her breast.

"No, Casey." Ross stroked the creamy slope of her shoulder, his voice shaking with denial. "Not here. If I kiss you there, I won't be able to turn back."

Casey looked into Ross's clouded eyes. "That wouldn't be so terrible...."

Dear Reader,

It is our pleasure to bring you a new experience in reading that goes beyond category writing. The settings of **Harlequin American Romance** give a sense of place and culture that is uniquely American, and the characters are warm and believable. The stories are of "today" and have been chosen to give variety within the vast scope of romance fiction.

Judy Harvey thought about the widow Cassandra Spencer for a year before committing her story to paper. Cassandra, a native Californian, inherits her deceased husband's partnership in a small advertising firm. The job presented no immediate problems, but Ross Allen—her partner—did!

From the early days of Harlequin, our primary concern has been to bring you novels of the highest quality. **Harlequin American Romance** is no exception. Enjoy!

Vivian Stephens

Vivian Stephens
Editorial Director
Harlequin American Romance
919 Third Avenue,
New York, N.Y. 10022

In Loving Regret

JUDY HARVEY

Harlequin Books

TORONTO • NEW YORK • LONDON
AMSTERDAM • PARIS • SYDNEY • HAMBURG
STOCKHOLM • ATHENS • TOKYO • MILAN

To John–my loving inspiration
Dayna and Jimmy–my living inspiration
and Jennifer–my darling pest

Published September 1983

First printing July 1983

ISBN 0-373-16023-2

Printed in Canada

Chapter One

Could she pull it off, meet this challenge? After a year of emotional regathering, was she ready to step out and make a play for the tantalizing carrot that was dangled before her professional palate the previous week?

Yes, on all counts! Casey averred stoutly. Her flashing brown eyes glittered with determination as they focused on the door to temptation, then flickered with startling sensitivity as they roamed on to the secretary ensconced to screen all visitation.

With a mischievous gesture straight out of the past, Casey interrupted the graying woman's preoccupied staccato with a quelling finger on the Off button of her electric typewriter.

Bev Kiley was around her desk in a flash. "Cassandra Spencer! How long has it been since you switched off my power to gain my attention?"

The deep affection between the two women was obvious as the smiling secretary hugged Casey to her breast.

"It's been two years since I last short-circuited your temper." Casey named the span of her absence, laughing. "And I can still recall every occasion when you yelled at me if I caused you to make a mistake."

"Two years!" Bev seemed to have trouble digesting

the declaration. "It doesn't seem possible you've been gone that long." She paused, motioning Casey into a chair, then resumed her own seat behind her desk. "It seems like only yesterday that you were the impetuous new bride of Quinn Spencer, blitzing in to terrorize my concentration, then demanding immediate audience with your husband. You came a long way in four years," Bev ruminated. "From the chairman's young wife and disciple to one of the most talented account executives we ever had at Spencer Ad. You were such a tremendous help to Quinn. I don't think he realized how heavily he had come to depend on your creative zeal until you were gone. What made you decide to give up your work, Casey?"

"Quinn wanted me to stay home." Casey still found it difficult to deliberate on her severance from the stimulation she had come to thrive upon and love. "It was hard, juggling two careers," she explained slowly, "and he wanted me to have more time to entertain, thought I could help him more at home—"

"Quinn's been gone just over a year, hasn't he, dear?" Bev broke in gently, consolingly, noting the slight quiver in Casey's voice.

"He died last June," she affirmed. Quinn Spencer had been cut down in his prime by a massive heart attack that extinguished his life and five years of marriage in one swooping blow. "It was so unexpected," she relayed unevenly. The fact that their last couple of years together had been so unrewarding, almost stifling, had only made it worse. "I've been sort of drifting this last year," she disclosed, her eyes darkly shadowed. "Rudderless, I guess you might say, looking for some kind of focus in my life to pull me back to reality."

"Is that why you're here today?" Bev ventured supportively. "Are you ready to shed your widow's weeds and step back into the fold, where you belong?"

Casey wrinkled her nose, casting a wry look down at the beige linen pantsuit, carefully chosen to foster a businesslike air but failing miserably to disguise her generous womanly curves. Hardly widow's weeds!

She confirmed Bev's conjecture. "I want to come back to work, yes. Driving down Wilshire Boulevard this morning was like coming home for me. Advertising is in my blood, and this building..." She hesitated, exhaling expressively. "I cut my professional teeth here at Spencer Ad; it will always be a part of me. I'd never consider working anywhere else."

"Spencer-*Allen* Ad." Bev added the necessary amendment, and when Casey quite noticeably stiffened, she reasoned softly, "Things went downhill that last year after you left, Casey. It wasn't easy for Quinn, admitting he needed help. It took a lot of consideration, overcoming years of prejudice and dividing the leadership in what had always been a family-run corporation, but the smartest thing Quinn ever did was take in a partner."

"Fresh blood, fresh money, fresh brainpower." Casey enumerated all that Quinn had gained, then darted an antipathetic glance toward the closed paneled door stenciled ROSS ALLEN, CHAIRMAN, SPENCER-ALLEN ADVERTISING. A door she must soon enter. "I know Quinn made the right decision, taking in a partner," she conceded grittily.

Before she could expand on her admission, Bev insinuated, "It was his choice of partners that always nettled, hmm? You've never cared for Ross Allen, have you, Casey?"

"I wouldn't say that exactly." Active dislike was more accurate since the day one Ross Allen had rubbed Casey the wrong way. "Omnipotent, all-knowing males are not my cup of tea," she observed dryly. Mentally she ticked off his other characteristics: overbearing, condescending, *arrogant!* Was she really going to venture into the irascible tyrant's lair?

"Did you know Ross is considering broadening his base?" Casey broached tentatively, thinking back to the chatty little telephone conversation last week when Ross had dangled the savory carrot. "He's looking for an assistant of sorts, I gather. Someone to share his account load and take over the reins of leadership when he's out of town." Or busy with his first love, Allen Modeling, she thought derisively.

"Is he, now?" Bev's impassive face gave nothing away.

Darn! Casey was hoping Bev would tip her hand and reveal what she thought her chances were of landing the plum position. "I've never held a post in top management," she brooded disparagingly. "And it's not as if I have to work," she felt compelled to establish. "Quinn left me comfortable financially...."

"But you want this job badly?" Bev surmised.

What she really wanted was to resurrect a partnership, but that might seem a bit presumptuous in these early stages. Quinn had left her his share of the business, yes. But not his years of experience.

"I know I can help Ross," she insisted, warming to the subject. "And he's expanded the horizons of Spencer-Allen Ad so widely these last two years, I can see where he needs a second pair of hands at the top...." She trailed off pensively, unaware of her old friend's amused scrutiny as she pondered, almost tasted the pungent flavor of challenge. Ah! To get her creative juices flowing again!

"Is Ross in his office?" Casey finally gave in to the inevitable. "My appointment is at nine thirty and I'm not going to get anywhere sitting out here, much as I'd rather dither with you than beard the lion in his den."

"Oh, come on," Bev scoffed. "You can be quite a

tigress yourself. If all else fails, just remind the boss that as the second largest stockholder in Spencer-Allen, your voice deserves to be heard."

And damn Quinn for ever letting Ross gain controlling interest, Casey thought uncharitably. She shuddered. Her agitation was so profound, she had sunk to cursing the dead!

Bev buzzed the inner office, announcing Casey's arrival, and a deeply resonant voice beckoned through the intercom, "Come into my office, Cassandra."

"Said the spider to the fly," she muttered under her breath, embellishing the gravelly enticement.

"Knock 'em dead" came the secretary's laughing encouragement as Casey rose and sucked in her breath.

If he doesn't slay me first, she echoed silently, one hand on the doorknob. She had to be insane to think she could ever work with—

"Oh!" she gasped, one hand over her galloping heart, as she charged headlong into a rock-hard, unyielding chest. "You startled me!" She flung the breathless accusation, backing away in wary retreat. "What were you doing, standing right inside the door like that?" In her haste to get on with things, Casey had burst right into the office, never considering Ross might meet her halfway. In *any* manner of speaking.

"I always open the door for ladies," Ross offered dryly. With calm authority he led her to a chair set at a right angle to his desk. His own chair he shunned, and instead he balanced indolently on the edge of the polished walnut desk, eyeing her with goading, amused toleration.

"Well, Cassandra? What can I do for you today?" One dark brow rose inquiringly. "I must confess, I was a little surprised when you called for an appointment. I seem to recall that we spoke on the telephone just last week."

Casey lifted her chin and, then steadying it, determined not to appear belligerent this early in the game. "That's why I'm here," she enlightened him. "Last week you mentioned you were thinking of taking on another m—" She stumbled over his word, *man,* substituted her own, *assistant,* then went on bracingly. "As a major stockholder in Spencer-Allen, I think I should have some say in choosing such an influential member of the staff."

"You have someone in mind?" Ross inquired drolly.

A perfect opening. "Myself!" she inserted boldly.

Piercing gray eyes darkened with interest. "I see." Whatever Ross thought of her sudden interest in company matters after an absence of two years, he was giving nothing away. "And when did you come to this decision?"

Last week, she almost blurted, but held on to her cool and maintained, "I've been thinking about it for some time. Since before Quinn died, in fact." A bald-faced lie, but Ross wasn't to know that. "Quinn probably wouldn't have agreed, though, lest you claim nepotism," she furthered the invention.

"But you're not nearly so hesitant, it seems. Having satisfied convention and maintained a year of wifely grieving, you've decided to come out of hiding."

"I have not been hiding!" The beast! Ross hadn't waited long to start taking verbal potshots.

"Hibernating, then," he conceded. "Under your parents' protective wing. In your little bungalow on the beach."

"You've been spying on me!"

"Keeping a watchful eye cocked," he corrected lazily. "Tennis, charity work, brooding on the beach..." Ross outlined her activities of the last year and chuckled. "The rich society matron routine. I knew it would pall in time and you'd wind up on my doorstep, begging me to rescue you from the doldrums."

Casey shot him a withering look. "I wouldn't beg you if you were the last thing in long pants."

"Ah, but then you've shut out all men, since your husband died," he declared smoothly.

Add ruthless to all of his other faults! Ross *had* been watching her, to know she hadn't dated since Quinn died. But, why?

Deciding to ignore that Pandora's box altogether, Casey went on righteously. "And you won't be rescuing me. Might I remind you, I have as much right to be here as you have!" She glanced pointedly around the impressive suite—Quinn's old office.

"Not quite." One incredibly long arm snaked out, and Ross captured her chin, raising her face to his implacable gaze. "As chairman of the board, and *controlling* stockholder, I make all the decisions around here, hmm?" As if to stress his superiority, he rose to his full measure of six feet four.

Not about to be intimidated, Casey scrambled to her feet and was instantly appalled at her stupidity. A tall woman herself, she disconcerted most men when she looked at them, for the most part, eyeball to eyeball. Not so the lofty giant who was smiling benignly from an easy six inches above. Casey had been so rattled when she careened into this—this ape a few minutes earlier, she had temporarily discounted his sheer physical magnitude. Ross Allen, she remembered with annoyance, was one of the few men who had ever succeeded in making her feel small and threatened and feminine.

"Why don't we move this little skirmish over to the sitting area?" Ross suggested dryly, easily perceiving her discomfort.

A no-nonsense arm guided her to an oatmeal-colored couch and adjacent tweed armchairs. Casey chose the couch and ground her teeth in vexation when Ross observed musingly, "Both seated, we'll be more equal. In size, anyway."

She watched in simmering silence as he shrugged out of his immaculately tailored tan suit coat, tossed it negligently on the back of one chair, then sprawled with careless grace into the other.

His long legs splayed in front of him, his fingers tented in mock reverence, Ross prodded, "You may commence, Cassandra. I'm all ears."

"I detest being called Cassandra," she shot back tartly. "My name is Casey. The only person who ever calls me Cassandra is my mother. When she's in a temper."

"So that's where you got your short fuse."

"I do not have a short fuse!"

Their gazes collided, one shimmering in fury, the other wryly amused, and Casey subsided into the couch cushions, forced to see the hilarity of her heated declaration.

"If I do have a temper, it comes from my father, not my mother," she imparted ruefully. "Dad is sort of like Mount Vesuvius. All but the most incautious back off while he's still shooting steam. If you keep pushing until he erupts..." The rest spoke for itself.

Ross smiled faintly, as if he found her disclosure in some way satisfying. "I'm glad to hear there has been one man in your life you were able to respect."

"I respected Quinn as well!" She responded with alacrity to his thinly veiled innuendo.

"Whatever you say." Ross shrugged in patent disbelief. "Suppose you get on with why you're here today. What is it you're asking of me...or offering?"

God! This man was impossible! Casey glared at Ross in seething frustration and then squared her shoulders.

He was not going to drive her away with his suggestive words or approach!

Dragging up all her inner resources, and keeping her voice as level and confident as possible, Casey launched into a fifteen-minute, for the most part uninterrupted, dissertation on her accomplishments during her four years at Spencer Ad.

Ross listened attentively, nodding occasionally when she mentioned various ad campaigns Quinn had allowed her to handle alone...and unhampered, she refrained from qualifying.

When she finally wound down from her carefully rehearsed vocal résumé, Casey found Ross studying her through lazy, half-closed eyes, the beginnings of a smile playing around his well-chiseled mouth.

"Fair enough," he drawled. "I'll take you on for a trial period, and we'll see how things work out. If we prove to be able to work together—and that's a big *if*, considering your hair-trigger temper, and the fact that I've grown accustomed to being in sole command—I'll set you up in the same kind of arrangement I had with Quinn. You make the decisions you think you're equipped to handle, and anything major we'll work out together."

He was offering the controlled revival of a partnership, something Casey had dreamed of eventually, but farther down the road, when she had demonstrated her ability. Considering her stockholdings, it wasn't anything less than she deserved, but still she was dazed. "Just like that?" she mused quizzically. "You don't want to check on any of my past work, see if I'm capable of handling this much responsibility? I haven't worked in several years, and when I did, Quinn always ran the show."

The low growl from nearby sounded almost like disgust. "Can you really be that naive?"

Casey stared at Ross in confused consternation, and his dry laugh echoed throughout the office.

"You were *carrying* Quinn, Casey! Quinn knew it, and so did damn near everyone else in the advertising industry. Eventually it began to eat at him, gnawing at his gut like some kind of insidious piranha, until pride and outright jealousy demanded that he remove you to the less-threatening position of young wife and social hostess." Ross shook his head, and there was no missing the disgust in his tone now. "Such a waste. Such a total waste of talent, shutting the door on a mind more innovative, more creative than his own!"

"I respected my husband!" Casey choked out her earlier conviction.

"In the beginning, when you were a fresh kid out of USC and Quinn was your older, worldly mentor at Spencer Ad, maybe you respected him," Ross allowed tersely. "But when the student began to outshine her inspiration, Quinn carefully closeted you in that palatial mansion in Bel Air. Out of sight, competition removed."

"It wasn't like that!"

"Wasn't it?" he persisted, undaunted. "I knew you were wasted with Quinn the first time we met. He was wary of you even then, but you were too young and idealistic to see it. Do you remember that night, Casey?"

"Yes." The admission came unwillingly. Twenty-two and only one year married at the time, Casey had been alarmed to the point of terror by the instant attraction that flared between Ross and herself. Such sensual awareness had never swamped her, not even in the marital bedroom. "You looked as if you couldn't wait to have me," she remembered accusingly.

"I couldn't . . . then. I've waited a long time, Casey." Potent words! Equally potent eyes looked her over in warm speculation.

"I was very young then, like you said," she cried plaintively. "And nervous, throwing a huge cocktail party for all of Quinn's impressive colleagues. Women were fawning all over you, the dynamic head of Allen Modeling. But you kept staring at me. I was flustered by your attentions, and—"

"Not looking for any extramarital alliances?"

"Precisely!" Casey jumped to her feet and cast him a venomous glance, unnerved by the direction in which they were heading. "And if you think I'm going to enter into any kind of a partnership other than a partnership of the minds, you're out of your arrogant black head!"

"Sit down, Cassandra," Ross reproved quietly.

"Go to hell!" she threw back, flinching when he shot to his feet to glare down at her like some kind of menacing Goliath.

One dark brow began a mocking ascent. "What's the matter? Don't you like being at a disadvantage?"

He was dead right! It irked Casey no end to have to look up at the beast. Even more so when he drawled, "I imagine you've spent the better part of your life looking down your pretty little nose at most men. Isn't it fortunate you'll always have to look *up* to me?"

Her fists closed with impotent rage. "Why, you . . . !"

"You're going to break a fingernail." Patiently Ross gathered her hands in his own, uncurling her clenched fingers. "And don't grit your teeth, either," he directed when she resorted to yet another habitual frustration reliever. Placing a heavy hand on either rigid shoulder, he pushed her down on the couch, this time depositing his own lanky frame right beside her.

"You're insufferable!" With all the dignity she could muster, Casey squirmed as far away as the arm of the couch would allow, her lips compressed in a thin, angry line.

"You have a beautiful mouth," Ross noted whimsically. "I'll wager your parents spent a fortune straightening those sharp little teeth."

"Then you'd lose your bet," she announced triumphantly and, without thinking, gave him just what he wanted—a wide, engaging smile. "I claim complete, unassisted credit for these." She ran a provocative tongue over perfectly spaced, toothpaste commercial white teeth.

"You don't get much assistance from anything, do you?" His eyes dropped suggestively lower, to the swell of rounded breasts thrusting tautly against the soft material of her knit top.

Heat rushed to her face, but Casey resisted the impulse to jerk her blazer closed. "Why do I get the feeling you lured me here today?" She was attempting to disarm Ross, but when he looked up in amazement, she added hastily, "To work, I mean. Can you deny that your phone call last week was a deliberate attempt to provoke my interest?"

"I threw out the bait, and you came up snapping. Just as I'd hoped you would," he admitted unabashedly. "You may have been lolling about on the beach while I pulled your husband's company back on the straight and narrow, but somehow I didn't think you'd cotton to the idea of a stranger stepping in to take up the slack when it came to the point that I needed help."

"You wanted me here?" The notion was strangely warming.

"Do you doubt it?" Leisurely, with pure male enjoyment, Ross began a visual exploration of her curves.

Casey took advantage of the brief respite to study the big man next to her under the protection of lowered lashes.

Their paths had crossed many times over the years after that initial contact. Quinn had been partial to using Ross's models, and Ross had been a frequent visitor, both at the office and the beautiful home he had alluded to earlier. A home not of her own choosing, being so opulently pretentious, she had sold it soon after Quinn died.

Her gaze slowly lifted. Not what you would call conventionally handsome, Ross was nonetheless a ruggedly attractive, compelling man. His midnight-black hair was prone to waviness and was allowed to have its own way, framing a deeply tanned face dominated by those dark, intimidating eyes. Heavy, frequently mocking eyebrows grew almost together above a well-defined, arrogant nose. Firm lips, for lack of a better description, were frank and wholly sensuous, full and very practiced looking. And they were quirking, she noticed, glancing up to encounter a hard, fixing stare.

"Like what you see?" he inquired.

"Passable." She shrugged, attempting cool indifference.

Ross chuckled throatily. "Like you, I live with what nature gave me. But that's pretty much expected of a man." His eyes narrowed on her bemused face, then flicked with casual disdain to the neat little bun corralling her glossy brown hair low on her nape. "Tell me, why do you go out of your way to play down your looks? You're a stunning woman, and yet you pull your hair back in an unbecoming knot and dress with an obvious effort to conceal your femininity."

"I dress for comfort," Casey replied stiffly, "not to pander to the roving male eye. What business is it of yours, anyway?"

"Oh, it's my business," Ross assured her, his voice hardening. "If you work for Spencer-Allen, you reflect Spencer-Allen, and I've never gone in for a woman trying to emulate a man. The bottom line is, I don't care for ladies in trousers and jackets, no matter how carefully chosen and well paid for. A female should look like a female, pure and simple. Especially a woman in advertising," he added judiciously.

"Quinn never objected to the way I dressed," Casey pointed out peevishly.

"I'm not surprised; he wanted you to blend in with the woodwork. Quinn was jealous as hell if any man so much as looked your way." Ross ran a distracted hand through his hair, demanding impatiently, "Aren't there any well-cut designer dresses hanging in your closet? The tailored business garb has got to go."

"Now, just a damn minute! I'm coming here to work, not act as some kind of fluffy window dressing. What I wear is strictly my own business. No one has ever told me how to dress!"

"Then it's time someone did," she was told firmly.

"You go to hell!"

"Do you want to work with me, Cassandra?" Ross asked with a heavy sigh.

"Are you issuing an ultimatum?" she countered.

Their eyes locked in a long, stormy battle. It was Ross who finally broke the silence, commenting harshly, "I have no objection to working with a woman in management, as long as she's confident in her role and comes across as one. I simply cannot countenance anything less than complete femininity in the gentler sex. Call it a carryover from my years with Allen Modeling."

"Of which you still maintain controlling interest as well!" she bit out sarcastically. "You see women as seductive dollies to be dressed up in skimpy little rags that take advantage of every inch of available flesh."

"Of which you're a bit overendowed right now," Ross put in wisely, calmly refusing to rise to her ire. "And that's another of my conditions. If you still want to work with me, chauvinistic devil that I may be, I want you to lose a few of those extra pounds that have accumulated while you've been lying out on the beach, underexercising, this last year."

That did it! "Are you saying I'm fat!" Jumping to her feet, Casey jerked off her blazer and stood before him, her hands on her hips, her eyes shooting fury as she glared down in her brief top and belted, formfitting slacks. "You just tell me where you see any excess pounds," she demanded tightly, turning in a circle.

"I didn't say you weren't well put together," Ross accorded humorously, "but the voluptuous look went out with miniskirts and spike-heeled shoes."

"Ooohhh!"

"How much do you weigh, brown eyes?" he queried indulgently.

"One hundred and thirty pounds. And before you say 'that much!' may I remind you I'm no diminutive debutante! I'm twenty-seven years old, and—and five feet nine inches tall!"

"Well, Grandma," came the mocking taunt. "How long has it been since you weighed yourself?"

"Quite awhile," she admitted. "But I've weighed one-thirty or less all my adult life."

The dubious quirk of his lips chipped away at her already ruffled composure. "Go ahead, call me a liar! If you had a scale anywhere, I'd wipe that cynical smirk off your face!"

His steady gaze flickered slightly, betrayingly, and Casey pounced. "You *do* have a scale somewhere! Where is it? In Personnel? The first aid station?"

Ross hesitated, then nodded slowly toward the private washroom adjoining his office. "This really isn't necessary," he began softly.

"I insist!" she averred, marching haughtily into the bathroom. Once there she was confronted with the type

of scale found in a doctor's office, weighted and re-
nowned for its accuracy.

Self-consciously she reached down and slipped out of
her low-heeled loafers, explaining haltingly when Ross
sauntered up behind her, "I—uh—never weigh myself
with my shoes on."

"Don't let me stop you," he drawled, rubbing his
hands in playful anticipation. "Take it all off if you
wish. I *love* watching ladies strip!"

"I'm sure you do," Casey voiced nastily. "But you'll
have to seek your entertainment elsewhere. I've had
enough excitement for one day." She turned a defiant
back on her cocky tormentor and stepped up on the
scale, watching pensively as Ross adjusted the balanc-
ing weights and nudged the indicator slowly upward.
When he passed one hundred and thirty, she groaned
and closed her eyes, afraid to look.

"My, my, would you look at that!" Ross whistled
through his teeth and patted her shapely derriere. "As
an educated guess, I'd say those extra pounds have all
settled right here."

"Ooohhh!" Casey swatted his hand away angrily,
only to have her shoulders firmly gripped.

"Stand still," Ross instructed. "Let's see how tall
you are. If you'll lie about your weight, who knows?"

Sure of her height at least, Casey stood straightly
proud. Hadn't she spent the better part of her adoles-
cence praying that her growth would stop before she
topped six feet?

"Well, it seems you do have *some* integrity," Ross
allowed musingly, settling the metal measuring arm in
her hair. "You're five foot nine and a half."

Smiling smugly, she stepped off the scale and pointed to a printed "desirable weight" chart taped on the
wall. Then, tracing her finger across the line of recommended weights for her height, she settled on the

middle category of 136–151. "You see! According to this, I'm right within my proper weight range." Not for the world would she admit to being appalled by those hateful five pounds that had somehow crept up on her!

"Wrong! You're looking along the column for a medium frame." Hard fingers encircled her wrist, easily lapping its delicate contours. "Frame size is determined by bone structure, most frequently measured by the size of the wrist. This is a dainty little wrist; hence, you have a small frame." Ross guided her finger to the first row for small-framed women. "One-thirty to one-forty is your desirable weight range, and you would be much more desirable at one-thirty...or less."

Casey ran her hands experimentally over her hips. "Am I really getting that well rounded?" Despite their antagonism, Ross was an unquestioned expert on the female form, and she wanted an honest opinion.

He smiled at her wide-eyed uncertainty. "Oh, I'd say you have a long way to go before you reach queen-size proportions. But I think you'll agree it wouldn't hurt to shed a few pounds. Say a nice round five? By the time you start work next Monday?"

"Are you suggesting or ordering?" she demanded warily.

The smile gave way to a teasing wink. "Let's just say we'll put you up on the scale Monday morning, and that will determine whether you're ready to start work."

"Why, you—"

Her angry retort was cut off as Ross consulted his watch and announced implacably, "We'll have to continue this little discussion next week. I have some notes to go over before my next appointment in ten minutes." With innate courtesy he waited until Casey stepped into her shoes and then, taking her arm, guided her back to where she had left her purse and blazer.

She was still smarting from the indignity of being *ordered* to lose weight when they reached the door to the outer office and it became apparent that there was no time for rebuttal. Somehow, despite her befuddlement, she managed to extend her hand and form the words "Care to shake on our alliance?"

"To seal our bargain?" Ross seemed amused by the idea. "I can do better than that, Casey." The proferred hand was pulled into his chest, and a warm palm slid caressingly around her nape.

Oh, Lord! What had come over her, to invite any kind of physical contact with this towering specimen of manhood! Breathing shallowly, Casey fixed her gaze on the immaculately turned knot of his brown satin tie. The hand at her nape exerted gentle upward pressure, and when she didn't respond, a thumb hooked under her chin, forcing her to look up.

"Forgotten the disparity in our sizes so soon?" Warm gray eyes swept over her startled features. "Relax," Ross chided. "I'll make this as painless as possible." Slowly, dizzyingly, he lowered his head, brushing her lips with tender, coaxing promise.

No man had been allowed close enough to kiss Casey since her husband had died, and even Quinn had never kissed her with such absorbed precision. Every rational cell in her brain screamed, *No! This man is dangerous! Don't let him get started on you; he'll put you into his sensual force field.*

Intellectually Casey knew she must resist, but emotionally she had been empty for too long... starved of all feeling. Just a moment's indulgence, that's all she would allow herself. Just long enough to discover the mystery that was Ross.

Her free hand went up to mingle in the dark hair above, and it was all the signal Ross needed as he pulled her possessively into his length.

The branding kiss seemed to go on forever, building in intensity until Casey shuddered and parted her lips, entranced. The final invasion of his warm, thrusting tongue was so shattering, she worked her trapped hand frantically loose and clutched at his neck with both arms.

Caution, pride, everything inherent in her nature, was forgotten as Casey responded with a passion too long suppressed.

It was Ross who finally slowed the involvement, bringing her down gently with quiet endearments and the soothing stroke of his hands.

"All this pent-up emotion," he husked against the shell of her ear. "It's been building for a long time, hasn't it?"

"Yes." Her answer came softly...and safely. She *had* been a married woman. There was no shame in admitting to physical longings.

"I knew." Ross drew back, cupping her face tenderly. "Five years is a long time to wait, but I knew you'd be mine in the end."

"Be yours?" she choked uncomprehendingly. "What are you saying?"

"I thought I was showing you." His hands came to rest on the wrists clamped behind his neck. "See how you're clinging to me? Would you like another demonstration of how perfectly we're going to fit together?"

Somewhere in the back of her mind a tiny seed of suspicion began to germinate. "You want me here as some kind of an office playmate?"

"Don't be absurd, woman!" Ross held her wrists captive as she tried to slide out of his embrace. "I want a partner in the office. A business partner. But away from work—"

"There won't be any 'away from work,'" she declared heatedly. "I'll make sure of that. I've had enough of belonging to one man, being *owned* by him, to last me a lifetime!''

"You married unwisely," Ross asserted quietly. "Quinn wasn't strong enough for you. Some women need a firm hand to shape them into their full potential."

Casey wrenched away from his grasp, muttering inelegantly, "Bull! That's chauvinistic pap at its worst!"

"We'll see." Ross laughed at her earthy outburst, taunting, "Just remember, you've got to look up the next time we put it to the test." His hands settled around Casey's waist, and he lifted her bodily...and *firmly* away from the door.

For a big man Ross was quick, but not quick enough for Casey to miss the universal thumbs-up for victory sign he flashed his pensive secretary.

"You knew about this all along, Bev!" Casey accused. Not waiting for an answer—amused guilt was written all over the older woman's face—she whirled on her heels and offered a fuming, over the shoulder, "I'll see you next Monday at nine. *If* I decide I can work with you two conspirators!"

"We start at eight now" came the unison chorus from behind.

"That figures," Casey muttered, shaking her head in weary defeat. Everything about this morning had contrived to throw her off-balance: earlier starting hours; a partnership handed back to the only surviving Spencer on a silver platter; then, unexpectedly, her mode of dress attacked; worse still, her body fitness slandered. And, oh, that artless submission in the arms of the enemy!

Only his secretary was left to see the satisfied glint in his eyes as Ross tracked Casey's departure.

"She's not going to be a pushover, you know," Bev warned dryly.

"Why, Mrs. Kiley, whatever are you talking about?" Ross retorted guilelessly.

"You don't fool me for a minute, Mr. Allen! You've had your eye on Cassandra Spencer for years. I must say, I admire your restraint, waiting a year to reel in the line. The question is, where do you want to land your prize catch in the end?"

Ross merely smiled, a wide, engaging smile that could mean almost anything, and Bev snickered to herself, "Casey, my girl, I think you may have bitten off more than you're willing to chew!"

Chapter Two

Casey was sure of it! The prickly warmth of the late August Southern California sunshine seemed to mock her as she trudged to her car, reminding her of the heated clinch of moments earlier. Of all the dicey experiments she had tried in her lifetime, mixing it up with Ross Allen had to stand as the pinnacle of stupidity! Especially after he had warned her, openly, that he'd been waiting for her for five years!

Well, you'll wait forever, buster! she vowed stonily, sliding into the stifling interior of her faithful MG. If Ross thought she was going to fall right in with his plans—right into his arms—now that she was unencumbered with a wedding ring, he could go pound sand!

She slammed her hand against the steering wheel to punctuate her vehemence and laughed when the warmth registered under her palm.

"You wouldn't hurt me, would you, little friend?" she chided the classically aging sports car that had been her cherished compatriot since graduation from high school. "You're just trying to warn me not to get my fingers burned. Now, the big man upstairs," she huffed, rolling down the windows to let out the trapped heat, "he'd like to see me go up in a poof of smoke. But he's not going to get the chance. Arrogant brute!

Firm handling, indeed! Like I was some kind of spirited filly that needed to be broken to the halter!''

Still muttering under her breath, Casey backed out of the parking space and looked up to find two neatly dressed businessmen waiting for her to pass, watching her lips form conversation with a nonexistent passenger.

"Slogans," she called out, and when they smiled in confusion, added, "I work up there, at Spencer-Allen, and the boss is a slave driver. I try out jingles in my free time. My car loves it."

With that she sped off, watching in the rearview mirror as the smiling men shook their heads and went on their way. *They probably think I'm a crazy broad spaced out on uppers,* she deduced hilariously, and then sobered. Great balls of fire! They were heading for Spencer-Allen! What if they were Ross's next appointment?

That morning was supposed to be her finest hour—like the emergence of a butterfly after its long chrysalis. It was rapidly degenerating into a three-ring circus.

Priorities! She had to set some priorities. A week! That was all she had to gear up for the specter of working beside the indomitable Ross Allen.

Blending into her accustomed spot in the fast lane of the San Diego Freeway, Casey let her mind wander back over the morning. So Ross had been keeping her under some kind of surveillance since Quinn died. Like a hawk reconnoitering its prey, she reflected grimly. Did that explain how he had sensed that she was ready to come out of her self-imposed exile? Was she crazy to put her neck in the noose he had so carefully constructed for her?

She loved advertising, exalted in the stimulating position that had been laid at her feet this morning, but why did Ross have to come gift wrapped with the deal?

How could she work creatively, *dispassionately,* alongside such a disturbing, provocative man?

"Damn!" she emoted, easing off the accelerator. In her anxiety Casey had been tailgating the psychedelically painted van in front of her. A quick glance in the rearview mirror revealed the distinguishing bubble gum machine—thus far not flashing its *gotcha* beacon—of a California Highway Patrol car two vehicles back.

Just what she needed—a ticket—on top of everything else! Deftly she switched lanes, breathing a sigh of relief when the patrol car exited at the next off ramp.

Relaxing for the first time in hours, she lifted slim, plucky fingers to release the bun at her nape. The arresting sight of a beautiful girl in her sports car, her long hair flying in the wind, caught the eye of many—most notably the young van driver as Casey pulled even with him.

A good-natured game of freeway tag commenced. When Casey sped up, so did the driver of the van. When she eased back, the youthful Lothario with his bedroom on wheels stayed right beside her.

Craftily she waited until the last minute to signal and move down her off ramp, not wishing to be chased and caught, but grateful for the temporary tension-relieving diversion. After the battering her ego had taken that morning, it was nice to know she still appealed to most males of the species.

Smiling, Casey pulled into the parking lot of Thrifty Drugs and went in search of some dieting inspiration. Never before forced into the distasteful routine of slimming down, she picked up several paperback books detailing various diet regimens, finally deciding on the highly touted low-carbohydrate reducing method.

Briefly she considered the vast array of diuretics and appetite suppressants, then dismissed them. Second only to her abhorrence of being sick was the idea of stuffing any unnatural, probably unhealthy and useless, pills down her throat.

Never had Casey's pink stucco cottage looked so welcoming when she finally drove up to it. Nestled next to her parents' much larger home, the stately Redondo Beach abode, where she had spent her formative years, Casey's private sanctuary had originated as guest house-cum-changing quarters. Her parents had gifted her with the thoughtful retreat the previous summer, opening their arms and their hearts when it became apparent that Casey needed some kind of haven in which to recharge her emotional batteries.

Once in her tiny green-and-white wicker-decorated bedroom, she began methodically shucking the by now sticky and oppressive tailored pantsuit that had seemed so appropriate when she had dressed earlier. Clad only in bikini briefs and a lacy bra, she stood subjecting herself to a long critical appraisal in the mirrored closet doors. Long, shapely legs rose dramatically to curve into rounded womanly hips. Her well-indented waistline was followed by a surprisingly narrow rib cage and proudly thrusting, globular breasts. At one time Casey had despaired that her breasts, like the rest of her, wouldn't stop growing until they reached gargantuan proportions. Fortunately, just as her mother had predicted, her growth had stopped somewhere in her seventeenth year, but not before she was blessed with an enticing whistlebait bustline and a stature that inspired awe in many and modestly heeled footwear in Casey herself.

A quick about-face in the looking glass disclosed the truth in Ross's maddening observation. Five pounds of excess Casey trailed the rear, inflating each sculptured hip with just a tad too much provocation.

Disgruntled by the revelation, she riffled through

her drawers, pulling out her usual summer garb of brief shorts and a halter top.

"Casey, Casey! Hey, Stretch, where are you?" The front screen door slammed, accompanied by the shrill of an urgent adolescent voice.

"In here," Casey called, adjusting the halter over her breasts.

A miniature whirlwind in the form of her young sister, Missy, flew into the bedroom. "Come on, give!" the exuberant teenager fairly shouted. "Did you get the job?" Ten years younger than Casey and what her parents laughingly termed "a little surprise package from heaven," Melissa Thorpe was Casey's constant shadow and privilege to many close, sisterly confidences.

"Oh, I got the job." Casey laughed at her sister's animated expression. "With a few conditions," she amended.

"What conditions?" Missy frowned, plopping down on the green-and-white floral bedspread.

"Well... Ross seems to feel I don't quite fit the part. He doesn't care for my taste in clothes, and he... uh... wants me to lose a few pounds."

"He *what!* There isn't a smidgen of fat on you anywhere!"

Casey wrinkled her nose affectionately. "So you say, but that's family bias talking. Ross thinks I'm a bit too well padded."

"And he wants you to go on a diet?" Missy was plainly incredulous. "I don't believe it. Ross seems like such a he-man. I can't believe he wouldn't appreciate your sexy shape."

"What would you know about Ross Allen, infant?" Casey chuckled. "You were only fifteen when Quinn and I threw that dinner party and invited you and Mom and Dad to meet Ross."

"Well, I wasn't blind" came the stiff retort. "I think Ross is dreamy."

"Dreamy! You're out of your teenage mind. The man's a shark. He eats little girls like you for breakfast. Even *I* have more sense than to get involved."

"We'll see," the younger girl replied smugly. "You're going to be working with him every day."

"Working is the operative word," Casey sniffed. "That's all I'm going to be doing, so don't go getting any matchmaking ideas."

"Oh, you!" Tracing an idle finger along the quilted lines of the spread beneath her, Missy changed course and prompted, "Tell me about this diet you need to go on. Did Ross make it up for you?"

"Certainly not! I *am* capable of thinking for myself, brat. Come on out to the kitchen with me, and I'll give you all the booty when I clean out my cupboards. If I'm going to succeed in this little undertaking, I've got to get everything fattening, illegal, and immoral out of the house."

Half an hour later Missy was weighed down with two grocery bags full of every imaginable goody. Religiously Casey packed up her Oreo cookies, pretzels, potato chips, rye bread, boxed cold cereal, half of a lemon chiffon cake, and, last but not least, her much-loved cheese-flavored tortilla chips. She drew the line at giving up her tomato and green chili salsa. No matter what the diet manual stated, she simply could not do without her favorite Mexican dip. If nothing else, she'd use it to camouflage stringy celery, she rationalized. If celery was allowed!

Shooing her sister away on the pretext of needing solitude to study her diet bible, Casey carried the dreaded book out to the beach and began to study in earnest. Not until she was sure she had absorbed the complete essence of proteins versus sugars—the allowed and the no-no's—did she go in to fix lunch, a huge salad of shredded lettuce, tuna, and the miraculously allowed mayonnaise. Milk was out, so she washed it all down with a can of diet cola and went back out to enjoy the rest of the afternoon soaking up sun, surf, and atmosphere.

Missy and her usual assortment of teenage friends were out on the beach, alternately squealing through a lively game of touch football and running down to the water to cool off. An inveterate people watcher, Casey was soon caught up observing the supple, near-naked bodies as they flitted about.

She had known most of these kids for years, and it was fascinating to watch each summer as the beautiful metamorphoses took place, transforming the girls into shapely goddesses and the boys to broadening specimens of future manhood. Most people would say the change was the most dramatic in young girls, but Casey enjoyed watching the boys' shoulders widen, their chest hairs sprout, and their arms and legs take on more muscle tone. If only she'd had a little boy of her own, to watch him grow, nurture his quest for self-mastery...

No! She would not be bogged down in that abysmal quagmire one more time! Flopping over on her stomach, she schooled her mind to wander elsewhere, and with frustrating predictability it zeroed in on her less than happy marriage.

It hadn't been all bad, she reflected wistfully. Sixteen years older than Casey and infinitely well bred, thanks to an upbringing in old Southern California money, Quinn Spencer came into Casey's life during her senior year at USC and literally swept her off her feet. Disregarding all contrary advice, her father's the most vehement because of the age difference, Casey and Quinn were married and had a beautiful, socially correct June wedding a bare one week after she was graduated from college.

For the first year she had seen everything through the rose-tinted blinders of newly wedded bliss. But by the second year of their marriage the bloom was decidedly off the lily as Casey strained increasingly to cope with Quinn's petulance in the office.

It came as a surprise to learn that his father had died just six months before their marriage, that up until that time, Rudolph Spencer had been the driving force behind Spencer Ad, but it explained many things.

After years of waiting in the wings, Quinn was drunk with the power of his inherited autocracy, his exaltation as the top banana. Not instinctively creative himself, he had to rely on other people to keep him rolling. But above all else, he had to be in charge! Unfortunately, probably due to his genteel upbringing, Quinn couldn't cut bait when the going got tough, and it fell to Casey and other innovative underlings to negotiate in tight corners, bringing in a contract here, saving another when clients tired of Quinn's flat, ultraconservative proposals.

Crawling out of the frying pan and into retirement in that mausoleum in Bel Air hadn't been the answer for Casey either. She needed intellectual stimulation the way most people needed to breathe. Eventually the vacuum of inactivity would have suffocated her, just as she had been suffocating for the last year. She needed out! She had made the right decision today in resuming her career. If Ross put up any roadblocks to her professional recovery, threw her any more curves, she'd roll right over him!

"Hey, Stretch!" A dark shadow loomed over her, dripping saltwater on her sizzling skin. "We need you to even up the numbers in a game of volleyball, and I'm choosing you for our side."

Casey squinted one eye open and looked up at Missy's latest boyfriend, a blond Adonis named Chuck. Last year, before he filled out, he had been "Chuckie" ... and thoroughly ignored.

Giving in good-naturedly, she allowed herself to be hoisted to her feet and hustled into a boisterous game of spiking the smooth white ball over the net and seeing who could render whom ineffective with a little sand kicked in the right direction.

By the time Casey went in to broil the steak she had left out to thaw for dinner, her stomach seemed to be pressed up against her backbone, so great was her hunger. The idiot blurb YOU'LL NEVER SUFFER HUNGER PANGS, emblazoned on the cover of her diet manual, was meant to sell books. Her stomach protested otherwise.

To her profound annoyance she stepped on the bathroom scales the next morning and found the merciless indicator stubbornly stuck at one-thirty-five. Thoroughly vexed, she decided to forgo breakfast and join the lively teenagers already out on the beach.

The young crowd, having been informed by Melissa that this was Casey's last week of leisurely companionship in their midst, steadfastly refused to leave her alone.

Over the next few days she alternately swam and starved, ran on the beach and starved, played football and volleyball and "who's going to dunk whom" and starved, always surrounded by Missy's faithful entourage. Probably, Casey decided, the contagious spirit of fun that began when her privacy was invaded by the vacationing youngsters had provided the impetus that finally snapped her self-destructive lethargy.

Melissa appeared at her door bright and early Friday morning, demanding that they go over Casey's wardrobe in preparation for "satisfying the big boss."

It was a tedious, disgruntling chore, sorting through

clothes that hadn't left their hangers in over a year, and Casey railed at the task. How she dressed ranked low on her totem pole of importance. Outward packaging she deemed superfluous. It was how you handled yourself and clients that mattered the most. Nothing would persuade her to believe otherwise. Designer dresses and Ross Allen be damned! Her wardrobe boasted none. She'd dress for comfort and practicality at work, just as she always had.

"I don't think Ross is going to be fooled for a minute," Missy sighed when Casey tried on her third skirt and tailored blouse in a row. "I thought he wanted you to look feminine."

"What do you suggest, frills?" Casey snapped, fingering the row of pearl buttons marching down the front of her silk blouse. "What's the matter with this outfit?"

"Nothing." Missy sighed anew. "You look every inch the efficient career person. You just don't look... womanly."

"Womanly!" she scorned. "The last thing I want to do is appeal to Ross on that level!"

Casey was to remember those words as she stepped back into the working world at precisely eight o'clock Monday morning.

Ross paced a wide path around her, taking in her appearance in the fashionable beige plaid skirt and color-coordinated cream blouse and jacket, her feet shod in the usual low-heeled pumps.

"Very functional," he murmured. His eyes lit on the sedate bun at her nape. "You certainly couldn't be classified as window dressing in that getup."

His condescending tone was goading. "What's the matter with the way I'm dressed?" Casey flared, shrugging out of the blanketing jacket.

"Nothing, if you were a respectable back country librarian. But you hardly look the part of a slick, fast-moving female ad executive. You'll have to dazzle our clients with your brains. You certainly won't get far on your looks if that's all your wardrobe has to offer."

"Oh, I don't think we'll have to worry," she shot back drolly. "You'll knock 'em all dead in your flashy five-hundred-dollar custom-tailored suits."

Ross's dark eyes narrowed on her defiant face. "You're so right! I learned to dress the part years ago. *You* have a lot of catching up to do!"

"If you think I'm going to pander to your every whim—"

"Save it" came the terse interruption. "How did your dieting go? Did you get those five pounds off?"

"My middle age spread, you mean?" She smiled smugly. There was no way Ross could accurately judge the shape of her derriere thanks to the cleverly chosen circular skirt. "Would you like to weigh me in?" she suggested sweetly, not the least concerned. She had hit the one-thirty mark yesterday morning, and skipped breakfast today just to be safe.

"Definitely." Ross rose to the challenge, waving her on to the bathroom. "Lead on. I can't wait to see if you've followed orders."

The man's insufferable! Casey seconded all of her previous character assassinations, furiously refusing to let "followed orders" get her goat. Fuming, she kicked off her shoes and trudged into the bathroom.

Incredibly, the miserable little indicator balanced at one-thirty-one, and all efforts to coax it down a notch tipped the scales.

"It was the Newburg sauce on the lobster my parents served last night," she bemoaned. "I tried to scrape it off. Really I did!"

"Not bad, though." Ross sounded sympathetic.

"Four pounds in a week. You just have one pound to go to reach my ideal."

"As if I care!" she gritted, stepping down off the scale. "Do you want me to go home and get back in training until I get that last pound off?" Her sarcastic offer tasted like bitter gall.

"Oh, I think we'll keep you around—one extra pound of upholstery and all," Ross proclaimed magnanimously. Lean fingers came up to cradle her clenched jaw. "Just don't slacken off, hmm?"

"You're all heart," she flung at him, backing away from his disturbing touch.

"And you're all prickles." He laughed, leading her back to his office. "Come on, my little porcupine. Let me show you to your office, and you can start settling in."

Casey shrugged out of his helpful clasp, piqued. "It may have escaped your notice, but I'm not a *little* anything!"

They were nearing a connecting door between Ross's office and a smaller one adjoining it, and she gasped disbelievingly. "You're giving me *your* old office? The one you used before Quinn died?" To his credit, Ross had never suggested changing quarters while Quinn was alive, but instead ran creative circles around his new partner in the smaller office Quinn himself had used while his father was alive.

"Of course this will be your office." Ross opened the door and pushed her inside, his dark head tilted inquiringly. "Where did you imagine I would put my second in command?"

"I don't know." That was the truth. The question hadn't occurred to her. "I—I used to have the office across the hall."

"Do you have some objection to working so closely beside me?" he queried, considering her thoughtfully.

"Of course not," she responded warily.

"Good. I want you where I can keep an eye on you."

That little challenge was a hot potato Casey had no intention of picking up. "Have you brought me any work to start on?" Perfect! She sounded polite but distant.

"Don't want to play this morning?" Ross parried, easily discerning her adroit dodge. "Ah, well." He shrugged philosophically and then sobered, suddenly every inch the auspicious leader of Spencer-Allen Ad. Guiding Casey to a desk only slightly smaller than his own, he saw her seated and motioned to half a dozen account folders stacked neatly to one side.

"I think you'll find I've allocated you several accounts that you actively solicited and signed during your first sojourn here."

Casey thumbed through the folders and nodded, pleased to see that she was to be in charge of the hotel account that she had worked so hard to corner her first year at Spencer Ad, as well as several equally impressive, familiar accounts.

"As you'll see," Ross went on, "I've also put you in charge of organizing and promoting the retarded children's home benefit drive coming up in October."

Her eyes widened, glowing with interest. The children's benefit, culminating in a wild bazaar-cum-Halloween extravaganza late in October, had always been Quinn's pet baby, and secretly she had always longed to get her own thumb into the adventuresome pie.

"Th-thank you," she stammered. "I don't know what to say."

"I'm sure you can handle it," Ross allowed quietly. "We showed an encouraging increase last year." He didn't need to add when *he* was running the show. "If you run into any snags, you can come to me any time," he offered, then added wryly, "Just remember, we don't line our pockets with gold on this one, but it's damn good community relations. I want it handled well, and more productively than last year, if possible. You bring that off, and I'll put you right at the top of my list of favorite people. Interested?" He cocked an amused eyebrow.

"I could be." She shrugged. Was she interested! To see respect and admiration reflected in the darkly dominating eyes above!

"Good." Ross smiled slowly, reading her intent more clearly than Casey would ever know. "I'll leave you to it, then. As you may have anticipated, Bev is going to take on the dual role of acting as your secretary as well as my own. I'll send her in now to make sure you have everything you need."

At Casey's vague nod of assent he afforded her a brief sardonic smile and disappeared through the outer door of her office. He was replaced momentarily by her new secretary and longtime friend.

Bev subsided into a chair across from Casey, her eyes alight with devilry. "So you finally made it to the office where you really belong. Personally, I think you should have been here all along. That way Quinn wouldn't have had to make that long trek across the hall when he ran out of gas—and ideas."

"He never came across the hall," Casey replied unthinkingly. "I always had to go to his office." When the impact of what she was admitting registered, she felt a discomfiting sense of contrition at the way she was condemning her dead husband.

Sadly, there was no fooling Bev. She'd seen firsthand how Quinn used people, how he'd practically suffocated Spencer Ad before he condescended to look for outside help.

Still, Casey felt compelled to admonish, "Quinn is

gone now, Bev. Whatever went on in the past is water under the bridge." She smiled weakly and then, remembering how Bev had seemed to be in cahoots with Ross in nudging her into this very office, added severely, "You're an old fraud, anyway. You knew I had this job sewn up when I came in last week, and you let me dangle on tenterhooks."

"That's the way Ross wanted it," Bev informed her ruefully. "He said it had to look as if it were your idea. That you'd balk if you thought you had been roped and hog-tied."

The last word came out in a snort of hilarity, and Casey sucked in her breath, unable to squelch the peevish retort forming on her lips.

"We'll see who's been hog-tied," she sputtered. "I was afraid that by my coming here last week, Ross would feel he was being...er...saddled with me. Ha! Little did I know. He led the horse to water, and lo and behold she drank. But if he thinks I'm going to swallow everything he dishes out, I'll—"

"Now, now, dear," Bev soothed. "Don't go getting in an uproar. The boss will have my head if you get in a snit your first day here." Quickly Bev changed to a neutral topic. "How about checking your desk to see if there's anything you think you'll be needing." She glanced pensively at her wristwatch. "Ross is a stickler about idle gossiping, and I really ought to get back to my own desk."

"When did you ever fritter away any time gossiping?" Casey scoffed, but relented and began dutifully pulling out drawers, examining their contents. "Pens, pencils, note paper..." She searched diligently and, when she was satisfied, lifted the telephone to receive a steady dial tone. "Everything seems to be in order, except—" She frowned thoughtfully. "Will you see if you can get me a calculator? Preferably one with a listing tape."

Bev snickered. "What do you need with an adding machine? With your brains, I would have thought you could do ten-digit multiplication in your head."

"Even *I* am not infallible." Casey grinned.

"One calculator coming up," Bev promised humorously, heading back to her own office.

Casey viewed the secretary's retreating back affectionately, then leaned back in the deep, well-padded swivel chair and cast an assessing eye around the office she had come to inherit. Indian-patterned geometric wallpaper adorned the wall behind a plush chocolate-brown sofa. Two oatmeal-colored armchairs sat at either side of the couch, and a heavy walnut coffee table completed the seating area. Resisting the impulse to kick off her shoes and try things out for comfort, she rifled through the folders on her desk and mentally geared down to concentrate on the work laid out for her.

Five minutes later Bev reappeared, a calculator under one arm and a cup of coffee in her free hand. "Two sugars, no cream. Did I remember correctly?" She set the steaming mug of coffee in front of Casey.

"Perfect." Casey was not about to admit that Ross had ordered her to diet. Besides, what harm could two little packets of sugar do? Probably just throw her carbohydrate level all out of kilter for the rest of the day. But then, she hadn't had any breakfast, she reasoned, lifting the aromatic brew to her lips.

A few preparatory phone calls revealed that Ross had been at work greasing her path, calling on accounts assigned to Casey, informing their clients that she would be handling their business from now on, and bestowing accolades as to her ability. Such consideration on the part of her new partner surprised her, and she was lost in contemplative thought when Ross strode breezily through the connecting door between their offices.

"Well, Cassandra? How did it go this morning?" He lifted one shaggy eyebrow. "Feel like you're getting back in the groove?"

"I'll survive," she murmured, staring at him pointedly. "Did you come in for something in particular?"

"Certainly." The amused shaggy eyebrow knitted with its mate at her cool tone. "I came to take you to lunch. Any objections? Purely business, I assure you."

"I wouldn't have it any other way," she inserted tightly.

Ross sighed heavily and shot her an exasperated look. "If we're ever going to get along, you're going to have to stop being so defensive. What's the problem now?"

A reasonable question. What *was* the problem? Surely she didn't imagine she could work with Ross every day without having to see him? "I thought you agreed to call me Casey," she scolded lamely. "I told you I don't care for Cassandra. Nobody ever calls me that."

"I beg your pardon," he dramatized. "Casey it is." Rubbing his chin, he observed musingly, "Somehow you just don't seem like a Casey. It sounds like a man's name. Don't you have any other nicknames?"

"No!" she negated in a flash. "Stretch" was an affectionate title reserved for a chosen few. And Ross wasn't one of them.

"Well then, *Casey*," he conceded, "hustle into the bathroom and freshen up, and we'll be on our way." He inclined his head toward the third door in her office...a door that Casey knew led to the same bathroom they had entered earlier from his office.

"We're going to share a bathroom?"

Ross chuckled at her scandalized tone. "I don't see why not. It's close and—" He paused, a wicked light flickering in his dark eyes.

Casey was still gritting her teeth when she climbed into the passenger seat of his surprisingly conventional Chrysler Cordoba. An unknowing smile curved her lips.

"You find something amusing?" Ross inquired drolly.

At that Casey laughed outright. "I was thinking that you don't seem the type of man to have such an elegant, yet middle-class vehicle." The soft velour upholstery caressed her, and she fingered it appreciatively.

"Thought I'd go in for something a little more impressive, like your classy MG, did you?" he hazarded shrewdly, watching as Casey's amusement changed to dismay. "That's right. I know what kind of car you drive. You'll come to realize eventually that there aren't too many things I *don't* know about you, Cassandra Spencer," Ross advised hardily. "And in answer to your observation, I drive a big car because I'm a big man. A height of six feet four and long legs aren't accommodated well in small vehicles. Neither do clients appreciate being folded in half like a pretzel. And...I don't think it hurts any of us to do our little bit to support the economy by buying American products, if you take my meaning."

Nonplussed, Casey could think of no suitable retort and remained silent until they reached their destination, a small, unpretentious seafood restaurant well known for its excellent cuisine.

"I'd suggest a drink at the bar," Ross murmured as they entered the restaurant, "but since you're reducing, I think we'll go straight in to lunch."

Domineering brute! Casey grumbled, and was incensed when, in trying to elude the guiding hand at the back of her waist, her companion's grasp wandered up to her nape and tightened warningly.

"Be still," Ross commanded. "When I take a lady to lunch, she stays with me."

Add possessive to domineering, she fumed. Unwilling to cause a scene, Casey allowed Ross to escort her to the table where the maître d' was waiting.

"I can recommend the chef's salad here," Ross vouchsafed urbanely as they each perused a menu. "It should fit in quite nicely with your diet, hmm?"

"Fine," Casey gritted. She was thinking more along the lines of the scrumptious-sounding seafood platter with a side of cottage cheese, so ravenous did she feel after skipping breakfast. But there was still that extra pound to get off. "I love salad," she maintained stoically, thinking that she'd consumed enough greens this last week to earn a gold plated rabbit hutch!

When the waiter arrived, Ross ordered the suggested salad for Casey and, to her utter consternation, the coveted seafood platter for himself. Shunning the wine list—probably because of the calories involved, she thought mutinously—he ordered them each a cup of coffee.

"Any questions about the material you went over this morning?" he prompted when their coffee had been served, and admirably refrained from commenting when Casey slapped aside the packet of sugar she had reached for instinctively and instead sprinkled a generous quantity of artificial sweetener into her steaming cup.

"No." She shook her head slowly. "And...uh... thank you for paving the way for me with a few well-placed phone calls," she added graciously.

"Common courtesy, my dear. You have...no questions?"

"Well...I *was* hoping you might fill me in on the tactics you used in upgrading the profits for the children's home during their benefit drive last year."

"A real challenge, isn't it?" Unselfishly Ross set about sharing his various strategies, and when their lunch was served, they attacked their food and the children's benefit with equal relish, blending ideas with the skill of two collaborators long accustomed to pulling for the same team.

Ross looked up just as Casey finished her salad, and found her gaze trailing longingly to his plate of toasted French bread.

"Didn't you have any breakfast?" he questioned perceptively.

"I...uh...no," she admitted self-consciously, and watched, almost drooling, as Ross generously forked several crab legs, two scallops, and a tempting chunk of lobster meat into her empty dish.

"Eat up," he advised humorously, shifting the little container of seafood sauce between them. "We can't have you withering away to nothing."

Never one to look a gift horse in the mouth, Casey wasted no time considering his sudden relenting as to her diet. Spearing a scallop, she moved to dip it into the tangy seafood sauce and then hesitated. It seemed so intimate, dipping into the same container where Ross had dipped, bitten, and then redipped. *Ridiculous,* she chided herself, plunging in. *If you are hungry, why dicker with sensibilities?*

And hungry she was again, soon enough. By the time the hands on her wristwatch had crept around to five in the afternoon, Casey's stomach was once again pressed up against her backbone. She simply was *not* cut out for skimpy meals, no matter what the provocation.

With the firm decision to stop for a substantial, if still carbohydrate-free, dinner on the way home, she picked up the files she had been studying on a successful ad campaign Ross had run recently for a competitor of her hotel account and headed for the file cabinets in the outer office.

Her partner was leaning against just the cabinet she needed.

"Find anything interesting?" Ross inquired blandly, leaning over to read the name on the folder.

"I'm not sure." Casey frowned. "This was a very slick campaign." It was a compliment, briskly delivered, but good work was good work!

"Why, thank you, ma'am." Ross inclined his head modestly, extending one hand to open the required drawer. His arm brushed against Casey's prominent breasts, and she froze, lightning heat flaring down the length of her body. Why did this arrogant devil have to have such a devastating effect on her senses? She felt like a flustered but aware schoolgirl every time Ross moved in too close.

"I beg your pardon" came the throaty drawl. "I guess I ... er ... underestimated your personal space requirements."

Casey flushed and was mercifully thankful that Bev had left for the day and was not there to witness her supreme embarrassment. "I can't help the way I'm built!" she cried defensively.

The folder was taken from her nerveless fingers, set atop the file cabinet, and encircling arms came up behind her shoulders.

"So indignant," Ross murmured, gazing down warmly. Lifting her chin, which was quivering and strangely acquiescent, he husked, "That's right. This is one of those times you have to look up. Let me kiss it better and show you what I think of the way you're built."

Just as she had done the last time Ross kissed her, Casey meant to resist. Her hands, trapped against his chest, set out to push away, but instead wandered up to wrap themselves around the strong neck above as she was once again swept away in a world of heady, dangerous sensations.

The pensive worry lines creasing her forehead were kissed away by his soothing lips, which blazed a trail down to the intoxicatingly bare skin behind each of her sensitive earlobes. And finally her mouth was captured, gently at first, and then with determined persuasion that denied all reason.

Casey shuddered and collapsed into a granite-hard frame as exploring hands roamed up and down the length of her arched back, finally coming to rest at the waistband of her flowing skirt.

"See how good it can be when you let a man show you the way?" Ross murmured into her hair. His nimble fingers went to work loosening the pins in her bun. "This beautiful hair and luscious body!" He pulled her close for one more lingering kiss and then smiled down engagingly. "Give in to me, Casey. Drop the prim exterior and come in tomorrow dressed as the soft, alluring woman I know you to be."

It was a command carefully sugarcoated as flattery, and Casey bristled at his practiced technique, pushing away from the calculating embrace.

How could she have been so stupid? Let down her guard so obligingly? "You conceited, pompous...! I won't be manipulated like some kind of mindless idiot!" She stamped her foot in vexation, drawing Ross's attention to her practical low-heeled footwear.

"And wear some decent shoes," Ross went on, ignoring her outrage. "Legs like yours should be shown off to full advantage. Don't you possess any high heels?"

"You don't put stilts on a giraffe," she flung back. All her shoes had low heels, a leftover concession to Quinn, who, only an inch taller than Casey, had made it clear early in their relationship that he didn't appreciate being eclipsed by a woman.

Ross folded his arms across his powerful chest and studied her through indolent, half-closed eyes. "I wouldn't say a giraffe," he corrected lazily. "More like a graceful gazelle." Anticipating Casey's furious retort, he cut her off with "Just see what you can do in the way of an improvement. If you don't come up to my standards, I'll settle the issue and dress you myself."

That unquestionable threat Casey refused to grace with an answer. Whirling on her heels, she stalked into her own office, furiously forming a plan of attack.

Chapter Three

Once she had satisfied her gnawing hunger with a huge porterhouse steak and an assortment of green vegetables, substituted for a baked potato, at a small fast-service family restaurant, Casey headed for her favorite department store to affect her transformation. No costly designer clothes were needed to produce the effect Ross wanted. Anything clingy and seductive would do, she decided with cynical belligerence.

Armed with several dresses she considered eminently suitable, she went on to the lingerie department in search of her mastermind purchase.

The secret armament in tow, she made an obligatory stop in the shoe department, intent on buying the highest platform heels she could find, and practically laughing herself silly at the young clerk's wary "Are you sure, ma'am? You might get a nosebleed way up there."

Melissa's reaction was much the same later as Casey stood modeling her new garb in her bedroom.

"The dress is really something," Missy effused, admiring the way the slinky red material clung to Casey's womanly shape. "But you look like a skyscraper in those elevator shoes. Are you sure you know what you're doing?"

"I'm sure," Casey replied loftily, turning sideways

toward the mirror to check the four-inch lift of the wooden platform heels.

"What have you done to your breasts!" Missy gasped.

"Minimized them" came the smug rejoinder. "Your dreamy Ross made a few choice innuendos as to their size, and I decided to fight fire with fire. What you see is the new me, suitably de-emphasized."

"What was the matter with this bra?" Missy demanded to know, fingering Casey's old, discarded white wisp lying on the bed.

"Too provocative." Casey lifted one shoulder dismissively.

"You're out of your mind! And I bet Ross will agree with me!"

"We'll see, little sister." Casey's eyes glowed with malicious anticipation. War had been declared!

When she entered Ross's office the next morning, it was to the accompaniment of a long, appreciative wolf whistle.

"God in heaven," he emoted. "I asked for femininity, and I got screaming sensuality. Where did you get that classy little rag?" His eyes wandered speculatively over the enticing red dress.

Casey had chosen the color deliberately. Like waving a red flag in front of a bull, she thought defiantly. "I take it you approve?"

Apparently Ross wasn't ready to go that far. "Well, it's an improvement, anyway. Except for the shoes, that is. I mentioned a more flattering heel. I don't recall recommending you buy something that makes you look like you're teetering on two launch pads, about to take off in orbit."

Casey lifted her chin haughtily, determined to resist his mockery. "I'm ready for the weigh-in any time you are."

"Confident little devil this morning, aren't you? By all means, lead the way."

She slipped out of the chunky shoes, which must have weighed a pound or more each, and headed for the scales, sublimely sure of herself. As she expected, she weighed in at exactly one hundred and thirty pounds.

"You made it. Very commendable," Ross murmured from behind her.

Squaring her shoulders smartly, Casey stared at her now trimmer sideways reflection in the wall-to-wall mirror over the sink.

Ross did the same, and his eyes widened in astonishment when he noticed her flatter, almost indistinguishable bustline. A string of savage oaths literally turned the air blue. "What in the *hell* have you done to your breasts!"

Such vehemence! Casey shivered convulsively under his wrath. In a tiny little voice that in no way resembled her usual confident tone, she told him, "Since you object to the voluptuous look, I've played down what there was an overabundance of."

"How?"

"With . . . with a brassiere known for its minimizing effects."

"Minimizing!" he rapped out. "I've got to see this miracle of engineering that cut Venus down to size!"

"No!" Casey made an instinctive grab for the front of her dress, trying to ward him off as Ross hooked his fingers under the elasticized neckline. "Get your hands off me!" she demanded indignantly.

"Be still!" he ground out. "I'm trying to make a professional evaluation, and you're as well covered as you would be in a swim top. It's this atrocity of a brassiere I'm trying to fathom. After years in the modeling industry, I thought I'd seen everything in women's lingerie!"

"Then go satisfy your curiosity with the plastic mannequin in the department store where I bought the damn thing," she gasped, struggling to break out of his hold as his fingers explored the intricate wiring of the formidable undergarment. "I won't be treated like this!"

"Damn ingenious!" came the grudging admiration. "But I don't like it. Breasts like these are meant to be admired, not bound into obscurity."

Casey's fruitless struggles only succeeded in bringing her closer to Ross, and the warm fragrance of masculinity combined with the magical spell of his questing hand flooded her senses, crowding out all thoughts of revolt. A low groan she finally recognized as her own escaped her throat and her lashes fluttered open, encountering an all-knowing stare. Powerless to resist, she allowed herself to be pulled into the enemy camp.

"God, Cassandra!" Ross slipped her dress back into place, his eyes roaming over her troubled features to settle on her nervously moistened lips.

She watched in helpless fascination as he lowered his head, lifting and shaping her nape to receive his hovering mouth. At the last minute she closed her eyes, afraid she would see male triumph and mockery reflected at her.

"That's right, close your eyes," Ross encouraged. "You don't need to see anything. All you have to do is feel. It's been too long since you've felt anything. Too long since you've been alive. Let me bring you back to life."

The first touch of his lips was so light, Casey almost melted with relief, certain she would be able to resist his strong male magnetism.

Ever so gently Ross played with her mouth, first coaxing, then nibbling, until her whole body grew soft and yielding in his arms. Drawing back slightly, he cradled her head in his hands and brushed his thumbs over her throbbing lips.

"Trust me, honey. I'm not going to hurt you. Just thaw you out a little. Think of it as a pleasant rebirth of your natural warm spirit. Necessary but painless." His eyes glittered with amusement and lusty intent. "Such a beautiful mouth, and so much more attractive when it isn't hurling insults. Show me what you can do with these enticing lips."

Casey shook her head in mute denial, but his hand tightened in her hair, overruling her, making her nod yes. This time the lips that descended were firm, much more insistently persuasive, and she began to squirm, desperately afraid Ross would push her beyond the exquisite warmth he had promised until she ignited into a roaring blaze.

Widening his stance, Ross flattened her restless hips with a quelling hand across her rounded bottom and pulled her intimately into his stirring length.

She stiffened when she realized the extent of his arousal, murmuring an almost incoherent "Please, Ross!"

"I am pleasing you," he growled. "Loosen up a little bit. It feels like I'm embracing the Eiffel Tower."

"I can't—"

Her words were cut off as, taking advantage of her parted lips, Ross's tongue entered her mouth with all the cunning of a patiently waiting predator.

Casey shuddered and allowed a much more experienced leader to take charge of the erotic confrontation, molding herself beneath Ross's directing caresses as he guided them to an all-consuming, passionate mutuality of discovery. A blackness as deep as the heated cavern of his mouth was threatening to overwhelm her, and her arms were clinging wantonly to his neck when Ross finally slowed the involvement, releasing the sweet moistness of her mouth with tender little kisses of promise.

For timeless seconds they simply stared into each other's eyes until slowly, self-consciously, Casey allowed her arms to disentangle from around his neck and fall to her sides.

"You're really something when you get going," Ross observed huskily. "Who would have thought you'd turn on so beautifully in my arms? Eiffel Tower indeed! More like the Towering Inferno!"

The dry, teasing note in his voice goaded Casey out of her sensual lethargy. "Was this all part of a predetermined plan to bring me to my knees at the great Ross Allen's feet?"

"Not in the office, anyway," he barked with a shout of laughter.

"Not anywhere!" she swore frostily, incensed now and mortified at the abandoned way she had responded to his advance.

"You're a stunning woman when you're aroused, brown eyes. Fighting mad or sexually alive, either way it's about time you came out of your shell. I'm delighted to have been the instigator."

"Don't be so damn smug. It won't happen again!"

"So confident," he taunted, eyeing her heaving chest. "You shouldn't make declarations built on such shaky foundations."

"And stop patronizing me! Who the hell do you think you are, Robert Redford? Just because I responded to you doesn't mean I'm—"

"Starved for sex?" he put in wryly. "Suffocated by your widow's weeds? Don't look so shocked, Casey. I told you, you've been hiding your vibrant colors for too long." Ignoring her derisive snort, he continued as if reasoning with a mulish child. "And about Robert Redford.... He may be one macho hombre, but his stature is a bit on the small size for you. You need a man you can look up to at all times."

"Well, don't look in the mirror," she bit out. "You've got to be the most overconfident, egotistical man I've ever had the misfortune to meet. I must have been out of my mind to think we could ever work together."

"We'll work together fine," he assured her lazily. "In fact, it's a shame you waited so long to come back. Despite what you may think, I would have welcomed you several years ago. Maybe with even more open arms, since you would have had a husband around to keep you in line."

"Oh!" Casey choked on his last words, delivered deliberately, she was certain, to get a rise out of her. "Quinn never 'kept me in line,' as you so ridiculously put it. As if I would stand for such a thing!"

"More's the pity," Ross drawled. "A firebrand like you needs a strong man to keep her on the straight and narrow."

"You're insufferable!" He had proposed this chauvinistic line of reasoning once before, and it was even more galling the second time around!

Ross grinned hugely, not the least disarmed by her causticness. "Ready to lay down your ammunition, brown eyes? I don't think either of us is going to come out the victor in this little shooting match. Let's call it a draw and declare a truce, hmm?"

Maddeningly the devilish man was right. Nothing further was to be gained by taking cheap shots at each other. "Whatever you say," she conceded, put out. Ross Allen needed to be taken down a peg or two, and she was just the woman to do it!

"I knew you were a bright gal," Ross assayed dryly. "Since you're being so reasonable, I know you aren't going to object to the introductory session I've scheduled this afternoon with an old friend of mine. My friend is a designer. A dress designer," he stressed. "We've worked well together in the past."

"I most certainly do object!"

"Ahhh, I was afraid it was too good to be true. Why make such a fuss? The company will spring for a new wardrobe."

"That's absurd!" she exclaimed, temporarily thrown off her mettle. "If anyone is going to pay for my working apparel, it will be me." *And on my own terms!* she thought defiantly, for in all honesty, Casey had been considering augmenting the meager offerings of her closet. She had shopped disinterestedly at best during the last few years, and more and more she was coming to realize how heavily Quinn had influenced her taste in clothing. The severity in cut and style that had pleased her husband during her prior tenure at Spencer Ad was becoming monotonously repetitive three years later, her disenchantment growing daily as she riffled through uninspired coordinates hanger by hanger every morning.

Yet the overstated sexuality of the clingy dresses she had purchased to taunt Ross were not her cup of tea either. What she needed, she owned slowly, was the talented insight of an artist who could define the real Casey. What she needed, she decided with sudden inspiration, was the masterful Sid Charles, the Dior of California designers. And even Ross Allen couldn't deliver the Wizard of Wilshire Boulevard in one day.

Feeling a jubilant sense of reprieve after her abstracted woolgathering, Casey turned to Ross and purred, "The only designer I'll ever consider working with is Sid Charles." The much-sought-after magician was probably booked months in advance, she thought smugly. And *she* wasn't going to do the running. Let Ross wrangle for an appointment! "When you've managed to procure a little time with Mr. Charles, let me know," she invited sweetly, flashing Ross a modestly triumphant smile.

"Will two o'clock suit you?"

"What?"

"Sid will be here at two," Ross specified with an unabashed grin, belatedly revealing the identity of his old friend.

"You set me up!" Casey's furious hiss had all the earmarks of a hot-air balloon suddenly pierced of its buoyancy.

No admission of guilt was needed, Ross's grin never wavered.

"I'll get you for this!" she threatened darkly.

"I quake at the very thought," he came back good-naturedly.

Resorting to an increasingly frequent habit of gritting her teeth, Casey whirled and stomped into her own office, slamming the door with a furious, infinitely satisfying gesture of pure childish rage.

She worked in concentrated silence all morning, stopping only for a fortifying and still low-carbohydrate lunch of broiled chicken from the company cafeteria.

At precisely two o'clock the intercom buzzed and she was summoned into the next office.

"Cassandra Spencer"—Ross motioned her over to his informal seating area—"meet Sid Charles. Casey asked for you specifically," Ross informed his old friend.

The pudgy little man's grin was infectious, and Casey returned his friendly greeting, extending her hand as Sid rose from the couch. The Wizard of Wilshire Boulevard looked much more suited to the role of Santa Claus, she reflected wryly. All he lacked was the red velvet suit. In her platform shoes, Casey stood an easy six inches over his rounded frame.

Sid gazed up worshipfully, obviously entranced at the notion of dressing such a stately spectacle of womanhood. "Enchanted, my dear." Accepting her hand, he pressed his lips above her wrist in the manner of an old-world gentleman. "It will be a pleasure dressing you," he said enthusiastically. His designer eyes roved over her assessingly. "Yes, indeed! A real pleasure."

"Did you bring that little item I mentioned?" Ross broke in.

"That I did." Sid smiled and reached into his pocket, pulling out a small tissue-wrapped parcel. "Thirty-four C, I think you said." He handed the package to Casey, his eyes moving searchingly to her bustline. "I should think it will make a vast improvement. I'm appalled at the atrocities these young women disfigure themselves with." He threw Casey an audacious wink. "You stick with me, young lady. I've been dressing ladies since you were crawling on the floor in a diaper."

Casey peered into the tissue-wrapped offering, and the lid flew off her temper. She rounded on Ross, incensed. To the shock of both men and herself most of all, she burst out with the uncharacteristically profane "Why you impertinent, sanctimonious jackass! Dammit, Ross! How dare you presume to ask a man I don't even know to bring me a—a *brassiere*!"

Ross was containing his laughter with the greatest of difficulty. "Crudity doesn't become you, Cassandra. Watch it, or you may find yourself hanging over the sink, getting your mouth washed out with soap."

"You dare!"

"Oh, I dare," he said, chuckling. His eyes narrowed on her furious features. "And I'll dare a lot more if you don't get a move on. Sid's time is valuable and he can't measure you accurately until your curves are displayed in their proper arrangement. Either you hustle on into the bathroom and change into that item you're holding, or sure as hell I'm going to give you a helping hand.''

Her head held high, Casey flounced off in a huff, not at all sure Ross wouldn't do as he threatened and affect the lingerie change himself. But she'd have a thing or two to say about the clothes they ordered, she vowed determinedly, standing before the mirror to view the flesh-colored seamless bit of froth the esteemed dress designer had deemed appropriate. The bra was so transparent and unrestricting, it was almost obscene. The clothes she ordered would *not* be so blatantly obvious!

When Casey stepped back into the office, she found Ross and his friend fingering bolts of many hued fabrics. Swiftly she found herself draped in an array of interesting possibilities. To her dismay she was soon caught up in the mood of creativity.

"Such beautiful long legs," Sid enthused. His eyes flicked down the length of her calves, stopping at her chunky high heels. "With the right shoes, the length of these coltish legs will flow beautifully with the line of my dresses." He kissed his fingers in a typically French gesture. "Just so."

Casey rubbed a silky mauve floral print between her fingers, a brilliant plot beginning to form in her mind. "Sid," she began tentatively, calculatingly, "isn't it a shame your forte rests exclusively with dresses. Think what you could do with a long length of leg and just the right fabric. The possibilities are challenging, wouldn't you say?" Carefully she molded the material to the shape of her leg.

The obliging little wizard rose quickly to her subtle challenge. "But of course, my lovely. Your head is beautiful but not filled with fluff, is that not so? In a pants costume you will be my pièce de résistance. Yes, indeed!" He rubbed his hands together, his eyes fairly gleaming with anticipation.

"Don't you think I'm a little too...fat, Sid?" Casey pursued, thrilled by the success of her inventiveness and greedily hoping to add frosting to the cake.

"Who uttered this sacrilege!" the little man demanded incredulously.

Like a kitten that has just feasted on a saucer of cream, Casey turned to Ross, unconsciously licking her lips as if she could still taste the sweetness lingering there.

Ross was leaning languidly against the edge of his desk, arms folded absently across his chest. His eyes reflected amusement and—yes—uncamouflaged respect for Casey's ingenuity. Trapping her flashing eyes in a fixing gaze, he murmured, "I agree, Sid. In her present shape my cohort is one formidable lady." He made no mention of her rigorous diet, but rather surprisingly added, "And a few tasteful pants costumes will make a welcome addition to her wardrobe, I should think. Most appropriate for the considerable amount of entertaining Casey and I will be called upon to do this fall."

Ross was at his urbane best, and Casey could not help but admire as he nodded and smiled at his friend.

"I think we're pretty much in agreement as to style and color," he continued. "Sid, why don't you jot down Casey's measurements and get back to me later in the week, and we'll discuss what you've come up with."

Get back to *him*! "Now, just a darn minute!" Casey jumped in. "I'm paying for all this, and if anyone is going to be consulted, it will be me!"

Sid had the grace to look uncomfortable, locating her waistline and sliding the tape measure down accordingly. "But, my dear," he inserted, "Ross is an unquestioned connoisseur. I've been dressing his women for years."

Casey's eyes bulged at *his women*, and she maintained a militant silence while Sid finished his calculations.

Ross saw the designer out and then sprawled lazily on the couch, eyeing her with open amusement. "All right, brown eyes, out with it. You're about to explode with whatever bee you've got in your bonnet."

And explode she did! "Damn you, Ross! I wouldn't be your woman if you were the last man on the face of the earth!"

A small smile played around his mouth and he inclined his head toward the plush chair at his right. "Sit down, Cassandra. I don't recall asking you to be my woman. Yet," he added meaningfully.

"Ever!" she indicated fiercely, flouncing down in the proffered chair.

"We'll see," Ross murmured dryly.

At that she reiterated, "We most certainly will not, you *beast*!"

They eyed each other in silence, dark masculine eyes full of mirth and brilliant feminine ones glittering with challenge and anger. Gradually Casey's fury gave way to something more akin to nervousness as she entreated, "I don't want Sid or anyone else to get the wrong idea about our relationship. And I can see where he might have. How did you make such an accurate guess about my bra size?"

"It wasn't a guess. Like Sid said, I'm a connoisseur of fine women. And when I get as close to one as I was to you this morning..." He let his words trail off suggestively, and Casey bristled.

"It won't happen again!"

"Time will tell. You weren't as unwilling as you like to let on." He waited for the full import of his words to settle and then added, "You and I are going to make quite a team."

"In the office I'm sure we will," she agreed tightly.

Then, remembering another disquieting observation Ross had made earlier, she prodded, "What was that little ditty you mentioned about you and I entertaining together? You wine and dine your clients, and I'll take care of my own!"

"And the important ones we'll entertain together." Ross was not making any pretense at suggestion; he was stating how it was going to be.

"You don't think I have the panache to entertain important clients alone?"

"My God, you're a perverse creature. Panache be damned!" he bit out. "I'm talking about practicalities, woman. Can you see yourself throwing ambitious parties in that little dollhouse on the beach?"

"I imagine my parents will be only too happy to let me use their home any time needs dictate," she replied coolly.

"But you won't. Any grand-scale entertaining will be done in *my* home, with you acting as my hostess."

"You have a suitably impressive abode?" she inquired drolly, knowing full well that Ross had a beautiful home in the fashionable Palos Verdes Estates area, not far from where she lived.

"I get by." He shrugged unimportantly.

Naturally! Ross was not given to boasting. From what Casey had heard, his home was a glittering showplace well suited to high-class social gatherings.

"You've been entertaining on your own for quite a while now," she pointed out logically. "I don't see why you need me all of a sudden."

"You don't see a lot of things," Ross declared enigmatically, and Casey had the strangest conviction that he was talking way over her head. "Didn't I give in over my long-time prejudice against women in pants? I can even see myself relenting to the point of allowing you to wear Sid's pants creations to the office occasionally, providing he lives up to his reputation and comes up with something agreeably feminine.''

Allowing rankled, and Casey was about to tell him so when Ross continued. ''Of course, I'm going to make sure *I* get something out of the deal.'' His confident smile was goading. ''Dresses will be the mainstay of your new wardrobe.''

''If they're adorned with flounces and frills, I'll take them home and recycle them into dustrags!'' Casey threatened heatedly.

''So ferocious.'' He chuckled, patting the couch beside him. ''Why don't you come over here, my tigress, and we'll see about dulling those sharp little claws.''

''Hell would have to freeze over first!'' Casey scrambled to her feet, alarmed at the prospect of finding herself in those dangerous, controlling arms once again. ''Just remember what I said,'' she implored. ''You can't have everything your own way. If I don't like your choice of outfits, I won't wear them. Or pay for them either!''

''I'll remember,'' he voiced dryly. ''You'll get second turndown on Sid's initial sketches. Scout's honor.''

True to his word, Ross called her into his office late Friday afternoon. Exhausted but supremely content after her first productive week back at work, Casey had all but forgotten their appointment with Sid Charles.

Ross's desk was covered with high-fashion sketches and assorted fabric swatches. To one side rested a second neatly stacked pile of designer drawings, and her brow rose inquiringly.

''The ones I didn't like,'' Ross enlightened.

And just where she wanted to start, Casey decided judiciously. To her chagrin she found that the small pile of rejected possibilities didn't appeal to her either. Not even one sketch.

''Ready to get down to business now?'' Ross smiled

knowingly, acknowledging her gesture of independence.

Just as Casey had anticipated, Ross had already made up his mind as to what suited his fancy, and the bargaining and trade-off session that ensued—coordinating fabrics with drawings, assessing winning combinations—was nothing if not lively and vociferous, to the point where poor Sid looked positively wilted by the time they were all in agreement.

"How much is all this going to cost me?" Casey interposed, almost as weary as Sid but secretly delighted with the new clothes she was ordering.

"For Ross, I make a special price," Sid declared proudly. "After all, I have been—"

"Dressing his women for years." Casey cut him off crisply. "But I am not one of his women," she maintained bitterly, staunchly. "This time your good friend Ross will *not* be footing the bill. This is a professional expenditure for which *I* will be paying." She arched a delicate brow at the flustered designer. "Now, how much?"

Sid named a figure considerably below what Casey considered equitable for high-fashion couture, but she shrugged philosophically when she encountered Ross's narrow-eyed warning, then extended her hand graciously to seal the agreement. She *had* gotten her own way, for the most part, as to how she would be dressing in the future. No use pushing her luck.

As soon as Sid left she made to retreat into her own office.

"Not so fast!" Clasping her elbow in a biting grip, Ross steered her back to his desk. "Sit down!" he barked. "You and I have a few things to discuss."

No sooner had Ross hunched into his own chair when he exploded into an angry tirade. "If you must turn your guns on someone, I'd appreciate it if you would steer clear of my oldest and most worthy of friends. I have never seen Sid at such a loss for words!"

"At least he knows where things stand as far as you and I are concerned," Casey retorted.

"Can you really be that thickheaded? Allow me to point out that none of my female employees have ever batted so much as an eyelash when I paid for their required wardrobes. By raising such a ruckus, you've succeeded in raising myriad unanswered questions in Sid's mind. 'My women,' to Sid, means the countless number of ladies in my working stables. Right now he's probably wondering where the hell you fit into the picture. Instead of seeing you as my business partner, he's probably got you pegged as my female paramour, chafing under the yoke of being dressed to fit the part."

"But I—"

"Didn't think," Ross concluded harshly. "You were too busy playing the independent, unconquerable career woman!"

"That isn't true," Casey averred quietly.

She was stunned by the bitterness evident in his tone, and even more bewildered when he grated, "Well, you'll have to deal with Sid's uncertainties by yourself next week. He promised to do a rush job and have a few things ready for preliminary fittings next Friday, and I'm going to be out of town at the time."

"Where are you going?" Casey asked with great interest, reeling at the discovery that she was going to be deserted after only one week in the harness.

"East" came the one-word, uncommunicative reply.

"Oh."

"Don't say you're going to miss me," Ross sneered. "You might choke on the unpalatable words."

On Saturday morning as she lounged on the beach, Casey pondered Ross's parting shot. She *was* going to

miss him, she admitted reluctantly. After their passionate skirmish in the bathroom early in the week, she had
found it increasingly difficult to focus on Ross as
merely a business associate. Curse the thought, he was
beginning to appeal to her on a much more personal,
primitive level, and it was courting disaster to consider
such an involvement.

Ross was too dangerous, too forcefully the dominant
male. And it was too soon! She needed time—years,
maybe—to recover from the shambles of a marriage
that had evaporated last year. If she could ever learn to
trust again, it would be a man of careful choosing. A
man who wouldn't pose any unnerving threats. A man
she could handle. A man the direct opposite of Ross
Allen!

Still, must they constantly be at loggerheads? Was
there no way she and Ross could meet each other halfway? Avoid any more ugly scenes like the one that had
mushroomed out of control yesterday?

Was it *she* who was stirring up the water? Casey ruminated later as she taxied her sister into town for a
haircut. Had she been stubborn beyond reason, antago-
nizing Ross at every turn?

It was an unpleasant hypothesis, a possibility that
Casey endeavored to banish from the forefront as she
watched Melissa's wispy curls submit to their once-a-
month shaping.

Her gaze strayed idly around the unisex salon, taking
in the industrious efforts of several busy stylists, and
then focused on an unlikely looking maestro creating a
masterpiece two chairs down from Melissa.

Excitement splintered through Casey's veins as she
watched the magical transformation. Glossy brown hair
much like her own was being coaxed, with each snip of
the stylist's scissors, into shiny, layered strands of exquisite animation. The overall effect was so daring, so

utterly breathtaking, Casey fingered her prim little bun and knew she must succumb to the pull of this challenge; knew she had found a halfway measure Ross would revel in and she would adore.

An exotic jungle creature stared back at her from the mirror some time later, half tame, half unbridled bewitchment, and Casey knew she had placed her trust well. Entranced, she nodded her approval as the stylist ruffled his fingers through his creation, demonstrating how the short feathered layers at each side fell instantly into place when released, flowing sleekly in line with the beautiful lioness pelt left in longer layers at the back.

Melissa's enchanted "Geez, Stretch! Is that really you?" gave eloquent testimony to Casey's potent new spell.

An olive branch had been fashioned that day, a stunning, uplifting concession to Ross. If he chose to accept the gesture in the self-rewarding, peace-making spirit it was given, Casey would be suitably gracious. But if he chose to crow over his victory, jabbing the needle into her submission on one of their bones of contention— her back-country librarian image—she would, quite understandably, be forced to be on the defensive. She would, Casey decided, simply point out that the stylist had layered the sides too short to be smoothed into a businesslike bun.

Casey entered the office with guarded trepidation on Monday morning. Either way Ross reacted, however, she was thrilled with her decision to update her appearance. The sleek tigress mane gave her a tremendous boost in morale, as did the many admiring glances that followed her entrance.

It came as a distinct disappointment to discover that Ross was spending the day at his modeling agency, but she geared up afresh to face him the next morning, knowing he would have to put in an appearance and chair the staff meeting scheduled at ten.

"You're not going to believe your new partner," Casey heard Bev preparing Ross in the outer office. "She's—"

"Transformed herself into a goddess," Ross breathed reverently, arriving at her doorway.

Whatever Casey had expected, it was not this open-mouthed wonder. "Do you like it?" she posed tentatively, turning in a graceful circle.

"Like it!" Ross found the verb inanely dilute. "It's gorgeous. You're gorgeous!" No crowing, no needling, just deeply absorbed male admiration. He did not choose to fathom her motive in pleasing him but simply continued to glory in the outcome, letting handful after handful of silky, feathered tresses float through his fingers.

"It was a true artist who did this" were his only added words, but they were poignantly sufficient, as was the lingering, appreciative brush of his mouth over Casey's smiling lips.

Meeting Ross halfway had proved more rewarding than she dared hope. Casey basked in his warmly approving regard as he escorted her to the staff room and set the stage for her introduction.

"No doubt many of you will remember Cassandra Spencer," he began. "Her reputation here has lived on during the years of her absence." Ross cleared his throat, every inch the top man in charge, demanding unqualified attention. "Cassandra is stepping into the position of second in command at Spencer-Allen. First in command when I'm gone, as I will be for the rest of this week. I trust you will all treat her accordingly." The hard gleam in his eye promised swift retribution should he hear otherwise.

Naturally there were smiles of assent all around. No one questioned the indomitable Ross Allen. But Casey was pleased to note that the smiles seemed warm and genuine, not prompted by intimidation. She breathed a soft sigh of relief. The staff had no reservations in accepting her leadership. Partly out of respect for Quinn, she was sure, but she would not let them down.

By Friday Casey had toured every department personally, determined to encounter as many employees as possible on a casual basis and establish herself as a friendly, sympathetic ear in management.

After her late-morning fitting session with Sid Charles, she treated herself to a two-hour lunch break, luxuriating, now that her weight had stabilized, in a sinfully decadent feast of lasagna, garlic bread, and a huge wedge of cherry pie.

Some attentive shopping came next. New shoes were an absolute necessity to go with the stylish wardrobe he was creating, Sid had discreetly insisted.

The silence from the office next door was almost deafening when Casey returned. Except for a few brief moments after the staff meeting Tuesday morning, when Ross had filled her in on what she could expect during his absence, there had not been one iota of activity in the large office next to hers all week, and Casey was anxiously awaiting the return of her mentor.

Her wistful sigh coincided with her secretary's quiet entrance. Setting a tray bearing Casey's afternoon coffee to one side on her desk, Bev grinned and commented astutely, "I see you're missing the boss as much as the rest of us."

"Ross hasn't even bothered to call," she dismissed lightly. "How could I possibly miss him?"

"He called this morning," Bev informed her. "You were on another line at the time."

"Oh." The disappointed note in Casey's voice completely belied her pretense of studied disinterest. "When is our esteemed leader coming back?"

"Late this afternoon," Bev retorted. "And you don't fool me for a minute, Cassandra Spencer! You've missed your counterpart, no matter how much you may pretend otherwise. Do you think I haven't noticed the magnetic attraction between you and Ross? The way you feed off each other's creativity? I never knew where I would find either of you last week; you were in each other's offices constantly, bouncing ideas back and forth, blending inspirations, discussing techniques that had worked in the past...." She paused, her shrewd eyes missing nothing as Casey flicked at an imaginary speck of lint on her skirt. "Come out of the clouds, girl! You and Ross are naturals together."

Natural what? Casey mused, tracking her secretary's disgruntled departure through an absentminded haze. Natural adversaries came to mind, and she smiled, realizing it was an oversimplification. She and Ross *did* work well together, just as Bev maintained.

A shiver of anticipation ran up her spine. Ross wouldn't fly all the way east without strong motivation. What juicy victory was he bringing home for Spencer-Allen?

Keyed up for the rest of the day, it was therefore somewhat of an anticlimax for Casey when Ross still hadn't put in an appearance by five thirty. If she lingered any longer, it would seem as if she were waiting for him and she was loathe to appear so anxious. Monday morning would have to be soon enough to hear about his adventures of the last few days, she decided dispiritedly, climbing into her faithful MG to head home.

Chapter Four

Casey was in her tiny kitchen the next afternoon, cleaning up after a snacking raid by her sister's always-hungry compatriots, when the telephone rang.

"Shirker!" a loud voice boomed when she lifted the receiver. "I came home yesterday bursting with my news, only to discover you were too lazy to wait around for me."

"Now, just a darn minute—"

"Save it," Ross fairly shouted. "I want to talk to you. *Today!* How long will it take you to get over here? I'm at home."

"I can't just leave," she protested laughingly. "I've got a beach full of teenagers here. My parents went to Balboa for the day, and I promised I'd stick around as unofficial chaperon."

"Bring the kids along!" he invited exuberantly. "I want to see you now! Have you got a pencil? I'll give you directions."

Instinctively Casey reached for a pad and pencil, furiously jotting down the careful instructions. As soon as Ross finished dictating she broke in, "But, Ross, I—"

The infuriating devil didn't even hear her out. With a solicitous "See you in about an hour," he broke the connection, leaving Casey to gape at the receiver.

"Got a problem?" Missy's boyfriend, Chuck, inquired, filching a Coke from her refrigerator.

"Six feet four of one," she said ruefully. "My... uh... partner wants me to join him for a little impromptu meeting, and I promised the folks I'd stick around and keep an eye on you guys." She paused meditatively. "Ross just lives up the way in the Palos Verdes Estates, and he said I could bring you along, but—"

"A cinch," Chuck agreed affably, snapping his fingers. "Hey, gang," he shouted out the door, "round up the vans. We're going for a little joyride." Grabbing up Casey's directions, he headed out to organize the caravan.

Casey barely had time to change from her skimpy, saltwater-faded bikini into a more chic, less provocative, one-piece swimsuit, grabbing a Hawaiian print coverup along the way, before she was hustled into Chuck's van.

To her acute relief, Missy's boyfriend drove at a surprisingly sedate pace in the lead, negating her fear that the three-van procession, sixteen teenagers and one ruefully consenting adult, might arrive at Ross's front door with a squealing police escort. The impetuosity of teenagers had long since earned her uncompromising respect.

At his urbane best, and not the least condescending, Ross led the lively group down to his tennis court, magnanimously unlocking his recreation room and offering free use of the tennis equipment, pinball machine, Ping-Pong tables, and pool table.

Then, with the uncanny ease of one leader spotting another, he sized up Chuck as the dean of the young group and murmured, "I trust you'll see things don't get out of hand, son?"

"Hey, man." Chuck grinned. "You can count on

me! This is one fantastic scene. We'll be careful. That's a promise!''

Reassured, Ross turned to Casey and smiled beguilingly. "Let's leave the youngsters to it, then."

She gave a visible start at his cryptic words.

"Relax," he chided. "Where we're going, we'll be able to see through the glass doors and into the rec room...and down to the tennis court as well." His warm gaze wandered with undisguised interest over her sarong-wrapped figure, up to the green straps of her swimsuit, then on to the windblown disarray of her exotic new hairstyle.

"My enchanting tigress," he whispered for her ears alone. "You're even more lovely than the vision I carried with me to New York." His fingers tunneled under her hair, snapping her swimsuit straps playfully as he turned her toward the patio. "Maybe we'll even join the kids for a romp in the pool later, hmm?"

Too bemused to protest, Casey smiled and allowed herself to be led up to the sun-room at the back of his house, a room that overlooked the whole of his property. Furnished much like her own bedroom, with white wicker furniture and the color green predominating throughout, it was a friendly, restful room. Once she had assured herself that the kids couldn't get into any unobserved mischief, Casey began to relax—temporarily.

It wasn't long before Ross pounced.

"Aren't you anxious to hear what I've been up to this week?" he demanded boyishly.

"The mind boggles at the possibilities," Casey teased, rolling her eyes heavenward.

"Well, then? Ask me!"

"What great coup did you accomplish this week, oh great one?" she said dutifully.

"Madison Limited," Ross supplied smugly, leaning

back in his seat, his hands folded in reverent anticipation.

He was not to be disappointed.

"What?" Casey shrieked. "The sportswear giant of the east? How did you hook that mouth-watering fish?"

Ross smiled with clear relish, delighted by her breathless response. "I hooked them, if I may be so immodest, with my immense personal charm."

Casey didn't doubt it for a minute!

"Also," he went on wryly, "with a lot of sweat and plain hard work. I've been studying their trends for the last year. As you probably know, up until now they've done business exclusively along the Atlantic seaboard. Armed with a briefcase full of carefully prepared ammunition, I descended to convince them the west couldn't survive without their leadership in the sportswear field. And our persuasive advertising, of course."

"Just like that?"

"Not quite," he admitted ruefully. "It took a lot of convincing, and in the end I had to agree to a weighty concession." His eyes narrowed thoughtfully on Casey's pensive face. "The upshot of the whole thing is, I agreed to a sort of . . . fashion show. A preview of what they will be offering this fall."

"When is this glittering event to take place?" she inquired interestedly.

"Two weeks from tomorrow."

Casey's eyes widened into huge brown pools, and he nodded. "That's right; it doesn't give us much time. That's why I wanted you over here today. We've got a lot of work to do between now and two Sundays hence."

"Where are you going to pull off this coup de grace?" she interposed, mentally calculating the amount of work involved.

"Right here." Ross grinned, waving an arm to indicate their surroundings. "Or rather, for the most part, out by the pool. I thought it would make an impressive backdrop. Next spring's sportswear displayed in the graceful environs of Southern California backyard affluence. What do you think?"

"I don't think you can pull it off with a scant two weeks' preparation," she said with great conviction.

"On the contrary," Ross disagreed. "With two of us working together, it should be a piece of cake."

"But I've got to get rolling on the children's benefit!"

"Do I seem like the kind of man who would make unfair demands?" His tone was placating. "You help me on this one, and I'll work right beside you when you need help with the children's drive."

So much for having that baby all to herself, Casey mused. Ross was not going to be swayed. "I've never organized a fashion show," she attempted weakly.

"Ah, but I have. And with my own modeling agency, and their very capable director behind us..."

"Won't they be booked, with only two weeks' notice?"

"Hey, brown eyes! Don't rain on my parade. Why do you think I opted for a Sunday? My models are dedicated, and at double pay they'd work for me on Easter Sunday if I asked them." He frowned meditatively. "I had to consider buyers as well. They're also likely to be booked with appointments weeks in advance. That's why I decided on a Sunday. It's a bit unorthodox, but for a chance to preview Madison Limited's debut west of the Mississippi, we'll get the buyers out."

At Casey's continued reticence, he conceded, "I'll admit we're going to be working close to the wire. But in this business you have to strike while the iron is hot. Madison felt that if he was going to break into the west, he would be at a disadvantage if he delayed any longer. In the garment industry orders are booked well in advance of the coming seasons."

"It is a challenge," Casey found herself agreeing. "And the setting is idyllic." She gazed admiringly at the beautiful grounds spread out below. Lush green grass and privacy-screening junipers and native shrubs rose dramatically from the tennis court up to the flagstone-paved pool and patio area. Huge clay pots filled with dwarf palms and lacy ferns were scattered around a swimming pool that could only be described as a rich man's dream. The pool wandered an impressive length of at least forty feet, curving around rock formations and flaring into exotic seating areas of sculptured underwater benches. The water, smooth as glass and extremely placid-looking with its lack of swimmers, was crystal clear with a bluish cast and looked extremely inviting.

"Like it?" Ross questioned huskily. Rolling to his feet, he reached for Casey and pulled her up beside him. "Come on, let's go down and see if the kids want to go for a swim."

Missy and her friends were only too ready for a cooling dip, and soon all forty feet of glistening water were alive and choppy with their antics.

"Shall we?" Ross turned to Casey and pulled his white knit sport shirt over his head. His hands went to the zipper of his slacks, and the suggestive way he tugged it down caused Casey to turn away in distress. Caressing hands dug into her shoulders as Ross leaned over to whisper, "A swim, Cassandra. I was just suggesting a swim. How you *do* go on!"

She was helped out of her concealing sarong and, through careful management, didn't look at Ross's near-naked body as he led her to the edge of the pool. Executing a neat little dive, she strove to put as much distance as possible between herself and her mocking host.

Soon the infectiousness of the noisy throng caught up with Casey and she found herself embroiled in a lively game of swimming pool volleyball after Ross produced a net and stretched it across the width of the pool.

Complaining vehemently about being shoved into the deep end while all her female counterparts splashed on the opposite side of the net in much shallower water, she was laughingly overruled when Chuck hooted, "Hey, come on, Stretch. Us big drinks of water have to stick together. Would you let us get beaten by a bunch of midgets?"

"Right, *Stretch,*" a husky voice drawled next to her ear. "You wouldn't want to be defeated by some diminutive debutantes, now, would you?" Ross taunted, wrapping his strong arms around her waist. Held so close, Casey could feel every rugged inch of him.

"Your serve, Stretch," Chuck insisted. "If you're half as good in the water as you are on the sand, the ladies don't stand a chance."

When Casey would have pulled away, Ross tightened his firm hold at her waist, and Chuck guffawed bawdily. "Hey, you guys, none of that! We're all just a bunch of kids. Don't put any ideas in our innocent heads."

A ball was shoved into Casey's hands and she hugged it to her midsection just beneath her breasts, negating the need to tread water as she wriggled away from Ross.

The frolicking in the pool continued for a full half hour until, pleading unfair tactics and outright exhaustion, Missy and her girl friends admitted defeat and hauled themselves out of the water.

Ross disappeared into the house, two able-bodied

male victors in tow, to return with a case of chilled Pepsis and assorted bags of potato chips and pretzels.

Every last morsel disappeared with startling rapidity until, reluctantly, the youngsters began to gather up their belongings.

It was then that Ross sought Casey out, his eyes softly pleading. "Stay and have dinner with me? We still have a lot to go over."

The invitation caught her off guard and she gnawed her lower lip indecisively. Her parents would be home by now, and Chuck would deliver Melissa back to their father's stern supervision. But to remain there alone with Ross? On his own turf, dangerously disabused of the trappings of civilization and *clothing,* Ross would stir any woman, and her own immunity had recently proved suspect.

"Just the two of us?" she posed warily.

"Tiny will be home soon," he cajoled.

"Who?"

"My housekeeper. So you see, we *will* be adequately chaperoned." He smiled at her unmasked relief. "Do we have a deal?"

Hesitantly Casey reminded him, "I don't have my car. I came in Chuck's van."

"I'll take you home later," Ross pledged.

What could she say? They did have a lot to go over if they were going to be ready for the fashion unveiling in two weeks' time. "Whatever you say," she agreed quietly.

"Now, there's an open invitation." Ross effected a mock leer. "There's just no telling where my imagination might lead me!"

Or mine, either, Casey seconded silently, unable to tear her eyes away from his trim, barely decent male physique. In a business suit Ross was a strongly compelling man. But near naked, the powerful muscles of his shoulders and upper arms bulging even unflexed... She shuddered and forced herself to look up. "If you're going to be difficult, I'm not going to stay."

"You're staying," he stated brusquely. Then, to give credence to his edict, he placed her determinedly in a nearby chaise lounge. "Wait here," he directed. "I'll see the little monsters out."

As the boisterous entourage made its way around the side of the house, Casey struggled to regain her composure at the high-handed manner in which Ross had hoisted her aloft, then dumped her on the lounger, as if she were a featherweight, dim-witted child.

Ross was just too bossy for words! The poor woman who finally landed herself with him would have to possess a will of iron and nerves to match.

Casey shook her head to clear her ridiculous musings and cast a rueful eye around the scene of destruction. The poolside area looked like a cyclone had hit dead center. Chairs and loungers had been pulled together at odd angles, pop cans surrounding them. Wadded-up plastic bags were everywhere, a generous sprinkling of their contents littering the paving bricks, having been soundly trounced and ground into broken little remnants of chips and pretzels.

"We'll have to get this mess cleaned up," Ross voiced from nearby, absently picking up litter along the way. "If Tiny sees this, my head will be on the chopping block."

Casey giggled, mentally conjuring up the picture of a burly manservant giving Ross a dressing down.

"It's no laughing matter," he roared. "Get moving, woman! Tiny is an institution around here, and you don't challenge institutions."

"I thought you asked me to stay and go over plans for the fashion show," she admonished, gliding jauntily to her feet. "I didn't know I was to be the maid."

Ross deposited the garbage in the middle of a deck chair and advanced on her, all teasing and male purpose. "Maid, huh!" Scooping her up in his arms, he made his way lazily toward the water. "Let's see how sassy you are when you're in over your head."

"Ross, *no!*" Casey squealed. But it was already too late. She barely got her gaping mouth shut when they both hit the water. She struggled furiously as Ross held her against him in water that was too deep for her but just right for his own lanky frame.

"Relax, *Stretch*." He drawled the teasing nickname, tightening his grip. "I'm not going to let you drown."

"Don't call me that!" she hissed. "Stretch is an affectionate nickname reserved for those who know me better."

"And you don't think I can be affectionate?" The hand at the small of her back moved down to her hips, pulling her still closer while Ross used his free hand to lift her chin. "Come here and let me show you how affectionate I can be. Then I can get to know you better, hmm?"

Before she could protest, Ross covered her wet lips with his own, drowning her in a deepness far more dangerous than water. Casey's resistance was only token at best. When she gave up her futile thrashing, he lifted his head and ordered huskily, "Open your mouth for me. I want to feel that spicy little tongue fighting me for possession."

"No." Another feeble protest.

"Yes," he insisted, squeezing her cheeks until her lips formed an enticing pout. "Now you're ready."

Hot breath mingled with her own as Ross placed his open mouth over her lips, and Casey wrapped her arms around his neck, giving in to the need for even more tantalizing closeness.

"Wrap your legs around me and let go of my neck,"

he exhorted, releasing her lips and holding her slightly away from his broad frame.

Wordlessly Casey complied and felt the straps of her swimsuit slide off her shoulders to be brushed down her arms, leaving her bare to the waist.

"God, you're beautiful!" Ross growled, leaning further away to admire the way her sculptured breasts floated on the surface of the water.

The action brought her even more tightly against his masculine hips, and she sucked in her breath when she felt his potent virility and then gasped.

"Haven't you ever swum in the nude?" Ross asked.

"No!" Her denial came out in a low wail, so greatly was she affected by the heated messages his evocative hands were sending to her straining hips.

"God!" he growled again. The intensity of his voice urged her to squirm closer, and he welcomed her crushingly as their lips met and parted by mutual agreement. So lost were they both in a world of sensual oblivion, they very nearly went underwater when a barking voice intruded.

"Young man! You get out of that pool this instant! I don't know what's been going on here this afternoon, but you're going to account for yourself!"

Ross turned his back on the intrusion, shielding Casey with his chest as he inched into shallower water so she could touch bottom. "Damn!" he muttered. "Attila the Hun." His breathing was raspy and uneven, in tune with Casey's shallow pants.

"And fetch the young lady out with you," the grating voice persisted. "When she's hitched up that bit of nonsense, that is!"

Casey squirmed to comply and was mortified when Ross took over the task, shaping her passion-swollen breasts into the fitted cups of her swimsuit.

"Tiny can't see anything," he chided quietly.

"I can damn well see what your hands are doing. Get out here this instant! I don't shock that easily."

To Casey's amazement, Ross grinned, seeming to acknowledge the upper hand of his challenger. "We're coming," he promised placidly, lifting her to sit on the side of the pool.

Her eyes flew up to examine this person who commanded Ross's respect, and she nearly slid back into the water when she realized it was a woman. Gravelly voiced, built like a drill sergeant, but a woman nonetheless.

Tiny subjected Casey to an equally thorough, narrow-eyed scrutiny, then turned to Ross. "Well? I'm waiting. What's the meaning of this colossal mess?" She swept an arm around the littered poolside. "I thought Cindy and her friends weren't coming until tomorrow."

"Cindy is my teenage niece," Ross said to Casey.

"Ross!" Tiny cut in impatiently.

"I had a little party for Casey's sister and some of her friends. We'll clean up the mess," he offered placatingly, looking hilariously like a repentant little boy.

"Darn right you will!" The graying woman appeared somewhat mollified. "And you're forgetting your manners, young man. You haven't introduced me to your friend."

Like Aphrodite rising, Casey scrambled to her feet, easily topping the formidable woman by at least two inches.

Ross came up behind her and grasped her shoulders. "Sorry, Tiny. Allow me to present Cassandra Spencer, my partner at Spencer-Allen."

The staunch disapproval dissolved somewhat as a strange light flickered in the housekeeper's eyes. "It's about time you brought home a suitable woman." Her eyes moved over Casey's wet form and then up to the towering hunk of manhood behind her. "And judging from the scene I just witnessed, you'd better marry the girl before the blessed event. I've waited a long time to hold your son in my arms, Ross Allen!"

"You're embarrassing Casey, Tiny," Ross declared musingly. "There hasn't been any talk of marriage."

Tiny gave a disdainful sniff. "Well, I've never seen a more perfectly matched couple."

"What about some dinner?" Ross suggested hopefully, resting his chin atop Casey's head.

"Might I remind you it's my day off!"

"Just a little omelet?" he coaxed. "And maybe some of your marvelous cottage fried potatoes?"

"I'll see about it," she relented, throwing a conspiratorial wink Casey's way. "*If* you get this mess cleaned up!"

"She's an old fraud, isn't she?" Casey guessed as soon as the buxom housekeeper was out of earshot. "All bark and no bite. Where did you find such a treasure?"

Ross turned to face her, smiling reminiscently. "Tiny has been with my family since I was a baby. When my parents died within a year of each other several years back, I bought this house, and just naturally brought Tiny along with me."

"Why naturally?"

"Well...Tiny considers me to be something akin to her last little chick. I couldn't just cast her adrift."

"Last little chick!" Casey giggled. "I see you more like a proud peacock."

"Be that as it may, Tiny still sees me as the baby of the family. And ever in need of guidance."

"You have brothers and sisters?" Casey had never considered the possibility.

"One of each." Ross inclined his head. "My brother, Rich, is a doctor, and the father of the niece I men-

tioned earlier. Suzanne, the middle child, lives in
Sylmar with her husband and an ambitious brood of no
less than five children." He smiled deprecatingly. "I,
alas, am the last of the lot, and sadly remiss in not
filling this house with the patter of little feet. Don't be
surprised if Tiny asks to see your teeth, or about the
state of your health in general," he warned teasingly.
"She's got her eye on you, there's no doubt about it."

Casey shifted uneasily, her gaze fixed unseeingly out
over the water. The subject of children made her uncomfortable. It always had.

"Don't you like children?" Ross queried softly.

Her malaise grew even more acute and she swayed
slightly, lost in painful reflection. "Of course I like children," she murmured with stiff precision, hoping Ross
would draw the obvious inference—that she had no
wish to continue in this sensitive vein.

He didn't. For whatever reason, Ross seemed intent
on digging through the ashes of her unhappiness. "But
you and Quinn didn't want any children," he said
gently.

Oh, God! Nothing could be further from the truth.
Casey began to tremble, suddenly deathly cold. "No...
I...we...Quinn died so unexpectedly...so young. I always thought we had plenty of time." Her voice broke
with emotion and Casey crumbled into the rough embrace that surrounded her fiercely.

"Don't," Ross groaned, fusing her against his chest.
"Don't look back, Casey. I can't stand to see you so
lost and vulnerable. I understand now. I never should
have brought it up."

You don't understand, her tender heart cried. But at
least Ross had dropped his painful probing, and for that
much Casey was silently grateful. Hugging his firm
waist, accepting his comfort, she had the strangest sensation of coming home, to be cosseted and protected. A

dangerous notion, she knew. She would just draw from his warmth for a moment and then move away.

"I'll tell you what." Ross tipped her head up, the soft brush of his mouth bringing her back to reality with a start. "Why don't I fix us each a tequila sunrise and we'll relax a bit before we start cleaning up out here."

Bemused, but not totally beyond reason, Casey knew it would be best to demur. The western concoction of tequila, grenadine, and orange juice was known for its potency. But Ross's tenderness struck a deep chord within her, and she found herself smiling in companionable agreement.

"Why don't you change out of that wet suit while I'm gone?" he suggested, releasing her to wrap a towel around her shoulders. He nodded toward a small dressing room. "Your sarong should cover you adequately."

True, she reflected ruefully, except for one small detail.

"I'm afraid I can't offer anything in the way of panties." Ross perceived her discomfort. His eyes twinkled with merriment. "Tiny's would go around you twice. I won't tell if you don't."

Casey wrinkled her nose. "You're a terrible man. Go and get me that drink. I think I'm going to need it to be able to put up with you tonight!"

"Your wish is my every command, *Stretch*." With that parting taunt Ross left her, and Casey shivered. This had been a most disturbing day!

Disturbing and, in the end, highly imprudent, she seconded on the way home, her head swimming dizzily from her foolhardiness.

The tequila sunrise had gone down like velvet, she remembered wistfully. All lingering traces of its potency had been dispelled by the exertion of blitzing through the pool area to restore its former order.

Tiny's dinner afterward had been superb, even if Ross did tease his guest unmercifully about the return of her lusty eating habits.

And they had accomplished a great deal toward making preliminary plans for the coming fashion event, working diligently in Ross's warmly inviting book-lined study. If only she had taken more care—covered her glass with her fingers as Ross topped the deceptively sweet contents absently after each cog in their plans fell into place. If only she had stayed away from the demon wine!

The closer they got to her little cottage, however, the less Casey berated herself. Benumbed by a pleasant, all-forgiving fog, she began to hum along gaily, if sadly out of tune, with the loving strains of Barry Manilow issuing forth from the stereophonic speakers all around her.

Ross cast her frequent sidelong glances, locating her snug little home without any help from Casey herself.

"Aren't you a talented devil." She giggled when he came around to open her door. "You've never even been here. How did you find this place so easily?" Her voice was noticeably slurred, her stance none too steady as he pulled her from the car.

"I've got talents you know nothing about." Ross chuckled, holding her waist with one hand while he leaned down to close the car door.

Past the point of ordinary caution now, Casey wound her arms around his neck and husked, "Do tell! What are these secret talents you've been hiding from your new partner?"

A long arm slid behind her knees and she was hoisted high in the air. "Come on, Cinderella. I think you've stayed too long at the ball!"

Casey giggled again, pressing her face into the

warmth of his neck. "Why, Ross Allen! What are you accusing me of?"

"At the very least you're tipsy. And I have a strong suspicion you're so sloshed, you're not going to be able to take care of yourself. I only hope I can get you to bed before you pass out on me."

"What kind of girl do you think I am?" she whispered seductively.

"Not that kind!" he rejoined sternly. "Now let go of my neck and fish your keys out of your purse. I can't do everything, you know!"

"Are you going to do...anything?" she broached with a provocativeness that would have mortified her while stone sober.

"I'd like to smack your hind end!" came the gritty response. "Why the hell didn't you tell me you couldn't hold your liquor?"

Casey groaned and covered her ears, sinking back against the pillows as they reached her bedroom. "Don't shout."

"I'm not shouting. And in case it escaped your notice, there are only two of us present at the moment."

"It sounds like a herd of elephants!"

"I'm sure it does," he observed a little more softly. "You're going to have one beaut of a hangover in the morning."

"Tell me something I don't know," she mewed, squeezing her eyes shut against the harshness of the overhead light.

"Hey! Don't go to sleep on me. You need to change into a nightgown."

"I will," she promised vaguely. "Just give me a few minutes and then I'll get up."

He turned to the door. "You have five minutes. If you're not finished by then, I'll come in and undress you myself."

"Wouldn't it be easier just to stay and do it now?" she posed appealingly, unsure of how she was going to accomplish the tricky maneuver by herself.

"Five minutes," Ross repeated, stepping out the door.

Casey rolled away from the sonic boom of his voice, pulling a pillow over her ears. She remained absolutely motionless until she was certain she couldn't delay any longer, but as soon as she opened her eyes she knew it was a no-go proposition. The room began to tilt, and she realized she was about to be violently sick to her stomach. A cold sweat broke out on her upper lip and brow, panic screaming through her shuddering frame.

"Roossss!"

Salvation appeared in the form of a huge shape blocking the doorway. "What in the world is the matter?" Ross thundered. "You sound as if you're dying!"

"I'm—I'm—going to be sick," Casey got out between gasping shudders.

Ross whisked her off the bed in a flash, arriving at the bathroom without a second to spare.

"I'm sorry," she tendered weakly when it was all over and he held her against his chest. "I *detest* being sick, and I didn't think I could make it by myself."

"Don't apologize," he ordered gruffly. "It was my fault. I knew you weren't going to make it. I never should have left you alone to get undressed."

"I'm so embarrassed," she muttered into his shirt. "And after you were so nice to me today."

His shoulders shook with silent laughter. "You're really going to hate yourself in the morning if I let you ramble on like this. Where is your gown? Let's get you into bed."

Casey waved a shaky hand toward the back of the door and then grabbed hold of his waist again, unwilling to stray from his rock-hard support.

With an easy motion Ross jerked the nightgown off its peg and tossed it over his shoulder. In the blink of an eye he had Casey's sarong off and the gown slipped over her nodding head. Like a father carrying an over-whelmed child to bed, he tucked her in, only to find his hand clutched so tightly, he was forced to remain.

"Don't leave me," Casey pleaded sleepily. "I hate being alone when I'm sick. Just stay with me for a few minutes...please?"

"My little vanquished queen." Ross sank down on the edge of the bed, brushing a stray lock of feathered brown silk behind her ear. "Close your eyes and go to sleep. I won't leave you tonight."

"I like it when you call me little," she sighed, obedi-ently closing her eyes. "You're the only man who has ever called me that without sounding ridiculous." Drowsy with contentment, she pulled his warm hand into the hollow between her breasts and snuggled in, too tired to notice the darkly possessive eyes gleaming down from above.

Not until he was certain she was asleep did Ross move from the bed, and then only to slide an over-stuffed chair from beneath the window over beside her. Commandeering one of her pillows, he stretched out his long legs and settled down for the night.

Casey stirred in her sleep several times, whimpering a wrenching, "Ross? You didn't leave me?" And as soon as Ross extended his hand she snatched it up greedily and drifted off, content once again.

The squall of sea gulls the next morning should have wakened her; they woke Ross instead. Sliding the chair back to its proper position beneath the window, he no-ticed an older couple walking along the shoreline and went out to join them.

"Mr. and Mrs. Thorpe?" He shot out his hand in

greeting. "Ross Allen. We've met once before, several years back."

"Yes," Blaine Thorpe remembered. A big, burly man, he shook hands firmly.

"No doubt you noticed I spent the night at your daughter's cottage?" Ross began slowly.

"Casey is a grown woman," a smaller version of her daughter interjected. "We don't question her...activities."

"I'm sure," Ross agreed quietly. "But she's going to be embarrassed enough without her family jumping to erroneous conclusions."

The older man sighed heavily, looking out over the rolling early-morning waves. "The idea you imagine us entertaining would almost be a relief. Muriel and I have been worried about our oldest daughter. She's been so...withdrawn. You're the first man she's brought home since Quinn died."

Ross nodded understandingly. "I had noticed the impregnable Fort Knox she's built around her emotions. And I wish I could take credit for unlocking the doors for her. But I'm afraid she didn't bring *me* home last night. In fact, it was quite the other way around. Casey had a little too much to drink last night while we were burning the midnight oil on an exciting new project for Spencer-Allen, and she was so pathetically sick when I brought her home, I couldn't bring myself to leave her."

"Oh, dear." Muriel Thorpe bit her lip worriedly.

"Has she always been this terrified of being sick?" Ross queried thoughtfully.

"I'm afraid so." Her father looked pained. "Casey had a terrible experience when she was just six years old. She was in the hospital. She'd had her tonsils out earlier in the day, and by nighttime she was doing so well—sleeping so peacefully—the doctors advised us to go home and come back in the morning; that she wouldn't be needing us." He shook his head remorsefully. "Poor little tyke. She was sick to her stomach all night, an adverse reaction to the anesthetic, and no one even thought to call us. I tell you! I almost tore that hospital apart when I found her in near hysterics the next morning!"

"And she's been afraid of being alone when she's sick ever since?" Ross was as outraged as Casey's parents had been years ago.

"Yes," Muriel agreed wistfully. "And then there's that strange metabolic intolerance she has for liquor. Her only two weaknesses, and you seem to have discovered them both in one night."

"Three," Ross amended obliquely. "Surely you've noticed her rockiness on the subject of children?"

"Casey discussed that with you?" At Ross's negative shake of the head Muriel's shoulders drooped. "I didn't think so. Casey never opens up to any of us. She's very sensitive about children, and I know it was a source of anguish during her marriage, but she never shares her personal feelings, not even with her mother."

"Muriel." Blaine pulled his wife close to his side. "You're getting maudlin. Let's go up and check on our oldest offspring. Ross?" He turned to the younger man questioningly.

"Of course."

"Honey?" A gentle hand nudged Casey's shoulder, and she lifted one heavy, tentative eyelid.

Three sets of speculative eyes looked down on her, her mother's the closest, and she felt like Goldilocks caught napping.

"I hope this isn't *Candid Camera*." She groaned and sat up on the side of the bed, holding her head in her hands. "I don't think I'm up to being seen coast to coast."

"Pity," her companion of the night before drawled. "I'm sure Allen Funt would be highly amused."

"He wouldn't have been last night," she muttered, gratefully accepting the robe her mother procured from the closet.

"You remember last night?" Ross queried, his tone indulgently amused.

"Some of it." Casey's eyes flicked betrayingly to the chair beneath the window.

Ross intercepted her wary glance and seemed to shoot back silently, "So that's the way the wind is shifting." But he allowed her to plead alcoholic amnesia rather than admit to her parents how often she had clung to him during the night.

Chapter Five

Often during the next two weeks Casey found the same speculative gaze trained on her, but Ross made no further effort to zero in on her vulnerable femininity. Discounting, that is, the day her new wardrobe arrived.

"I want to see everything on you," he insisted, carrying the myriad boxes into the bathroom. "We have to decide what you're going to wear to the biggest fashion unveiling of the year."

"I thought I would be wearing one of Madison's creations," she mused spiritedly.

"You're not one of my models," came the cryptic reply.

"Since I'm going to be allowed to wear my own clothes Sunday," she began, modeling the outfit she had purposely saved until last, a simple white jersey jump suit daringly belted in maroon suede and falling into beautifully draped folds at both front and back neckline, "I thought this would be an appropriate selection."

"Pants," Ross muttered deprecatingly.

"You were the one who agreed to pants outfits for entertaining," she reminded him frostily. "And we *are* representing a sportswear firm, in case you have forgotten!"

"I have a memory like an elephant." Ross grinned wolfishly. "You, for example. I remember every little thing about you!"

"Beast!" To her relief, he dropped the teasing banter and suggested she bring the children's drive data into his office so they could work together for the rest of the day.

Without the support of Ross, his housekeeper, Tiny, and the amazingly capable woman who ran his modeling agency, Casey was certain she would not have survived the pace, organizing a major fashion event in two short weeks.

But survive she did, standing up to take full accolades Sunday night with the immaculately dressed, white-summer-suited Ross—accolades from no less than the head of Madison Limited.

"You two make quite a pair," the grizzled, grandfatherly man pronounced. "A real brainstorm you had, both dressing in white. A perfect foil for my more colorful creations!"

"Did you plan it in advance?" Casey asked mellowly a long time later as she and Ross lounged in comfortable solitude beside the deserted backlit pool. "Both of us dressing in white, I mean?"

"To the point of calling Sid to make sure the number you're wearing tonight would be ready when he sent over the rest of your things," he agreed, equally mellowly.

"You're a sly devil," she accused softly. "Always thinking ten paces down the road."

"I try to be." Ross studied her through lazy, half-closed eyes. "If a man waited for Muhammad to come to the mountain . . ." He shrugged expressively, patting the space beside him on his lounger. "Why don't you come over here, and we'll do a little mutual congratulating on the success of the day?"

"I don't think so," Casey demurred, shaking her head.

"Scared?"

"Cautious," she substituted wryly.

"Too cautious. You can't hold out forever. Someday I'm going to get you to admit the attraction we feel for each other."

"I may never come around to your way of thinking," she warned. Her voice held more certainty than she really felt.

"You'll come around," he assured her calmly.

His implacable tone was annoying. "I *do* have a mind of my own!"

"And it works a little more slowly than mine," he agreed evenly. "That's why I'm giving you plenty of time."

And rope, to hang myself with, she thought worriedly.

"Hey, come back!" Ross snapped his fingers when she drifted into a brooding silence. "I didn't mean to send you off to the deep six. I have some plans I want to discuss with you before you go home tonight."

"I'm listening," Casey murmured drowsily. He probably wanted to discuss business, and she was really much too tired.

"I want you to go up to my cabin at Big Bear with me next weekend."

"What!" She shot straight up in her chaise lounge.

"Strictly business," he declared blandly, chuckling at the dark drifts of rage climbing up her neck. "I'm going to take a client and his wife up for the weekend, and I want you to come along as my hostess. I did mention that you would be called upon to fill that position occasionally. You did beautifully today."

"Who's the client?" Casey asked guardedly. If it was a hip young swinger, Ross was going to get a definite no!

"Cal McCoy," he responded breezily. "Ever heard of him?"

"The hamburger king?" He had her interest now! "I didn't know he was one of our clients."

"But then, you're still learning, hmm? You *will* come along as my hostess?"

The ball rested squarely in her court, and Casey's mind was in a whirl trying to dredge up everything she had ever heard about Calvin McCoy. Around sixty, balding, happily married. A family man, if memory served.

"I'll think about it," she hedged.

"That's my girl!"

The whole of the next week passed in a blur as Casey worked diligently to catch up on the accounts she had neglected during the flurry of activity before the fashion show.

On Friday morning she arrived at the office with a carefully packed suitcase and a distinctly fuzzy head. Probably the result of an unusually heavy workload, she rationalized. She *had* been a lady of leisure for the past few years, and the last couple of weeks had been hectic. The time spent in the mountains relaxing was starting to sound like heaven.

They left for Big Bear right after lunch. The McCoys, she discovered, were to meet them up on the mountain. She and Ross were to go on ahead and lay in provisions.

Never could Casey remember having been so tired. Traffic along the San Bernadino Freeway seemed to tighten the lanes to hair-raising proportions, and she squeezed her eyes tightly shut, drifting off into a much-needed nap.

Who would have thought she'd sleep the afternoon away? Cramped, achy, and thoroughly out of sorts, Casey woke to find that they were parked in front of their apparent destination.

"Is this dinky little thing it? I was anticipating a showplace fit for a king—an advertising king."

She knew she was being a crab and was instantly contrite when Ross murmured, "My parents bought this cabin when they were first married. It's been in the family for years. My brother and sister and I share it equally, now that the folks are gone."

"I'm sorry." Her apology was hoarse and strained. "It's just that I'm so tired..."

"Flushed, too," Ross noted dryly. "I hope you aren't coming down with something." His lips quirked devilishly. "Or anticipating some kind of wild, partner-swapping sexual romp all weekend?"

"I'm anticipating a long rest, nothing more." She sighed wearily, too pooped to rail at his mockery.

"Come on in, then, and let me show you to your bedroom. It sounds like you're going to be needing it, *scrooge.*"

Casey wrinkled her nose and followed him inside. The charming, thoroughly old-world cabin raised her spirits—for a while, anyway.

A cozy living room and each of three bedrooms were filled with Early American antiques, each bed covered with a handmade patchwork quilt crafted locally. The family atmosphere was relaxing—and reassuring.

They made a quick trip to a supermarket in town to stock up on provisions, and had a beautiful london broil marinating for dinner, when she questioned, "What time are the McCoys supposed to get here?"

Ross frowned and consulted his watch. "Cal said they'd be here by six at the latest. I hate to think of them driving on strange mountain roads after dark."

"Mind if I take another little nap, then?" Stifling her third yawn in as many minutes, Casey stretched out on the comfortable wing-backed sofa. "I'm awfully tired."

"And such sparkling company, too," Ross chided, reaching behind her to pull the heavy, ripple-marked afghan down from the back of the couch and spread it over her.

"Just wake me when they get here," she muttered

into the throw pillow he slid under her head. "Or sooner, if you want any help preparing dinner."

When Ross finally woke her it was dark, and Casey was shivering in spite of the afghan. She sat up groggily and instantly noticed that they were still alone.

"I'm afraid I have some bad news." Ross sat down beside her, squeezing her shoulder gently.

"They're not coming, are they?" she accused gratingly, backing away from his warm gaze and caressing hand. "They were *never* coming! You planned this little excursion in a deliberate attempt to—to seduce me!"

"That load of crap doesn't even deserve a denial," Ross bit out grimly.

"Where are our guests, then?" she hurled suspiciously.

"Cal's wife came down with the flu," he informed her tersely. "Under the circumstances, I could hardly demand that he drag her up here just to satisfy your irrational code of ethics."

"And how did you ascertain that piece of information? There isn't a phone anywhere in this cabin. Did Mr. McCoy send some kind of magical brain wave through the air?"

"I went down to a phone booth and called him while you were asleep," Ross informed her tightly.

Casey eyed him doubtfully, and he exploded, "Come on, call me a liar, if you dare!"

"It just seems too pat." She sighed, rubbing her aching temples. "Like you planned it all in advance... or...or something." The idea sounded feeble, even to her own ears.

"Give me credit for a little more class than that!"

They glared at each other, both clearly put out.

"Come on." Ross finally rose and reached for her hand. "Let's go and have some dinner. There's no sense in going hungry just because our guests failed to arrive."

"I don't have much of an appetite," Casey said glumly.

Ross turned on her, eyes ablaze. "For God's sake! If you're going to be such a wet blanket, we'll leave right now! I was going to suggest it in the morning, anyway. Much as we both need a relaxing weekend, I was afraid you were going to kick up a fuss."

"I am not kicking up a fuss," Casey enunciated slowly, angrily. "And I'll eat your damn dinner." *If it chokes me,* she vowed silently, not at all certain her stomach was going to accept food. "We'll see about tomorrow—tomorrow." The way she felt right now, she might be dead by then, so badly did she ache all over.

The thin slices of rare, succulent steak Ross placed on her plate swam before her eyes drunkenly, and Casey couldn't suppress her shudder at the thought of swallowing such bloody meat.

"Don't you like your meat rare?" Ross demanded impatiently, placing a steaming baked potato next to her meat. He nudged the salad bowl a little closer. "Somehow I knew you'd find fault with my single-handed effort."

"You don't have to rub it in that I didn't help," she snapped back. "And I wasn't complaining about the meal. I just like to be sure my meat isn't going to squirm when I cut into it!"

Ross swore under his breath and began scooping the strips of steak off onto his own plate. "Since you're so squeamish, let me give you some end cuts. They're charred to perfection, just to Your Majesty's liking."

Casey tried her best to repair the damage and sound charming with "The dinner looks delicious," then put her foot in it with "You went to a lot of trouble for just two people."

"I didn't know we would be dining solo," Ross reminded her coldly.

The rest of the meal passed in painful silence. Every bite of meat Casey put into her mouth seemed to swell into a huge, unmanageable lump. The baked potato loaded with sour cream went down easily enough, even if the salad seemed disagreeably slimy. The cherry cheesecake Ross served for dessert was so smooth, it presented no problem. She didn't even have to chew. Determined not to be accused of grumbling, she made sure to scrape her plate clean.

She didn't want to be accused of shirking either, and insisted on doing the dishes—alone, since Ross had prepared dinner.

Ross slammed out of the cabin, and Casey didn't hear him return until a long while later when she had finished in the kitchen and retired to her bedroom to climb wearily into her nightgown.

Too tired even to brush her teeth, she fell into bed to be haunted with dreams of drowning in a ten-foot-deep cherry cheesecake. She woke in a cold sweat, the proud owner of the stomachache of all times.

The edge of the bathtub was unforgivably hard, but she spent a teeth-chattering hour there, sitting next to the toilet, praying that her stomach would empty itself. Anything would be better than the pressure building up inside her wretched body.

Finally, in desperation, she gave up her vigil and trudged back to the bedroom, only to find her bed drenched with perspiration and freezingly uninviting. There *was* a vacant dry bed, she remembered. When the reason for its being empty dawned on her, she groaned, covering her face with her hands. Calvin McCoy's wife had come down with the flu, Ross had said. And *she* had been aching all day. A sure symptom of the same thing!

She simply would not be sick there, she vowed, clutching her churning stomach. Not with Ross so angry with her. Maybe it was just overindulgence at dinner. Glancing at the clammy bedclothes, she headed once again for the bathroom, determined to rid herself of one monumental stomachache. But she began to shiver so wretchedly that, when she hadn't had any relief in ten minutes, she shuffled miserably back to bed.

A towering giant joined her as soon as she slid between the sheets.

"What the hell is going on?" Ross demanded raggedly. "You've been wearing out the floorboards. Can't you get to sleep?"

"I've been to sleep," she informed him, teeth chattering. "I just can't get *back* to sleep. I feel a little... strange."

The bedside lamp was clicked on, and Ross flung back the covers, issuing forth a diatribe of curses that would have made a beefy truckdriver blush. "You're drenched in sweat and shivering like crazy. Why the hell didn't you call me?"

Uncertain whether he was disgusted or genuinely concerned, Casey mumbled, "I didn't want to bother you. It's just that I'm—"

"Sick as the devil!" Ross decreed, feeling her feverish brow. "We've got to get you into a dry bed and a fresh nightgown."

"I didn't bring any other nightgowns," she revealed unhappily.

"Damn shortsighted, wouldn't you say?"

"Well, I don't wet the bed," she retorted peevishly. "And I could hardly be expected to know that I'd turn up sick. I'll bet you didn't even bring *one* pair of pajamas, much less a handy change!"

"You're so right, little lady. I sleep in my shorts. Would you like me to strip you down to your panties?"

Casey's stomach took a violent tumble at his taunting words and she made a mad dash for the bathroom, finally accomplishing the inevitable. A considerably less mocking Ross was waiting at the door, definitely concerned now.

Slipping a supportive arm around her waist, he led her to his own bedroom. Too wrung out to protest, Casey allowed him to seat her on the edge of the bed and watched dazedly as he jerked his undershirt up over his head.

"It will be warm and dry, as is my bed," he pointed out gently, pulling her upright once again.

"Don't look," she pleaded when he reached down to the hem of her gown. "Just do it and don't look." Sick as she was, she could still beg for her modesty.

"Don't be a little prude," Ross chided gruffly. "If you're as sick as I think you are, I'm going to see a lot more of you before the weekend is out." With all the nonchalance of an old country doctor, he pulled the soaked gown over her head and slipped his body-warmed T-shirt in its place, forcing her boneless arms through the sleeves. "Now climb into bed. You're as cold as a marble slab."

But not for long! No sooner had warmth stolen into her veins when it raged out of control, and Casey was soon burning up, thrashing wildly and throwing off the bedclothes. The blanket was allowed to remain at her feet, but firm hands pulled the top sheet insistently under her chin, holding it with dogged determination when she struggled.

"You're starting to sweat," a low voice observed patiently. "If the cool air hits your perspiring body, you're liable to catch a chill."

"You put on a shirt," she noticed fuzzily. "I must have drifted off."

"You've been asleep for several hours," Ross confirmed. "During which time I also put on shoes and socks. If my hunch is right, you woke because your stomach is about to protest again, and I don't want to pick up any splinters in my feet if I have to rush you to the bathroom."

"I made it by myself the last time, didn't I?" Nothing seemed clear anymore.

"You did. But your temperature has shot up a good two degrees since then. I doubt if your legs will even support you—now."

"Well, we're about to find out!" she wailed, fighting out from under his restraining arm. Lightheadedness hit her before she made it halfway across the room, and Ross scooped her up, muttering savagely about stubborn, independent women.

This time he did not wait politely outside the bathroom door, and Casey was ever so grateful for the strong arms that carried her back to bed. Another dry T-shirt was produced. Then, miraculously, she seemed to sleep for the rest of the night.

Or did she? Casey worried, waking with the morning sun to find Ross sprawled out on an absurdly short rollaway cot right beside her.

"Morning, my little pest," he greeted sleepily.

"Oh, no," she groaned. "Did I make a nuisance of myself all night?"

"You slept like a baby." At her audible sigh of relief he went on teasingly, "A miserable, fretful baby. Kicking and squirming and pulling at your poor nightshirt. You seemed intent upon wearing it up around your neck. I lost track of the number of times I had to sit and hold your hands just to keep you decent."

An embarrassed search under the covers located the item in question, wadded up around her waist. Every bone in her body protested as Casey wiggled to pull it down. Her anguished moan filled the room. "I feel like

I've just gone ten rounds with Muhammad Ali. Did you beat me as well?"

"Don't think I wasn't tempted." Ross chuckled, swinging to his feet. "Even in your sleep, you're as stubborn as all get-out. If I didn't have seventy pounds on you, I'd be nursing a few bruises."

"What are we going to do?" Casey voiced her worries. "It looks as if I have Mrs. McCoy's flu!"

"Stay up here and weather it out, I imagine." Ross folded the rollaway cot in half and pushed it into a corner. "I'm certainly not going to attempt that long drive off the mountain with your iffy stomach."

Casey shuddered. "Don't remind me. There can't possibly be anything left in my stomach. If I have to be sick, I'm just going to lie here and ache. I refuse to make any more visits to the bathroom!"

It was a weighty resolve, unfortunately destined to failure. The small glass of orange juice she attempted a short while later threw her system into violent revolt, and the tiny sips of water and fever-reducing aspirin Ross insisted she try set off world war three as the vengeful grip of Montezuma's revenge joined the onslaught.

"Even your hands sliding under me hurt," she whimpered late in the afternoon when another bout of intestinal cramping doubled her over and Ross made to rush her to the bathroom. Pathetically weakened, she clung to his neck, miserably aware that no one, not even her mother, had ever cared for her in such a personal way.

When Ross laid her on the bed, she clutched at his hand, her color heightened by more than the fever. "I'm sorry to have dragged you into this." Her apology came in a breathless little rush. "I've never been so embarrassed in my life."

"Ah, love." Ross shook his head, eyeing her tenderly as he pulled up the covers. "I know all about your quiet little terror when you're sick. I'm just glad I was here to take care of you. Much as you may loathe the idea, sometimes only a man will do. Isn't it fortunate you fit so beautifully in my arms? That your Florence Nightingale should be so much bigger and stronger—a perfect physical match?"

His last words were delivered warmly, and she shivered under his watchful gaze. One shiver led to another and, as had happened many times during the afternoon, she was soon unable to stop, huddling miserably under covers that felt like ice blankets. "So cold," she got out between violently chattering teeth. "I'm never going to be warm again."

The desperation in her voice spurred Ross into action. "You need a doctor," he stated definitively, "and I'm going to get you one."

Hard hands settled around her shoulders, tucking the blankets around her more snugly. At her wild look of panic he added understandingly, "I won't be gone long, honey. Your little stomach upheavals clock out to be about an hour apart, and I'll be back long before then. Just lie quietly and try not to think about being alone. I'll be as quick as I can, but I want you examined tonight!"

There was no arguing with that tone of voice, and Casey nodded resignedly, acknowledging the wisdom of a clearer, unfevered mind. But as soon as Ross left, the shivers intensified into massive, quaking shudders, so tragically bereft did she feel without the security of his comforting vigilance. The twenty minutes he promised were actually more like fifteen, but they seemed like an hour. Damning herself for being such a baby, Casey tried valiantly to get her jittery nerves under control.

Ross, when he returned, wasn't fooled for a minute

by her tremulous show of bravado. Rocketing to the side of the bed, he scooped her up fiercely, blankets and all, into the warm protection of his arms.

"Were you sick again?" he asked roughly, pushing her face into his chest. "God! How I hated leaving you."

The tension in his body was unmistakable. Casey struggled with the bedclothes, pulling them out of the way as she pressed her body more closely against his warmth. "I wasn't sick again, but don't go away anymore, please!" With trembling fingers she unbuttoned his shirt, burying her face in burnished skin that seemed almost as warm as her own.

"Hey, little mole." An amused voice chuckled into her tangled hair. "What do you think you're doing?"

Past the point of caring now, Casey slid her arms around his solid waist, hugging his bearish strength possessively. "You feel so good...so warm. Just hold me like this, please?"

Her nightshirt had worked its way up to her waist, a fact which registered dimly as Ross gripped her burning skin and shifted her more fully into his length. But if he was disturbed by her half-naked state, he gave no notice.

"I'll hold you, love. At least until the doctor comes."

"You got a hold of one?" Casey wasn't the least surprised. Once his mind was made up, Ross could accomplish anything.

"Uh-huh. And he lives not far from here, so he'll be here before you know it. Now hush up and let's get this shivering under control so he can take a look at you."

Delicious, soothing hands moved under her shirt to stroke down the length of her narrow back. "God!" Ross husked, "for a big girl, you're built so delicately." As if to accentuate his point, he slid her smaller, yielding frame higher against the bulk of his own, flattening her feminine curves against his brawny chest.

The hand behind her nape held her head immobile in the hollow of his shoulder, and when eventually the shivering began to subside, Casey remained thus. Tomorrow, when her vitality wasn't at such a low ebb, she would take positive steps to reassert her self-sufficiency as an adult woman. Right now she felt too languidly content to worry about letting her arrogant partner find her so weak and submissive... and childlike.

The squash of tires in the gravel outside finally heralded the arrival of the medical man, and Casey was gently disentangled and settled back into bed.

"We've got to get you decent," Ross offered in explanation as his hands slid under the blankets to locate the bunched material riding up at her midriff. One hand turned her on her side while the other smoothed the knit T-shirt down over her hips, and at this Casey did flush—with mortification. Where was her pride? Her innate modesty?

She was still indignantly ruffled when, expecting a kindly old country doctor congenial enough to agree to a house call, she found herself confronted with a young, sun-bronzed edition of a very tall Dr. Kildare— followed closely by the slightly loftier Ross.

And if she thought she was going to be left in privacy for the examination, she was in for another surprise. To her acute discomfort, Ross remained present the whole time, describing in remorseless detail the gravity of her intestinal distress.

"Sounds like a virulent case of influenza," the unlikely-looking doctor proclaimed, gliding a thermometer under Casey's tongue.

Forced to keep her mouth shut on the fragile instrument, she was left ignored and unconsulted while they discussed her condition as if she were a fractious child.

"The most important thing is to see that she gets

plenty of liquids," the doctor warned. "While the fever rages, it's important that she replace the fluids lost through perspiration. Do you have any fruit juice?" he demanded of Ross.

"Yes." Ross nodded affirmatively. "But I can't even get her to drink water. Everything that passes her lips she loses, one way or another." He grimaced at the last observation. "I'm afraid all these frantic dashes to the bathroom are wearing her out."

"Keep a bucket beside the bed" came the practical advice. "If it's just an upset stomach, that should suffice. The only time I want her out of bed is when there's no other choice. Is that clear?"

As crystal, Casey thought mutinously. Only with the greatest of effort did she keep from biting down on the thermometer as another bout of shivering set in.

To his credit Ross noticed her discomfort immediately, jerking the thin piece of glass out of her mouth and deftly deciphering the tiny markings. "One hundred and two," he announced his findings, watching as Casey huddled deeper under the covers. "What do you suggest we do about these chills? The only time Casey has been warm today was when I held her in my arms." He cocked a questioning eyebrow at the doctor. "Any objections?"

"Not if you're willing to risk coming down with the same thing your wife has."

Wife! Casey very nearly let her tongue get trapped between her chattering teeth. Before she could form a denial, the two men departed, no doubt to discuss privately her treatment, she thought crossly.

It seemed like an age before Ross returned. When he did, he was carrying a jug of orange juice in one hand and a small basin and drinking glass in the other.

"I am not going to drink that," she declared unequivocally, glaring at the pitcher he set on the bedside table.

"Not all at once," Ross agreed. "But you are going to drink some of it, starting with a few sips right now." He glanced at his watch and then Casey's tight-lipped face. "It's been well over an hour since you were last sick. It's possible you may be on the mend. If not..." He shrugged philosophically, indicating the small emergency basin resting on the bedside table.

He had that determined look again, Casey noticed as she glared up balefully. Well, let him! Nothing was going to pass her lips while her teeth were clanking together like agitated typewriter keys.

"I guess we'll have to do something about the chills first, hmm?" Ross went on implacably. "Then I'll see about getting you a plastic cup, in case you bite down, or have a temper tantrum and throw it at your poor nurse." Disregarding Casey's glowering look, he bent and untied his shoes, slipping in beside her before she could grasp his intentions.

"What are you doing?" she gasped as he lifted her quaking body into his length.

"Following orders." His amused observation gave way to the even more goading "I had my wife's treatment clearly laid out for me, and I intend to follow the instructions to the letter. First we get you warm, then we force liquids."

Smug, arrogant beast! Casey began to thrash wildly, and had her kicking legs captured firmly under a heavily muscled thigh. Enraged by his easy domination of her, she began to beat impotent fists against Ross's chest. "Why did you let the doctor think I was your wife?"

A quelling hand grasped her wrists. Ross used his free hand to wrench her chin up. "I didn't let him *think* you were my wife, I *told* him you were. What in the hell was the man supposed to think when he found us alone together, and you dressed in my undershirt?"

No wonder the doctor had not insisted Ross leave

while he examined her. He thought they were married! Weakly she tried "You could have told him I was your—"

"Partner?" he hazarded sardonically. "Bed partner would have been the more logical conclusion. Even you were thinking along those lines last night."

And so she was, Casey remembered with a little flush of shame. "You wanted to ... protect me?"

"Of course I wanted to protect you." Ross sighed heavily, his next words muffled into her hair. "I've wanted to protect you since the first night I saw you, five years ago, languishing under Quinn's passive ineptitude. I've waited a long time, Cassandra Spencer, but I've finally got you right where I want you. Under my protective wing."

Protective wing! Hah! Under his thumb was more like it! Ross was a powerful man, used to ruling with an iron hand. Casey began to wiggle, desperate to escape his securing hold.

Ross merely laughed, stilling her squirming body in a scissor grip between the long power of his legs. "Why struggle?" he taunted softly. "You've been mine since the day you walked into my office and offered up your ... services. It was only a matter of time before I was able to convince you what a great team we're going to make, in *and* out of the office."

"You're crazy," she hissed, dazed by his possessive declaration and equally possessive embrace.

"Very likely"—he chuckled—"to take on a firebrand like you."

"You are not going to take me on!" The very idea was preposterous! "We are never going to have the kind of—of relationship you're suggesting!" It would be no relationship but wholesale war, each of them battling to see who could come out on top. Casey was sure of it!

"Never is a long time." Ross chuckled again, enraging her still further. "I'm a patient man, and I've been waiting for years. You'll be mine eventually. And glad of it."

"I won't!" she insisted, into his shirt, where Ross pushed her mutinous face.

Clearly not in the least concerned with her indignation, but only her health at the moment, he chided, "You're getting yourself all worked up, and you can ill afford it right now. Come closer and stop all this dithering."

"I can't get any closer," Casey choked. "You're suffocating me as it is!"

Indulgently Ross shifted so she was lying on her back, his legs sprawled over her hips and a heavy arm curved over her waist. "That better?" His tone was gently mocking. "As soon as you quiet down, we're going to try a little of this nice refreshing orange juice."

It was a double-edged threat, she reflected morosely. If she continued to struggle, she would be forced to lie with him. And if she acquiesced, her stomach was going to be bombarded with that deceptively placid-looking orange poison.

Eventually her body decided the issue. The shivers subsided, leaving her too weak and achy to imitate any fake shudders in order to escape the hateful drink.

Ross lifted her then, supporting her shoulders as he moved the glass relentlessly toward her lips. Casey turned her head aside at the last minute, only to have it wrenched firmly into a hard shoulder.

"Drink," Ross commanded, squeezing her cheeks lightly. "I don't want to have to hurt you, but I want your mouth open *right now*!"

Casey's mouth flew open at his stern injunction, and he smiled at her startled obedience. The man was a tyrant! Not until half the juice was consumed did he move the glass away, and she buried her face weakly in his shirt.

"I think that's enough for now." Ever so gently he lowered her back to the pillows. "Let's see how it sits on your stomach, hmm?"

It didn't. Violently, unforgivingly, the citrusy drink was rejected. "If I have to drink something, couldn't it just be water?" she wailed, clutching her burning throat. "Orange juice is so acidic!"

"Sorry, love." Ross was full of remorse. "I didn't think of that." The sickening orange juice was swept away, to be replaced by a pitcher of cool water.

"We'll try this later," he soothed. "Right now you look wiped out. Why don't you close your eyes and try to get some sleep?"

Casey accepted the suggestion gratefully, drifting off in an alternately heated and freezing doze. Gnawing cramps finally woke her, and she found herself once again held within the hard circle of masculine arms. Ross seemed to be asleep himself, but as soon as she attempted to jerk upright, he was galvanized into action, sweeping her up with all the agility of a resting but aware mountain lion.

"How could there be anything left in my system?" she begged to know when he laid her back on the bed. "I'll never eat again!" she shuddered, thinking of the huge meal she'd put away the night before.

"I'll remind you of that when you've recovered," she was wryly told.

Swaddled once again like a baby, she flared up angrily, "Don't be so damn condescending! You were the one who demanded I lose weight. You ought to be dancing a jig at this latest development."

"That was a lousy crack," Ross gritted, but then checked himself, as if he saw the humor in the situation. "At least you're getting some of your sparkle back. Let's see if you're up to a little water."

"I'm not!" Never had Casey been more certain of anything.

"We'll never know unless we try, will we?" Ross was undaunted, stubbornly insistent. A small amount of water was poured into the promised plastic cup, then he sat down beside her. "I'll subdue you if I have to," he threatened when she flinched away from his grasp. "Now sit up here and take it like a lady!"

She did so... grudgingly, and gave it back just as grudgingly ten minutes later. "See!" Casey turned an accusing gaze on her tormentor. "It's not going to work. Why don't you just leave me alone? I'm going to die anyway."

Ross feigned deep wounding. "And brand me a failure as a nurse? You're going to get better if I have to drag you every step of the way!"

Casey turned her back on his mockery, her tongue dulled of its usual sharp edge. With taunting persistence the chills returned, and soon the warmth of a large, covering body. Drenched with perspiration, she woke several hours later, achy, but somehow relieved of the urgent tension in her lower body.

An exploratory hand settled on her forehead, brushing damp, sleep-tousled hair out of her eyes. "Your fever is peaking," Ross observed with satisfaction. His hand moved lower, checking the clinging, moisture-soaked nightshirt. "Let's get you changed into something dry and see if we can get some aspirin down."

He left, to return moments later with a towel, a fresh set of sheets, and a look of quiet authority. Setting his load aside, he slipped his hands under Casey's heated body and lifted her to sit on the side of the bed, pulling the T-shirt over her head before she had time to protest. Brisk, impersonal hands chafed the absorbent towel over her nakedness. Then, miraculously, yet another dry T-shirt was produced, this time from the antique maple dresser a few feet away. Ross had to step around an obstacle to reach the dresser, and for the first time Casey noticed that the rollaway cot had been stretched out once again beside her.

"Why didn't you sleep there?" she demanded to know as Ross pulled a lavender-scented shirt over her head and then placed her down on the cot. "And whose T-shirt is this?" She sniffed at her shoulder.

He shot her a sardonic glance and began stripping her sickbed. "The shirt is mine. I keep a few things up here in case I ever run short over a long weekend. And as to your other question..." He rubbed a thoughtful hand over the stubble of his evening beard, his lips curving into a teasing smile. "You were calling for me so sweetly, I couldn't resist. Did you know you mutter in your sleep? Very revealing!"

Casey didn't care one whit for his taunting tone. Cautiously she tendered, "What...what did I say that was so revealing?"

"Never you mind, sweetheart." Ross popped a silencing thermometer under her tongue. "Your temperature is spiky enough without my revealing how indiscreet you've been in your sleep!"

Casey's eyes mirrored her shocked astonishment, and Ross laughed softly under his breath. "You just asked me to hold you," he relented. "You were shivering again and you wanted a little warmth."

But she had cried out for him, and that was disquieting. "What does it read?" she asked shakily when he plucked the thermometer out of her mouth.

"A hair over one hundred and two," he slanted down at her.

"How much of a hair?"

Ross merely shrugged and replaced the thermometer in its case on the bedside table.

"Ross!"

"One-oh-two point five, Miss Nosy," he grated against her ear, lifting her into the freshly made bed. "You're a veritable little furnace, that much I can attest to personally. Now, let's see what we can do about putting out the fire." Cradling her face into his shoulder, he reached for the glass of water. "Open up, big eyes. We're going to pour some water on the flames."

"More like oil to fan the fire," Casey muttered, her teeth clenched and resisting. "My stomach seems to be recovering, and I don't want to tempt the gods." Mulishly she refused to open her lips.

"You're tempting me!" Ross thundered. "Open your mouth, *right now!*"

Where's your backbone, girl? Casey wondered as she opened up like an obedient sparrow. *Are you going to let this man gain the upper hand?* Swallowing convulsively, she looked up at Ross's stern face, half expecting him to tip the whole glass of water down her throat.

"That's better." He nodded, surprising her with his gentleness. "Just a little bit at a time, now." Slowly, coaxingly, he persuaded her to sip until she had managed what he wanted—the whole glass of water.

At first Casey expected it to come right back up, and her eyes were glued fixedly on the little plastic escape valve lying on the bedside table. Then, gradually, almost imperceptively, her stomach muscles unclenched and she began to relax, breathing in a long, restoring draft of air.

"I think I'm going to make it." She sighed, closing her eyes and clutching for she knew not what.

A warm hand was placed on the bed, and she snatched it up greedily, as if it were a lifeline, eliciting a deep, richly amused chuckle.

Chapter Six

"You changed your clothes" was the first thing Casey noticed when she opened her eyes the next morning. Ross was standing beside the bed, his damp hair attesting to a recent shower. "And you've had a shower, too," she accused irritably.

"I've also had some breakfast," Ross noted wryly. "Are you going to complain about that, too?"

"Sorry," she muttered. "I wasn't complaining. It's just that I'm so *hot*," she fretted, plucking at her sticky shirt.

"You can say that again! You sweated all over me last night, among other things."

"What...other things?" she phrased delicately.

Ross roared with laughter. "Spilling your water, cursing me for holding you too tight, begging me to come back when I left, kicking, scratching, cuddling, strangling—"

"I didn't throw up anymore?" she interrupted inelegantly.

"No." He shook his head, then added dryly, "Nor suffer any more spells of the trots." Casey shuddered at his earthy observation, and he went on, grinning. "You've become quite a little exhibitionist, though. When you weren't trying to burrow under *my* shirt to better enjoy my warmth, you were pushing me aside and trying to pull your own shirt up over your head."

"You accused me of that before, and I don't believe you," she said, affronted.

"No? Then we'll just allow you your own way tonight and see if you don't wake up stark naked tomorrow morning, hmm?"

"I'm not going to be sick tomorrow, am I?" Casey's voice wavered with misery and uncertainty.

"Time will tell."

"But we have to leave! This afternoon!" she began urgently. "We have to be back at the office tomorrow."

Ross was shaking his head even before she got the words out. "We're not going anywhere until you're better. And *I've* got to get back to work," he corrected. "*You* are going to take a few days off to recuperate once I get you home. Now, simmer down! Spencer-Allen won't topple to the ground without their leadership. I'll call Bev tonight and tell her to expect me when she sees me. Who do you think anchored the ship when I was out of town before you signed on?"

"I was just—"

"Overreacting," Ross pronounced. His voice was heavy with irony. "God save me from dedicated female executives." Leaning down, he scooped her up in his arms. "We're going for a little ride. I've got the bed made up fresh in your room."

Casey stiffened, clinging to his neck like an anxious, about-to-be-deserted child.

"Hey, don't choke me to death," Ross chided, loosening her stranglehold. "I'm not abandoning you, love. Just bringing you to drier quarters. This room catches the morning sun, I thought it might be more cheerful."

"And tonight?" Casey was horrified to hear herself plead.

The moment was fraught with tension. Ross could

easily have pressed home his advantage, crowing about how much she needed him—wanted him. He didn't. Instead, he allowed softly, "I won't leave you, Casey. Today or tonight. We'll go back to my room and the little nurse's cot later."

"Oh...okay, then," she breathed as he lowered her to the bed. With an economy of movements Ross changed her into another fresh, lavender-scented T-shirt, smiling at her unspoken question.

"I've got an untapped reserve of these." He fingered the ribbed neckband and cuffed her chin lightly. "Enough to see you through the next day or so, anyway."

As the day wore on Casey came to be a believer. Her fever raged and finally broke, and countless times yet another nightshirt was produced as first one was dribbled with the much-less-disagreeable apple juice, then untold others succumbed to her relentless perspiration. Still others became clogged with the soothing lotion Ross slathered over her aching body as the virulent influenza worked its way out of her system.

And through it all she remained meekly acquiescent, unwilling to ponder whatever construction Ross was going to put on her surrender to his complete takeover of her physical needs. It was just because she was sick, she reasoned. As soon as she was back on her feet, she would fight off his dominant mastery.

Tomorrow was soon enough to start asserting herself, though, she decided when darkness fell and they were once again in Ross's bedroom. Tonight she could be forgiven for being weak. Once again she opened her arms, pleading for the security of his closeness. That Ross was becoming far too important to her she recklessly refused to acknowledge.

Ross gathered her up easily, murmuring softly, "At least your body knows where it belongs, even if your peevish little mind is working overtime to deny the notion." He laughed at her startled expression, pushing her flushed face into his chest. "Go to sleep, love. You can rise to the challenge later, when you're back up to par. I don't savor victory over a defenseless opponent."

The rich amusement in his voice lulled her to sleep, too spent, too utterly exhausted to worry about the import of his words.

Warm fingers finally roused her, curling sensuously around her breast. Casey brushed the intrusion away irritably, but it returned with dogged persistence until her eyes blinked open, encountering a roguish grin from above.

"I just wanted to make sure your heart was still beating," Ross teased, sliding his hand away to check her brow. "You were sleeping the sleep of the dead. Or innocent," he added with a slow drawl. "How do you feel? Your fever seems to be down."

Tentatively Casey stretched her arms and legs, expecting to find aching soreness, but instead finding an equally disturbing weakness. "Better," she decided, "but not quite up to a ten-mile hike."

"How about a little jaunt to the bathroom?" Ross suggested drolly. "You must be at least a quart over full, what with all the liquids I've poured down your throat since I carried you in for relief during the night."

"Oh!" Casey was mortified at what he was implying, unable to remember even drinking during the night, much less any trips to the bathroom.

"Now, don't get all uptight. How can you possibly feel embarrassed by what you don't even remember?"

Unmollified, she demanded, "What time is it?"

"Four o'clock."

"In the afternoon?"

"The sun doesn't shine at four in the morning, love.

Look around if you don't believe me. You've slept most of the day away. It's late in the afternoon—Monday afternoon."

Casey slipped around him, aghast at how much time she had lost. Stubbornly uncooperative, her rubbery legs refused to support her, and she subsided meekly on the side of the bed, chagrined and more than a little humiliated when her doleful glance upward elicited an amused query.

"Not quite as independent as you thought you were, smarty pants? Come on, let your trusty nurse help you one more time. I'm going to miss all this. You're so sweet and clingy when you need me!"

"I can walk," she bit out crossly when he slipped an arm behind her knees. "Just give me a little support until my legs remember how to perform the catchy maneuver."

"Certainly," Ross quipped, moving his arm up to her waist.

Their progress was maddeningly slow. Ross forced her to follow his sedate pace.

"I'll be all right now," she told him when they reached their destination. "I won't need your help in the bathroom. Ever again!" she added with sharp emphasis.

"Just don't lock the door," Ross warned, eyeing her narrowly. "I don't want to have to kick it in if you get into trouble."

"I'll be all right in my own room tonight," she declared shakily when she emerged and found him waiting right outside the door.

"You might be," he agreed, "but you won't be given the opportunity to find out."

As he slid her between the sheets—in *his* room—he queried, "Think you could manage some toast for dinner? If we leave here tomorrow morning, it won't be until I've satisfied myself that you can keep food down and your stomach isn't going to turn over in squeamish revolt."

"I'll eat some toast." *If it kills me,* she added silently.

"I thought you'd see things my way." He nodded, suppressing a grin. "Unruffle your feathers and lie back and relax. I'm going to do a few chores and then see about dinner. Maybe you wouldn't mind if I join you and have dinner on a tray in the bedroom? I'm getting damn tired of my own company in the kitchen."

Casey shrugged noncommittally. "Suit yourself. I didn't realize you found my company so entertaining." She cast him a surreptitious glance through lowered lashes and found his arms folded across a wide chest shaking with mirth.

"Your wit is returning. That's a good sign." With a hearty chuckle he pivoted away, shaking his head at some private amusement.

As it turned out, the amusement was well warranted. By the time he returned, Casey was thoroughly fed up with *her own* company, and craving a little attention.

"Shove over," Ross commanded briskly. "There was only one serving tray, so we're going to have to share."

"You're having *two* dinners," she noted amazedly when he slid in beside her and removed the foil from two silver trays.

"Honey, I'm a big man," Ross returned with a wolfish grin. "These little seventy-nine-cent wonders I unearthed from the freezer just won't fill me up, TV dinners being what they are."

One piece of toast was removed from a steaming stack of many more. Ross placed it on a small saucer and handed it to her with all the aplomb of a head waiter. "Your dinner, love. This"—he tapped a frosted glass at the side of the tray,—"is your before dinner, during dinner, and after dinner cocktail."

"Apple juice," she scorned. "And you're having a beer!"

He grinned at her caustic tone, then began spreading a thick layer of strawberry preserves over a piece of toast he had commandeered for himself. "Want to effect a trade?" he offered magnanimously as Casey looked from his toast to her own.

At her dazed nod she found herself holding what appeared to be a much more delectable meal. Her dainty little bites soon proved absurdly unsatisfying, and she gave in to what at any other time would have smacked of wholesale gluttony, literally inhaling the remainder of her toast and licking her fingers with relish before turning an envious gaze on her companion's dinner. "What are you having?" she demanded, sounding for all the world like a jealous, wheedling child.

Her eyes followed, mesmerized, as Ross waved his fork clockwise over each steaming compartment. "Salisbury steak, mashed potatoes, peas and carrots, Dutch apple dessert." He moved on to the other tray. "Meatloaf, French fries, corn, more Dutch apple dessert. And more toast." The fork waved upward. "Would you like another piece?"

At Casey's vigorous nod he reached for a piece at the bottom of the stack, still appealingly warm. "Jam as well?" He shot her a brief glance, his knife held aloft in anticipation.

"Please," she agreed demurely. "And...do you think I could have a bite of salisbury steak? My appetite seems to be returning."

"Fancy that!" The rich gravy was scraped off a carefully cut section of requested meat and it was popped into her waiting mouth. There was positively no missing the look of amused satisfaction on Ross's mocking face. He was deliberately tempting her appetite.

"What's in that little bowl off to one side?" Casey demanded suspiciously.

"Jell-O" came the amused, one-word answer.

"Jell-O," she sneered. "Just the thing I'm sure you crave to top off a meal." Typically sickroom fare. Bland, uninteresting, intended to sit well on a balky stomach. "I hope you enjoy it," she enjoined sarcastically, reaching for a spoon. "*I'd* rather have your Dutch apple dessert."

"No doubt you would"—Ross laughed—"but you aren't going to. It's a bit rich and spicy for your delicate constitution." Another piece of steak was forked into her surprised mouth before he turned his attention to his own dinner.

At least she had her thickly spread toast, Casey consoled herself, chagrined to find the spurned Jell-O sounding more and more enticing.

In the end she was served with a small bowl of the shimmering dessert, feeling ruefully as if she'd had to wrangle for the treat, while all the while she was wholly aware of having been set up.

Ross popped his head in the door when he had finished the dishes. "I'm going down to phone Bev and let her know we should be returning tomorrow. I'll call your parents as well. They were pretty concerned when I talked to them last night and told them how sick you'd been. You'll be all right," he prompted. "Is there anything you need while I'm out?"

"No, nothing, thank you." Except a bath, and she would accomplish *that* as soon as Ross was safely out of the way.

How much time did she have? Casey worried when she heard his car pull away. Fifteen—twenty minutes? Forcing herself to remain calm, she made her way slowly to her own room, amazed to find that her small cosmetics case seemed to weigh a ton. "I'm weaker than I thought," she mused aloud when she reached the bathroom, and was furious when she had to expend added energy retracing her steps to Ross's bedroom to fetch a clean T-shirt.

At least five precious minutes were gone by the time she started to fill the tub, sprinkling a generous portion of bubble bath crystals under the stream of water. Her shampoo and hair conditioner were lined up on the edge of the tub, a towel placed strategically on the folded-down toilet seat, and a box of bath powder set out on the sink. Securing her lank hair out of the way with a barrette, she sank into the tepid water, intent on eradicating all traces of sickroom grubbiness from her sticky body.

Ah, bliss! Languidly she stretched out a long leg, using her toes to nudge the hot water back on. The bathroom began to fill with steam as she soaped herself and breathed in the heavenly fragrance of clean skin and aromatic bubble bath. Giddiness swirled in front of her eyes when she sat forward to turn off the water, and she leaned her head against the edge of the tub, sliding her arms along either porcelain side for balance. She'd just rest for a few minutes before lathering her hair, she decided shakily.

"Casey!" The bathroom door flew open, crashing into the side wall with an explosive, ominous thud. "What the hell is going on in here?!" Ross coughed and waved his arms through the dense fog of steam. "Damn it, woman! Are you all right?"

Casey's eyes blinked open, held even more firmly than the murderous grip Ross had on her chin. And that traitorous part of her anatomy was quivering, as if she were a naughty child caught in some dastardly deed. Curse her stupidity in not locking the door!

"I'm all right." Even her voice quivered. "Will you get out of here so I can finish my bath!"

"You're finished!" With a furious shake of his head Ross released her chin, sweeping the plastic bottles off the edge of the tub. The tiny window over the toilet was slammed open, and he began methodically jerking the bathroom door open and shut, clearing the steam.

Casey watched, dazed by his ingenuity, as the man-made draft dissolved all her bath bubbles. Two hands collided as she reached for the towel. Naturally the stronger, masculine hand emerged victor in the ensuing tug of war.

"Christ almighty!" Ross swore. "You'd try the patience of Job!"

The window was slammed back down, the towel thrust over his shoulder, and he glared down with deadly intent. "Come on, you ridiculous infant, let's fish you out of there!" Thrusting his hands under her armpits, he lifted five feet nine of dripping, blushing, indignantly protesting womanhood out of the water.

"You're insufferable!" Casey seethed as he set her down on the bathmat and began implacably towelling her rosy body.

"Sit," Ross commanded, indicating the folded-down toilet seat.

"I'm not a dog!" she cried. Her bottom made sharp contact with the wooden seat, aided by two impatient hands pushing angrily on her shoulders.

"Don't move, Cassandra! I'll be back in a minute."

Damn it all! Every time Ross was annoyed with her he resorted to Cassandra, just as her mother did. Come to think of it, that was just how he was acting—like an outraged mother hen.

Dreaming up all manner of bitter invectives to hurl at his arrogant head, Casey could only stare, bewildered, when he returned, bearing her freshly laundered nightgown.

"I'm not totally insensitive," he grated as her eyes flew up to his grim face. "I figured you would want a bath tonight, and I planned to supervise, sedately, from outside the door.''

"Oh.''

His eyes narrowed and hardened with irritation. "Yes, 'oh'! And what happens? As soon as my back is turned you have to flaunt that infuriating self-sufficiency, climbing into a sweaty steam bath! You look like a god-damned boiled lobster!" With an exasperated flick of his wrist he shook out the folds of her nightgown.

"I wanted to put on some bath powder," she attempted feebly.

"Well? Get on with it, then. The night isn't getting any younger!"

With him standing there, like some kind of angry Goliath!

"For heaven's sake, Cassandra! Your body doesn't hold any mysteries for me." Swearing under his breath, Ross pulled her upright and whisked the towel away, patting the furry powder applicator up and down the length of her body.

"You don't have to get *physical*!" she protested when he finished with a startling pat on her rump.

"Honey, I'm only restraining myself with the greatest of effort," Ross evinced, lifting the gown over her head.

The sensuous feel of the feminine garment whispering over her bare skin lessened the sting of his hand. "Thank you for . . . for washing this," Casey offered appeasingly. "I won't know how to act in my own nightgown.''

"Don't let it go to your head," he shot back harshly. "You've got yourself so damn overheated, I'll probably have to strip you down before the night is out!"

Her shoulders drooped. There was no pacifying Ross in the mood he was in tonight. "I'll just br-brush my teeth and then go to bed," she mumbled unhappily.

"Think you can manage it without gagging?" It wasn't a humorous question; just a cold, cynical demand.

"I won't ask you to hold my head if I can't," she retorted, stung.

"Hell's afire! I think I liked you better when you were sick. At least you weren't quite so blasted stubborn!"

"If I'm stubborn, you're impossible!"

"However impossible, you've needed me these last few days," Ross stated inflexibly. "Are you woman enough to admit it?"

Was she? Casey's failure to respond immediately sealed the doom on an already ruined evening. Once he had seen her back to bed, Ross turned with a sharp "I'll be out in the living room, in the unlikely event you should want me for anything."

"You aren't going to—to sleep in here?" she tendered miserably.

"Does it matter?"

There was a long, poignant silence. Half of Casey wanted to admit how much she had come to depend on this big man. The other half was paralyzed with indecision.

Ross sighed, long and heavily. "I'm just going to tackle some paperwork I brought along. You'll have your nurse, for one more night, anyway."

And with that he went out, leaving Casey to cringe in wonder at the bitterness in his tone. Had all the tender care Ross bestowed on her these last few days suddenly become repugnant to him? How could a man claim to want you on the one hand, yet find you so annoying, exasperating beyond reason? And why did it hurt so much, having Ross mad at her?

There could be only one reason. Ross was getting too close. Slowly, inexorably, he had worked his way under the tight curtain she'd erected around her frozen heart. And this weekend the curtain had come tumbling down, leaving her weak and open and vulnerable. After a year of innuring herself to all pain, it ached to have to feel again. A miserable, wrenching ache clawed at her heart and brought the prick of hot tears behind her eyelids.

Surely she wasn't going to let the enigmatic man in the next room reduce her to tears? But that was just what happened. Huge, scalding tears welled in her eyes and brimmed over to track a glistening trail into the hair at her temples. When she could no longer contain the sobs that threatened to carry into the next room, Casey hunched over on her stomach and gave in to a storm of pure emotion such as she hadn't known in years.

It was because she had been sick, she thought despairingly. Illness always brought back a feeling of desperate solitude, leaving her open and touchable. And she hadn't been touched in years—not in any meaningful way.

Quinn had been her husband, yes. But never her intimate—not in any way other than physically. Only her mother and father had ever glimpsed the sensitive inner core of her that Ross had laid bare this weekend. Because her defenses had been down, Casey had allowed herself to reach out for comfort from another breathing, reacting human being. And when the door slammed shut in her face, it was like so many closed doors echoing out of the past. So many years of having to stand alone, the invulnerable fortress of a woman who was Quinn Spencer's wife, and later his widow. Beautiful, too intelligent for most people's comfort, Casey gave off a touch-me-not aura that was as fragile as it was deceptive. And she was paying for it now.

If she had to be brought down from her exalted

perch, if she had to be branded a fraud, why did it have to be the indomitable Ross Allen who accomplished the feat? Would he laugh at his victory now, if he could see how far she had fallen—reduced to ignominious tears like a typical weepy female?

Did it really matter what Ross thought of her? The painful truth was that it did, too much. After that last agonizing year with Quinn, Casey wasn't ready to jump headlong into a commitment with Ross. She couldn't surrender to him completely. Not yet. But it hurt to have to give up the closeness, the vitality of spirit they had begun to share.

Earlier she had fantasized about losing herself in his arms for one more night. She was not blind to the way they fit together so perfectly when Ross thought she was asleep, the way he molded her yielding body into harmonious accord with his own. And it felt so right— as if it were preordained.

And now Ross wasn't even speaking to her. Because of some petty, insubstantial grievance, she was to be denied her last night of cosseting. If she reached out to him and he spurned her.... It was unthinkable. She cared too much, and the knowledge brought a fresh crop of tears.

So deeply had Casey sunk in her pain, she missed his footsteps as Ross approached the bed.

"Casey?" He groaned deep in his throat, his suffering seeming to match her own. "God, love! If I've done this to you, I'll never forgive myself."

A long string of self-directed curses followed and then he was beside her, sweeping her into his arms in a gesture of fierce protectiveness. "I ought to be quartered and hung out to dry," he pronounced harshly. "Don't, darling. Don't cry like that. You can't hate me any more than I hate myself."

When nothing he said seemed to have any effect on

Casey, he simply held her close to his heart. Gradually the gasping sobs subsided into hiccuping shudders, and she lay limp and spent on his chest.

"I hurt you, didn't I?" he inquired abjectly. "Leaving you alone while I tramped off to the living room to sulk with my offended male pride."

Casey sniffed miserably, whispering, "I—I don't understand."

A handkerchief was produced and Ross ordered gruffly, "Blow your nose and let's see if I can explain."

Like a self-conscious child she complied, to be rewarded with a conciliatory pat on the bottom. "That's a girl. I've been a bear, haven't I?"

"Just because I took a bath," she agreed brokenly.

"I guess it seems that way, hmm?" Ross smiled tenderly and cradled her face in the hollow of his shoulder. "But you see...I was going to play the gallant knight tonight, escorting my patient into a perfumed bath, dazzling her with the gift of her own nightwear, then wooing her with a challenging game of Scrabble I unearthed in the hall closet. I got used to you depending on me, honey. When I came home and found you fluttering your independent wings again, I was furious, and I...reacted badly. Forgive me?"

Who could resist such a heartwarming plea? "I forgive you." Casey's voice was still wobbly at best. "Will you stay with me for a little while? Just until I..."

"Feel better?" Ross stiffened momentarily. "Honey, you feel awfully good to me right now. And you're not so sick that you can't be held accountable for your actions. If I let you sleep next to me tonight—" He broke off, groaning when he saw the wary, pleading look from below. "I'll stay, if you promise to behave yourself."

"I will." Casey's trembling fingers went to work on the buttons of his shirt.

"That's not behaving," Ross growled. "What do you think you're doing?"

"I like to rest my cheek against your warm skin, not your shirt," she imparted huskily.

"You remember that much, do you?"

"Umm."

"Do you remember how you tangled your legs up with mine?" A heavy thigh settled between her lower limbs. "Or how you pressed your breasts up against my chest once you had it bare?" He finished unbuttoning his shirt and jerked it out of his pants, pulling her next to his brawny chest. "I think it's about time you discovered what you've been doing to me, rubbing this sexy little body up against me while you slept."

"Don't," Casey whimpered when his fingers slid through her hair, lifting her face to his own.

"Don't what?"

"Touch my hair. It's so filthy." She was breathless in anticipation of his hovering lips.

"But the rest of you is so clean!" Obligingly Ross released the back of her head, burying his face in her neck. "That better?" he husked, nibbling the lobe of one ear and the scented skin behind. "You smell like a baby. A powdered, pampered baby. Are you going to let me pamper you a little more tonight? I want you so badly!"

"I—I—" No words would come as Casey gazed into the blazing fire of his eyes.

Casually, as if he had all the time in the world, Ross lowered his head to play with her mouth, nibbling, stroking with his tongue until Casey began to writhe restlessly for more meaningful contact.

"I want you, Ross," a deep voice prompted. "Say it. I want you, Ross. You've said it enough times in your sleep." Caressing fingers worked up under her gown to settle around one full, throbbing breast. "See how madly your heart is beating? Listen to it! Tell me how much you want me!"

"I want you to make love to me!" It came as a low moan...the closest Casey could come to admitting what he wanted to hear.

"That wasn't so hard, was it?" Ross brushed his thumb over her willing mouth. "Keep your lips parted for me now, and I'll give you the proper kiss you've been waiting for."

Proper, hot, and moistly welcoming, for when it came, his kiss engulfed her completely, and Casey was lost under a spell as old as time and as intoxicating as heady wine. Not until Ross was satisfied that she was completely involved did he lift his head, and she clutched wildly at his hair, wrenched by the sudden loss.

"Let's get you out of this piece of fluff and bare all the way down." He chuckled at her expectant expression, brushing the thin straps of her nightgown down past her shoulders. "Those elusive flashes of pink skin you've shown me these past few days have been pure hell. It's only fair that I pay you back. Before the night is out I'm going to know every inch of you. Every sensitive dimple and curve." Supporting her shoulders, he slid the thin covering down to Casey's waist, drinking in her loveliness for a long minute before curling his fingers around her hips. Eagerly she lifted up, and the gown was slipped past her feet.

"You need to shave your legs." The chuckled observation seemed to come from a long way off as Ross began to explore the lissome length of her.

"I was going to use my electric razor after my bath," she managed breathlessly.

Ross didn't seem to be listening as he moved up to her shapely thighs. "Ah, but your skin up here is smooth and silky, like a baby's behind." His fingers moved higher, exploring the tufted warmth above. "But babies don't have this kind of silk, do they?"

Casey's hands were busy with the fastenings of his remaining clothes. Naked skin against naked skin seemed desperately imperative.

"Not so fast, my lovely." Ross gathered her hands in one of his own, pressing his knee into intimate contact with the center of her desire. "I have yet to enjoy these beautiful breasts, and they're just begging for attention. See how your nipples strain against my palms? What do they want?"

Casey could take no more of his verbal seduction. "They want to be kissed, Ross! How long are you going to torture me?" The last words came out in an agonized groan as his teeth rolled around one granite-hard tip and then moved on to the other. "Let go of my hands!" She was panting now, twisting and churning beneath him. "You're driving me crazy!"

"And about time, too." Lazily Ross released her hands, framing her face for another long, drugging kiss. "You've been driving me crazy for days. It's only right that I return the favor."

Her eyes were glazed, her breathing shallow and raspy, when he finally moved away to step out of his clothes. As soon as he lay down beside her she tugged desperately to finalize the embrace, but Ross was clearly in control. As in all things, he took his time, putting off the moment of final commitment until they were both incoherent with desire.

"Now tell me what I want to hear," he demanded, hovering over her at the moment of ultimate possession.

"I want you, I want you. Please!"

Ross moved with passionate confidence to bring them to completeness. They made music, they soared, and still he held back, postponing his own fulfillment until Casey passed the gates of ecstasy and drifted into the world of abandon beyond.

"It doesn't get any better than that." The hoarse words breathed into her neck brought Casey gently back to earth.

"It's never been as good as that," she couldn't help seconding.

"It will be, love. That was act one of a two-act play. Having you once just dampened the flames. I'll want you again...soon."

Drowsily content now, she murmured, "I've never made love more than once a day."

"More like twice a week and never on Sunday, hmm?" he deduced wryly. "That's about the national average for married couples." His teasing tone suddenly turned serious. "You haven't made love since you were widowed, have you, Casey?"

"You could tell?" she whispered feelingly.

"Umm. So much passion locked up for so long. And when I found the key!" Ross shook his head in sheer masculine appreciation.

"You're not too bad, yourself," she rushed, "for an old man of thirty-four."

"Old man! I'll give you old man!" Ross sprawled her on her back and began to wreak havoc all up and down Casey's soft, unresisting body. "We'll start here, with an appetizer," he growled against the curve of her neck, "and work down to something more substantial to nibble," he husked, tonguing one engorged nipple. "By the time I get to your toes, this old man should have recharged his resources enough to move on to another main course. Are you with me?"

"All the way." She giggled at his devilish whimsy.

And all the way they went...languidly...all sense of urgency gone the second time around.

"You could become addictive," Ross growled just

before he drifted off to sleep, his arms and legs entwined with hers. "I can see myself tumbling you on the couch in my office, and on the couch in your office, and—"

"And Bev could see you, too," she cut in prosaically.

"Ah, a woman of infinite practicalities."

"I try to be." And for hours, long after Ross fell into a peacefully content, bear-hugging sleep, Casey *did* try to be practical.

What implication was Ross going to put on her surrender tonight? From the beginning he had been arrogantly confident that she would be his. And when the moment of showdown came, she had given in, without so much as a token resistance. Like a snowball, melting in the Mojave Desert, she mused worriedly.

The hand resting on her stomach stirred and closed around her hip, pulling her more tightly into his furnacelike heat. Even in his sleep Ross was a dangerously possessive man.

What demands was he going to make on her now? Ross knew that she wasn't promiscuous. She shuddered. Even the word was ugly—base and degrading. And yet, he had taken her to his bed as if it were his natural, God-given right. Ross was not the type of man to go in for meaningless one-night stands. So what was he looking for? An affair...*marriage*?

The second possibility was frightening, sending shivers of alarm up her spine. Maybe it was best, she decided resolutely, to let tomorrow take care of itself. Ross was like a large predatory animal. He would swoop and declare his intentions eventually.

Chapter Seven

Ross was up well before Casey in the morning. He had his shower, secured the cabin, then whisked her away without even so much as a mention of the passion they had shared the night before.

The only thing she could discern from his manner was that he was still impossibly bossy, overbearing, and above all else, *possessive*. That much was demonstrated with annoying thoroughness when they pulled up in front of her parents' home.

Muriel Thorpe was out the door to help her daughter from the car before Ross had time to cut the ignition. "My poor darling," she crooned, wrapping a comforting arm around Casey's waist. "To be sick, and so far away from home!"

"Ross took good care of me, Mama," Casey felt compelled to put in—with an embarrassed blush.

"I know, dear." The older woman smiled apologetically at Ross as he joined the procession, Casey's suitcase in one hand. "But when Ross told us how sick you'd been, well—" She broke off, noticing the dark color flooding Casey's cheeks. "You should have had your mother with you!"

Ross chuckled under his breath. "But instead she had a fussy mother hen, hmm?" The knowing wink he slanted down at Casey turned her knees to jelly, and she slumped in her mother's arms.

The suitcase hit the porch with a jarring thud, and an insistent arm slid behind her knees. "Lead the way, Mrs. Thorpe," Ross instructed. "I've had a lot of practice carrying your delightful offspring." Lowering his voice for Casey's ears alone, he growled, "Stop squirming, love. What is your mother going to think if you put on such a show of ingratitude after *all* that I've done for you?"

"You didn't tell her everything, did you?" she rebuked, burying her scarlet face in the curve of his neck.

"No, but I will, if you don't stop struggling, *right this minute!*"

"What are you two whispering about?" Muriel interposed worriedly. "Is Casey feeling poorly again? She looks flushed."

"I'm all right, Mama." Casey glared at her implacable captor. "Ross is just being overprotective, as usual, aren't you, nurse?" She bit out the last word with ill-concealed sarcasm.

"Cassandra!" Her mother gasped at her biting tone.

"Did you ever paddle this brat when she was a child?" Ross queried indulgently. "The tongue she's got on her!" He shook his head, smiling benignly from mother to daughter. "Sassy as all get-out. I tell you—"

"Don't!" Casey pleaded, wrapping her arms around his neck as if to cut off any more provocative words. "You're a brute! Why don't you go back to work and leave me in peace?"

"I wouldn't blame Mr. Allen if he put you over his knee right now!" Muriel bustled in. "Such ingratitude! I know what a trial you can be when you're sick, young lady!"

"Casey has thanked me already, haven't you, love?"

The audacity of the man! Casey sucked in a strangled breath. Her mother had no way of knowing about last night, but still!...

"As you may have noticed," Ross went on urbanely,

"your daughter hasn't regained her sea legs as yet. If you'll just lead the way, we'll get her settled up in bed."

"Damn it! Quit talking about me as if I weren't even present!" Casey snapped.

"Watch it," a deep, goading voice warned. "As soon as we get you undressed I may follow up on your mother's invitation and—"

"You're leaving as soon as we get upstairs!"

"Are you asking me or telling me?"

"Please, Ross!"

"Please, Ross!" he mimicked her furious hiss, watching as her lips compressed in a tight, angry line. He followed her mother lazily, one foot after the other rising on the carpeted stairs as if the burden he was carrying were negligible. Stopping to see which room Mrs. Thorpe entered, he turned his dark gaze downward. "If I leave straightaway, are you going to be a good girl and mind your mama today?"

"Yes!" she flung back, incensed by his ordering tone.

Quirking lips came down to seal the bargain, long and lingeringly, leaving Casey so shaken, she scarcely noticed they were moving again.

"I want Casey to rest in bed today." Ross turned to her mother after depositing his bundle on the turned-down bed. "I'll be back this evening, and we'll see how she's doing. If she's obeyed orders, taken it easy and not given you any trouble, we'll see about her getting up tomorrow."

Who the hell did Ross think he was, her guardian? How *dare* he presume to issue orders as to her care! "Now, just a darn minute..." Casey began.

"She'll probably fret about washing her dirty hair," he went on through the interruption, "but don't leave her alone in the bathroom. She tends to get a little over-confident."

"You!..."

"Since you're coming back to check on my daughter later, why don't you stay and have dinner?" Muriel suggested, ignoring Casey just as Ross was doing.

"That's very kind of you," he accepted suavely. "I've been living on TV dinners these past few days."

"I'm sure Tiny won't let you starve." Casey finally got her two cents in, then felt a twinge of shame. Ross had been living on TV dinners because of her. All the gourmet food they had purchased for a weekend of entertaining was packed up in a cooler on the backseat of his car.

"Do you have some objection to my dining with your family?"

"I—I—no." Put that way, she sounded like an ungrateful monster.

"Will seven thirty suit you?" Muriel inserted.

"Sounds good." Leaning down, Ross planted his hands at either side of Casey's startled face and brushed a slow kiss across her unsuspecting lips. "If you've been good, you might be allowed downstairs for dinner." His voice was low, too low for her mother to overhear, and before Casey could form a suitably cutting retort he lowered his head for a harder, branding kiss and then he was gone, Muriel Thorpe following close behind.

How many hats could one man wear on his swelled head? Casey fumed. Lover, business partner, disciplinarian— She choked on the last one. When Ross returned tonight, she'd buzz his ears off for the way he had ordered her about in front of her mother! Whatever her mother was going to make of the little scene she had just witnessed, Casey shuddered to think.

Muriel was gone for what seemed like an age, returning to perch on the side of the bed and cast her daughter a long, thoughtful glance.

"Mr. Allen is interested in you, isn't he, dear?" No subtlety; she just barged right in. But that was typical of the entire Thorpe family.

"Now, Mama," Casey began cautiously, "you know how rough it's been for me since Quinn died. I'm just starting to get my life back in order. I'm not ready for a man. It's too soon."

Her mother looked doubtful. "Mr. Allen seems like a highly perceptive man. I'm sure, knowing what you've been through, he won't push you too far, too fast."

He pushed me all the way last night, she longed to cry, but that would have been sheer fabrication. She had given herself to Ross willingly...deliriously.

Trading on her recent illness, Casey brushed a distracted hand across her brow, hoping, if she managed to convey weariness, that her mother would drop the tasty bone she was worrying.

Thankfully Muriel took the bait. "You're tired, dear," she sympathized. "Would you like to take a nap, or maybe have a bath and some lunch first?"

"A bath, I think." Casey sighed, ever so grateful that Ross hadn't stripped her down in front of her mother. She wouldn't have put it past him. "My hair is positively yucky." She grimaced, anxious to restore her regal lioness mane to its former bouncy splendor. "I'm going to have to shampoo it at least three times to get it clean."

"We'll have to blow it dry, too," her mother added. "Ross was very firm that you mustn't go to sleep with a wet head."

"What else did the great man decree?"

"Now, dear. He was just being—"

"High-handed, as usual," Casey gritted.

Propped up in bed sometime later, her hair freshly washed and *dried,* her body shrouded in a ridiculously prim calf-length granny gown her mother had procured from her cottage, Casey waited in stomach-growling anticipation for her promised lunch. Her appetite was coming back in spades. The meager helping of toast Ross had allocated her for breakfast had long since ceased to satisfy.

"Did you bring what I asked for?" she asked eagerly, mentally devouring the bacon, lettuce, and tomato sandwich, cheese-flavored tortilla chips, and chocolate ice cream she had requested.

A walnut lap tray was deposited over her outstretched legs. "I brought what you're allowed to have," her mother advised.

"Allowed!" Whipping the silver covers off the serving dishes, Casey stared in angry dismay at a plate of softly scrambled eggs, an English muffin, and, as an apparent peace offering, three plain vanilla cookies. "I want what I asked for," she demanded, slamming her fist on the tray like a disgruntled child.

"Mr. Allen said you would probably throw a tantrum. If your stomach proves to be able to handle a bland lunch—"

"I know! You and the dictator will see about letting me have dinner with the grown-ups." The very idea, lining her mother up in his corner!

One look at her mother's determined face told Casey that was just what Ross had done. Sulkily she poked at the tufts of eggs, weighing the pros and cons of outright revolt. At the very least she'd suffer anguished hunger all afternoon. And there was a distinct possibility Ross might order her served the same menu for dinner—in bed, like a stubborn infant.

Her grumbling stomach finally won out, and she consumed every morsel on the tray in fuming silence, mentally jabbing at Ross's authoritative person with each mutinous stab of the fork.

The annoyingly satisfying meal left her heavy-eyed with drowsiness, and her mother beaming with satisfaction. The tray was removed, the curtains drawn, and a nap imperiously ordered—by Ross Allen's mouthpiece.

The bedroom was in darkness when she finally woke to the murmur of voices in the hall. A hand brushed the wall switch, bathing the room in the soft glow of two bedside lamps, and then Ross was at her side, trailed by the obviously excited Melissa.

"We thought you'd never wake up," Missy informed her sister smartly. "Ross has been here over an hour, and we checked on you twice, but you never even stirred."

"Feeling better?" Ross drawled, smiling down from his lofty height above.

"Much." Casey squirmed, feeling like a pinned butterfly under two pairs of watchful eyes.

"Grab your sister's robe over there on the armchair," Ross directed Melissa's way. As soon as the younger girl turned to comply, his hands snaked under the bedclothes, locating Casey's twisted nightgown. She lifted her hips automatically, allowing Ross to smooth the flannel material down over her thighs.

"A pair of pajamas would be a godsend," he muttered. "You're a positive menace in anything else." Assured that she was decent, he thrust the covers aside and lifted her to sit on the side of the bed.

"I want to talk to you," she gritted as he slid a pair of fuzzy slippers on her dangling feet.

"Later." Ross ignored her wrathful tone altogether. "Your mother has dinner ready, and we're all hungry. You can save your histrionics until after dinner. Understood?"

"What are you two whispering about?" Melissa demanded, handing the robe to Ross.

"Nothing," Casey grumbled. "Ross is just being difficult. As usual," she added caustically when he pulled her to her feet.

"I think it's so romantic, the way he took care of you while you were sick." Melissa sighed dreamily, watching as Ross eased the formfitting quilted robe over Casey's stiff, uncooperative arms, then belted it snugly at the waist.

"Romantic!" Casey dismissed the suggestion with a derisive snort. "Get your head out of the clouds, Missy. There's nothing romantic about being sick."

"Cranky, isn't she?" Ross accorded. "Dinner will probably go a long way toward improving her disposition." Whether by habit or design, he stooped to lift Casey in his arms.

"I'll walk," she insisted with great dignity. There was no way she was going to let her family see her being carried downstairs by this domineering hulk of a man!

"Suit yourself."

By the glint in his eye Casey knew that Ross was irritated, but she moved on ahead, following her sister with slow, determined strides.

Too many days in bed, that's what it was, she decided with consternation when her legs began to wobble halfway down the stairs.

A hard, steadying arm came up behind her waist. "You are by far the most obstinate female God ever put on the face of the earth!" Ross grated in her ear. "Now put a smile on that beautiful face and act as if you're grateful for my support. If your parents weren't looking on..."

"Ross wanted to carry her, but Casey wouldn't hear of it," Missy informed her parents smugly, joining them at the base of the stairs. "You should have overruled her and swept her up like Rhett Butler." She giggled up at Ross.

"Ross did, this morning, dear," Muriel remembered with a wistful sigh.

"So I did." Ross smiled. His hand maintained its visegrip on Casey's waist as he turned to her father. "Lead the way, Blaine. Sleeping Beauty here has kept us waiting long enough. I'm sure Muriel can't keep dinner holding much longer."

So it's Blaine and Muriel now, Casey noted dismayingly. And her parents were calling Ross by his first name as well. Ross hadn't wasted any time, ingratiating himself with her family! He'd been there over an hour, Missy had said, which meant they'd had plenty of time to sit and chat while she slept.

Clearly her parents were impressed, she realized as she was seated next to Ross at the round dining room table, bedecked with the best linen and china. Her mother was humming as she carried the serving dishes out from the kitchen and placed them on the large lazy Susan centered on the table. And Ross and her father were conversing with the easy camaraderie of longtime friends.

"I carved the meat in the kitchen to speed things up." Muriel smiled apologetically at her husband and revolved the lazy Susan until the platter of succulent sirloin roast stopped in front of Ross. "You're our guest, Ross. Why don't you get things started?"

Melissa, the ridiculous infant, was gazing at Ross as if *he* were the main course, Casey noted irritably. "You're such a *big* man," Missy effused. "I'm sure you must have a big appetite."

"Go bury your head in the sand," Casey muttered, praying that no one else had picked up on the sexy innuendo.

"Children, children," Blaine interceded. His eyes narrowed on first one daughter and then the other. An old, usually effective silencer. "Not at the dinner table, please."

"Spoken like a true, long-suffering father." Ross laughed, reaching for the proferred platter of meat. "I'll bet these two firebrands have caused many a case of indigestion, tussling at the table during their growing-up years." He winked at Casey, served himself with several slices of roast, then placed the exact piece she was coveting on her plate. "Here you go. A nice end cut." Extending his arm across her, apparently forgetful of the lazy Susan, he made to pass the platter on to her father.

"You're too kind." Casey was furious! Grabbing the fork off the platter as it went by, she stabbed the other browned end cut and slammed it down on her plate. "I'll have both pieces, you—" She choked off when she saw her father's thunderous face.

"I'll have both end cuts, since nobody else likes their meat well done," she finished with a dry swallow.

"What's come over you?" her father asked.

"I don't think Casey appreciates a helping hand," Ross supplied dryly, and then, ignoring his own observation, spooned a small helping of browned roast potatoes onto her plate. "I've been tempted to apply one where it might do the most good, but then she's been sick." He shrugged dismissively, pivoting the center server to reach for two crescent rolls. After carefully buttering one, he placed it on Casey's plate, followed by a helping of peas. Then, covering her clenched fist, he squeezed gently until she uncurled her fingers and guided a fork in between. With a quiet "Eat your dinner now," he directed his attention to his own brimming plate.

Oh! To have her dinner dished up for her like a brainless two-year-old! Casey's hands shook so badly, she made a miserable botch of trying to cut what was undoubtably a tender chunk of roast beef.

With a smooth movement Ross reached over and, ignoring all rules of mealtime etiquette, cut one entire piece of meat into small, manageable pieces. "See if you can handle this, and then we'll see about the other piece," he directed quietly. "I think your eyes may have been bigger than your stomach."

The hard, penetrating glance he shot her compelled Casey to obey, and she waited in breathless anticipation, literally daring anyone to comment on what they had just witnessed.

Wisely her parents demurred, knowing how she hated being dictated to. Not so the impulsive Melissa.

"Do you believe it?" she chortled. "Stretch letting a man tell her what to do? Why, Quinn wouldn't have dared—"

"Melissa!" Two strident voices intervened, Muriel's winning out over her husband's. "Close your mouth right this minute or you'll leave the table. With your father close behind," she added, glancing at her husband's grim face. Sisterly taunting had never been allowed at the dinner table.

"Thank you, Mama," Casey got out through clenched teeth. "It seems I have *one* friend in my corner."

"Ah, but it's such a tight corner," Ross inserted, just as if he had to.

"That's exactly my point," Melissa persisted. "It's about time Casey let some man storm the barriers, and I think you're just the right man for the job."

"That's it!" Casey threw down her fork and sprung angrily to her feet. "Either she leaves, or I will."

"Why? I haven't said anything we aren't all thinking."

"I'm thinking I'm going to lift a skirt and wallop some hind end," Blaine's voice boomed. He fixed his youngest daughter with a hard stare. "Do you control that runaway tongue, or do we go into my study?"

"I'll be quiet." Missy's eyes dropped sulkily to her plate. "But I still think—"

"You've had my final warning." Turning to his other daughter, Blaine rapped out, *"Sit down!"* and Casey sat—immediately, without question.

The rest of the meal passed in grateful silence. No one, it seemed, was willing to lift the lid on the tempest Missy had insistently brewed.

"Am I going to be allowed to stay up for a while tonight?" Casey posed sarcastically and to no one in particular when they rose from the table.

All eyes turned to Ross. To her chagrin Casey's as well.

"If you're going to simmer down, yes," he decided with a slow nod. "You've got yourself so worked up, you scarcely touched the beautiful dinner your mother served."

True. She hadn't done justice to half the food on her plate, including the second piece of meat she had defiantly commandeered. "I'll do better with dessert," she promised as they moved out to the glass-walled family room, a no-nonsense arm once again encircling her waist. "What are we having for dessert, Mama?" she asked, subdued.

"One of your favorites, dear." Her mother was beaming. "Cherry cheesecake. I made it especially for you."

"Ooohhh!" The huge cheesecake that had threatened to drown her a few nights back swam before her eyes, and Casey squeezed them tightly shut, swaying slightly.

"Bad connotations." Ross pulled her into a shuddering heap on his chest, resting his chin atop her shiny head. "We had cheesecake the night she became sick," he explained. "I'd love a piece, but for my friend here"—he eased his hand under the glossy curtain of her hair—"I think something a little lighter, for the next few days, at least."

"No more of those dry, tasteless cookies," Casey pleaded. "I want some ice cream. Chocolate ice cream, with cherries and marshmallows and nuts on top, like you used to fix when I was little."

The back-and-forth movement of the chin across her hair heralded a negative response. "Vanilla, no cherries, no marshmallows, no nuts."

"I know what I want!" She attempted to pull away, but the hand behind her neck only allowed a few inches of movement.

"Want to see what I've found to be effective in dealing with your oldest problem child?" Not waiting for a response, Ross lowered his head and captured Casey's lips—warmly, but gently, cajoling her out of her little sulk.

"Wow! Would you look at that!" Melissa breathed worshipfully. "No man has ever kissed me so tenderly."

"No *man* has ever kissed you at all," her mother corrected. "You're still going out with boys, and will be for some time yet. Come out to the kitchen, young lady, and help your father and me bring out the dessert."

As soon as they were alone Ross abandoned his restraint and pulled Casey more fully into his arms. He made no effort to tighten the embrace, merely worked his own brand of magic over her softly willing lips. The hand at her nape slipped under her jaw, exerting just enough pressure to pry her lips apart for more intimate invasion, and it was all the signal Casey needed. Memories of the night before impelled her closer and Ross groaned, guiding her more tightly against his stirring length.

"What would Melissa think of this?" he husked, the

evidence of his arousal thrusting tautly against the front of her robe.

Casey responded with all the latent passion inborn in her nature, pressing her lips into the warm V of bare skin at his throat, and her hips into his promise.

"God! You'd have it, too, if we were alone," Ross growled, lifting her face to his calculating perusal. "You know that, don't you?"

"I know." She could only nod helplessly.

"Well, you'll have to settle for this instead." Locking her head in place, he crushed her mouth under a wave of sensual oblivion.

"Ross...they might come back," she whispered when he finally lifted his head. "Any minute," she added with imploring feeling.

"I know, love. I know." His eyes searched the room, settling on the couch, and he shook his head regretfully. "Definitely not there. If we sit down, we'll *lie* down. Let's go out on the patio and hope the ocean breeze will effect some kind of magical restoration."

Once they were outside and Casey still clung to him, he chided softly, "You've got to let go of me or it's not going to work."

"I know." Perversely she clung tighter.

"Damn this robe!" His hands roamed up and down the length of her inaccessible body. "Damn this house, and your family for being here. I don't have any rights here."

It was *rights* that did it, jarring Casey back to reality with a start. Slowly, with a smoothness that belied the violent beating of her heart, she allowed her arms to slide down to her sides, waiting until Ross released her rather than struggle for complete withdrawal. They were heading into turbulent waters, talking about rights.

She made a fleeting attempt to steer Ross into safer channels. "Listen!" She cocked her head to one side to better hear the sounds in the distance. "The sound of the waves is so gentle and soothing. Even when it's too dark to see the water, the ocean always lulls, always challenges you to go on."

"Pure escapism." Ross moved up behind her, wrapping his arms around her shoulders. "What are you running away from? Me, or all men in general?"

"I didn't run last night," she reminded him, but her words sounded hollow.

"You gave me your body, yes," Ross agreed softly. "And you were beautiful in my arms. Is that all you have to give?"

If I try to give you any more, I'll destroy myself, she thought desolately, yet could not answer him.

"Damn it, woman! Don't freeze up on me!" Ross shook her roughly and turned her into his arms. "If you can't talk, at least you can feel. That much we know. Give me your mouth and *feel!*" His lips came crashing down, wildly, bruisingly, willing her to accept and not question, feel and not think, and she gave in to the exquisite pull of his mastery with an intensity that was as shocking as it was satisfying.

Later, as she slipped into bed, it occurred to her that she hadn't castigated him for his outrageous laying down of the law earlier.

She smiled crookedly at her omission. Ross had been the model of beguiling charm when they returned to have dessert with her family. All thoughts of recrimination had fallen by the wayside. Even the tension-filled moments out on the patio might never have been, so lighthearted and relaxed was the atmosphere when they went back inside.

Maybe that was the key, she decided musingly. She couldn't risk losing Ross; he was the vital force that had prodded her, angered her, literally commanded her to rejoin the living. But if, somehow, she could keep things light and easy—draw from his strength without hurting him...Could she be that selfish?

Casey pondered the question at length over the next few days. To please her mother, she remained up at the big house and allowed herself to be fussed over. Missy came forth, suitably repentant, if not convinced of the magnitude of her wrongdoing, with a carefully executed pledge to stay out of her sister's personal affairs, and was welcomed back into Casey's affection with open arms. Strangely Ross remained absent, checking her progress by phone without descending to issue any more outlandish guidelines as to how she was to convalesce.

By Friday she felt so much her old self, nothing could dissuade her from going back to work. Ross was not expecting her until Monday, and Casey was prepared for the lash of his tongue and untold reprisals when she stepped into his office.

What she got was a slashing grin, the most raucous of wolf whistles, and a betraying sigh of relief.

"You're back sooner than expected," Ross observed conversationally. The smile in his eyes said, "And I'm delighted to see you."

"Honestly!" Casey ignored his tentative greeting and remonstrated, "You wouldn't ask for help if you were going down for the third time."

"What are you doing?" Ross chuckled at her righteous air as she began riffling through folders on his desk, plucking up an eventual armful.

"Taking back *my* workload. You said you were handling everything nicely; no fire drills, nothing pressing!" There was so much work spread out on his desk, the top of it could no longer be seen.

"Have lunch with me." A complete non sequitur,

but then, Ross was adept at ignoring her when it suited his purpose.

"What about all this work we need to catch up on?" she reminded him briskly.

"With both of us here to handle it?" He lifted one shoulder negligently and moved around his desk until he was standing a mere hairbreadth away. "You need to be taken out to lunch. You look so regal today, so alluring!" He fingered the delicate shell neckline of the daffodil-yellow dream of a dress Casey had chosen so carefully to complement her dark hair and eyes.

"This little creation is Sid at his best." Delicious shivers ran up her spine as his hands traced the length of the back-closing zipper, then came to rest on her hips. "Did you wear this especially for me?" he asked huskily. "Knowing it was my favorite? Would you be so daring?"

"Conceited man!" With the folders hugged to her breasts, there was no way they could get truly close, but Casey slithered away in trembling agitation. "What time do you want to go to lunch?"

Her studied nonchalance was ridiculous, and the taunting "Twelve thirty, chicken!" sent her scurrying into her own office.

Whether in an attempt to dazzle her, or simply because of the atmosphere and class, Ross chose to dine at the famous Brown Derby restaurant. It wasn't Casey's first visit to the one-time beanery, but she was impressed as always by the early California elegance, hacienda style, as they made their way through thick arches to be seated in a dimly lit booth.

"I'll have the veal scallopini," she decided as soon as they were alone. There was no point consulting the menu. She knew what she wanted.

"You've been here before." Ross managed to look boyishly crestfallen.

"Of course," she tinkled in return. "Did you imagine I could have worked on Wilshire Boulevard for several years and *not* eaten here?"

"I'll have to try harder the next time," he decided with mock gruffness. "Where haven't you eaten?"

It seemed like a frivolous question, so Casey answered frivolously. "Oh... Scandia, La Scala, Perinos..." She giggled and went from the ridiculous to the sublime with "Hamburger Hamlet, Clifton's Cafeteria, the new McDonald's..."

A large brown hand came up in teasing surrender. Deftly Ross changed course. "Veal scallopini, hmm? Your stomach's back up to par? No lingering effects from last weekend?"

Casey searched his face to see if the question held any underlying meaning. Seeming to find none, she answered flippantly, "Yes! You should be pleased. I'm down three pounds. Two more to go, and I'll hit the bottom rung on your weight chart. A svelte one-twenty-five."

"You're teasing, of course?" Not sure that she was, Ross growled, "You lose any more weight, and Sid will strangle you. All those beautiful clothes, hanging on a skeleton."

Her lips curved in a sexy little smile. "Are you suggesting you were wrong, Mr. Allen? That my ideal weight may be a little more than you estimated?"

"Looking for a fight, love? Don't start something you can't finish" came the enigmatic advice. Warm eyes looked her over thoroughly, mockingly, and Casey flushed, dropping her gaze.

From playful banter she had let herself slide into the age-old feminine gambit of flirting. Subtly, but provocatively as well.

A clapping tribute sounded from across the table. "Bravo!" Ross taunted. "That's the Casey I've come

to know so well. Back out of the kitchen when things
get chancy and it looks like you might get burned. Rise
only to the challenges you can meet. Nothing ventured,
nothing gained—or lost.''

"I don't know what you mean." Casey pleated her
napkin nervously and had her chin wrenched up firmly.

"You know what I mean." Ross sighed. "But I'm
not going to push it. If you have to force something,
it's not worth having." His fingers stroked over the
faint red marks he had made on her chin. "We'll play
things your way for a while. Nothing too heavy; just
slow and peaceful. It won't be easy," he grunted. "I'm
a product of the jet age, and to drop back to a horse-
and-buggy pace—"

Casey leaned forward and covered his mouth with
gentle fingertips. "You'll make a gallant old-world
gentleman." It was an attempt at gaiety while her heart
was aching dreadfully, and at that moment Casey acknowledged that she loved Ross as she had never loved
in her life. Her eyes were soft and dewy with the revelation.

"Woman!" Ross barked. "If you don't turn the
promise in those beautiful brown eyes somewhere
else, I'm going to commit a scandalous deed, right here
in front of all these people!"

She lowered her gaze instantly. Her heart in her eyes,
she had been devouring him visually.

Ross emitted a bearish, rumbling growl from deep
within his chest. Unmindful of the very audience he
had mentioned, he leaned forward and took her mouth
in a kiss so hard and hungry, it was almost as if he were
trying to store up the taste of her. And when he would
have released her, Casey pulled him back to complete
her own memorization.

Chapter Eight

During the next few weeks, Casey found herself drawing from those memories repeatedly. She and Ross
lunched together often, frequenting several of the elegant as well as everyday establishments she had jok-
ingly professed to have missed in the past. To all
outward appearances they were still the same two
people, and on a business footing they still meshed
beautifully, as testified by the ease with which they
complemented each other sewing up the last-minute
details on what was by now a mutual effort—the children's bazaar just a few days away.

However, their magnetic spark, their intense awareness of each other, was suffering like a magestic bird
that wanted to soar, but had had its fluttering wings
clipped in denial.

When Ross gazed at Casey now, it was not with
casual intimacy, but tightly leashed calculation—and
frustration. His hand would come up in an instinctive
gesture to brush back a wispy lock of her hair, then
retreat to straighten the knot of his tie. After he helped
her into a jacket, he shoved his hands in his pockets,
lest he forget himself and turn her around to do up the
buttons. When they walked, his hand remained at the
back of her waist, never around it, or up at the sensitive
skin at her nape.

It's what I want, Casey reminded herself. But her body knew differently. She missed the blanket of ownership Ross had been quietly drawing around her. Without it she was beginning to freeze.

They drove out together on Saturday to the west L.A. children's home. Everyone participating in the Halloween extravaganza was to come in full costume, and with a touch of wry impudence, Casey rented southern belle and old country squire costumes for herself and Ross.

Ross was resplendent in his snug-fitting finery, but Casey was the unquestioned queen of the ball. All eyes were on her graceful beauty as she made her way between plywood booths set up on the wide, grassy field, checking on the supply of apples for bobbing, prizes at the dart and balloon game, and sales at the craft boutique. She was constantly shadowed by sweet little children tugging at her bouffant skirt. All of them were afflicted by some cruelty of nature, but they were so preciously dear! One little Mongoloid toddler was so persistent, her flattened features so worshipful, Casey found herself carrying the child on her hip when her stubby little legs couldn't keep up.

Most of the time Ross was busy at his own self-appointed tasks, lugging cases of soda to the concession stand, steering befuddled parents to ticket booths, and generally overseeing the perfect coordination of the day. But often Casey found his dark gaze focused on her, broodingly thoughtful.

They talked quietly on the way home, both immensely proud of the way the fund raiser had turned out.

"You were beautiful today," Ross husked, cutting the ignition as they stopped in front of her cottage. He stretched a long arm along the back of the seat. "Don't go in for a minute. Let's just sit out here and talk."

"What do you want to talk about?" she asked wistfully. The full moon bathed Ross in its soft glow, and from the serious expression on his rugged face, Casey thought guardedly that it might have been wiser to retire into her cottage. She was sure of it when she heard his next words.

"The children today," Ross began quietly. "They lined up behind you like so many little chicks following their busy mama. The fact that they were retarded didn't bother you a bit, did it?"

"Of course not. Children are children. The fact that they were special just makes you want to hold them that much closer. They were so free with their emotions, so open and angelic."

Ross chuckled, his warm gaze almost a caress. "The little tigers were on their best behavior today. Kids are kids, honey. They have their good days and their bad days. Wait until you have a brood of your own, you'll see." He eyed her consideringly and smiled. "You'll make a wonderful mother. You're a natural with children."

"Other people's children." Her voice was dull. Mentally and physically, Casey felt a desperate need to withdraw. Ross was probing too deeply... and dangerously.

The arm behind her shoulders descended, and with a muttered curse Ross pulled her into his arms. There was a furious shifting of positions as he slid out from beneath the steering wheel, and then Casey was lying across his lap.

"Get your head up here, you ridiculous turtle!" he gritted. "You are *not* going to duck back into your shell. Why are you so skittish about showing human emotions? Every time I get a glimpse of the real woman beneath your marble facade, you scramble to resurrect the Great Wall of China. I'll bulldoze it down if it's the last thing I do!"

"Please, Ross." Casey felt herself being drawn into the vortex of his anger, his very nearness sending her senses swimming. "You said you weren't going to push me," she reminded him breathlessly.

If anything, his grip tightened, prohibiting normal respiration. "Push you! I'd like to strangle you! What is this fixation you have about children?" He shook her gently. "And why do you keep dodging and feinting, denying what we feel for each other?"

"I'm not denying it. I just don't know—" She faltered, unable to go on when she saw the harsh glitter in his eyes.

"What don't you know, love?" His tone vibrated with feeling. "You know how much I want you. How much longer are you going to hold out?"

"No more," she whispered fervently, pulling his head down. "I—I want you, too." With every fiber of her being she wanted him, needed him. "Do you want to—to stay with me tonight?" she posed with unaccustomed openness.

"Of course I want to stay with you," he growled fiercely. "And it would be beautiful... tonight. But tomorrow..." He shook his head regretfully. "Tomorrow, and the day after that? What then? You're like a brilliant military strategist. For every step you take forward, you drop back two in retreat."

"What is it you want of me?" she pleaded softly, uncertainly.

"I want all you have to give. Is that asking too much?"

Casey could only stare, lost in his fixing gaze. "Let's go inside," she tried again. "Everything is so much clearer when you hold me."

He laughed, a low, mirthless rumbling that echoed beneath her ear. "We've already established that you're mine physically. Perhaps too well."

She gave a visible start, and he pulled her closer, locking her head immobile when she would have buried her face in his neck. "This holding pattern isn't going to work, Casey. If our relationship is going to grow, you've got to give it room."

"I know." And she did, only too well. But could she handle the kind of relationship Ross wanted? He was playing for keeps. Did she dare take the risk? That she loved Ross she had admitted days ago. But she had loved once before, and in the end it hadn't been enough. Doubts, fears, insecurities, all chased across her expressive features.

"Trust me, love. Is that too much to ask? You trusted me up at the cabin."

"But I had no choice...then."

"You want more time, is that it?"

At her bewildered nod Ross gave a deep growl of impatience. "You've got it, then. I leave to go on vacation next Friday. I'll be gone for two weeks, and when I—"

"You never mentioned anything about taking a vacation," she cut in agitatedly.

"Didn't I?" he mused.. "It must have slipped my mind. I always take off for two weeks before Thanksgiving. Skiing in Vermont. I went to college back east," he explained.

"I—I—didn't know," Casey stammered. The thought of two weeks without him was devastating.

"When I get back, I want no more of this vacillating from you," he reproved sternly. "Now, bring your mouth up here and give me some fresh memories to draw on."

With the mere touch of his lips she surrendered beyond reservation. If this was love, this intense desire to be one with a man, she could drown in the sensation, so great was her need.

Her hands came up to stroke the dark hair above, clutching feverishly, almost desperately, when a bold tongue mingled with her own, darting and exploring with artful precision.

The bodice of her dress loosened, aided by nimble masculine fingers tugging at the front lacings. Casey's warm, kittenish purr degenerated into a strangled moan when her bare breasts were lifted and encircled by warm, kneading fingers.

"Do you have any idea how many times I've wanted to do this these last few days?" Ross questioned hoarsely. "I know every inch of this luscious body intimately, and the knowledge is driving me wild!"

The gentle roll of his thumb and forefinger across her nipple produced an exquisite sensation, and Casey surged upward urgently, wanting the loving caress of his mouth.

"No, honey." Ross stroked the creamy slope of her shoulder, his voice shaking with denial. "If I kiss you there, there will be no going back." Instead, he captured the sweet separation of her lips, ardently, dominantly, until Casey quivered with unfulfilled longing.

"You'd better go in," he decided long minutes later. "Before this old country squire chucks his honorable intentions and takes this wench to his bed."

"Would that be so terrible?" Casey whispered at her front door, wriggling against him provocatively.

"Tonight, yes." A hearty swat on the behind stilled her movements. "Thanksgiving weekend." His reminder was almost a threat. "Be ready with some answers for me then!"

The days of the next week literally flew off the calendar until, suddenly, it was Friday, the day she had been dreading.

"You're going to do fine," Ross stated positively.

They were going over the accounts she would be handling during his absence, and Casey looked pensive and drawn.

"I don't know," she began miserably. "It's so much responsibility...."

"Honey? What is it?"

No answer.

"If I had any doubts as to your ability, I wouldn't leave you alone," Ross pursued. "But you're as well suited to leadership as I am."

Maybe. But I've grown accustomed to your leadership, in all areas, she wanted to cry. "I'll be all right," she offered listlessly.

Ross shifted in his chair, a thoughtful frown creasing his brow. "Interested in a little stimulation while I'm gone?"

Fat chance. Ross was the only stimulation in her life. Without him she was back to square one—empty and unfulfilled. "What kind of stimulation?" she inquired with lackluster interest.

"This." Reaching into the top drawer of his desk, Ross withdrew a thick account folder. "Miracle Bakeries," he enlightened, and Casey frowned uncomprehendingly.

"I've heard of them, but they aren't one of our accounts, are they?"

"Not yet," Ross agreed flatly. "I've been working on them for two years." He indicated the density of papers in the folder and nudged it toward Casey.

"And... ?" Mild curiosity stirred.

"I've drawn a blank. No results. Nothing. They run a tight ship, and I haven't been able to find the gangway."

"You want me to give it a go?"

"I'd like to turn the damn thing over to you. Permanently," he added with harsh finality.

Casey took wry note of the shortness in his tone. Obviously Miracle Bakeries was a thorn in her partner's side. "You don't take defeat easily, do you?" she perceived slowly.

"Right!" His terse one-word answer was accompanied by a dark, unfathomable glance. "Keep that in mind when I get back."

"I will." There was no mistaking the underlying meaning in his cryptic remark, and Casey shivered. Ross wanted her, and he meant to have her. Period.

"Come here." He rolled his chair back from the desk and patted his knee.

"Fraternizing in the office?" she remonstrated drolly. "I'm surprised at you, Mr. Allen!"

"Get over here and don't give me any lip!"

Perched on his lap, she teased, "If I don't give you any lip, how can you accomplish what you have in mind?"

"Impudent wretch! You talk too much."

"My lips are sealed." She pressed her mouth into a tight line—for as long as it took Ross to will it to part.

Their lighthearted banter and gentle farewell stayed with Casey for days after Ross's departure. Well into the next week, she could still taste the kiss he had pressed on her with lazy persuasion, branding her as his own.

God! Why couldn't she have gone with him? Casey had never been on skis in her life, but it would have been heaven, having Ross all to herself for two weeks.

Bev broke into her reverie late one afternoon after Ross had called to see how she was faring, and Casey was lost remembering the warm caress in his voice.

"You miss him, don't you?" the secretary posed softly.

Casey grimaced. "Is it that obvious?" The only thing

that had kept her going without Ross was the challenge of trying to convert Miracle Bakeries. A challenge that, thus far, had netted a big fat goose egg.

"Yes." Bev nodded. "It's that obvious." Casey's bleak expression spoke for itself. "Ross is more than just your mentor...your intellectual spur. You're in love with him, aren't you?"

"Yes," came the quiet admission.

"What are you going to do about it? He wants you, honey. And Ross isn't a patient man. He won't wait forever."

"I know," Casey admitted weakly.

"What happened that weekend up at Big Bear? You went away antagonists and came back like two wary animals, tiptoeing around each other as if you were both about to explode."

"We went away hating each other," Casey began haltingly, "and came back—"

"Lovers," Bev deduced gently. "But you're wrong about one thing. Ross has never hated you. Teased you, maybe, baited you to distraction, but hate— never!" She shook her head with great certainty.

He will when he gets back, Casey thought desolately. *When I won't play ball on his diamond, he's going to be furious.*

Chapter Nine

For a while it seemed that she might be wrong.

Ross called for her the Saturday after Thanksgiving, the personification of affable geniality as he escorted her, much as she had been escorted during her teenage years, to an early-evening movie along Hollywood Boulevard.

His mood seemed unusually expansive. So expansive that once they were seated for dinner in the exotic Polynesian restaurant Don the Beachcomber, Casey marshaled her valor and attempted, "I'll have a zombie." A potent combination of light and dark rum and fruit juices, the intoxicating concoction was a favorite at the Beachcomber.

A frown darkened his features for the first time all night. "Trying for Dutch courage?" Ross chided. "I'll have a zombie, and you can have a nice glass of fruit punch. If you're good, I'll give you a few sips, but you are not going to get snockered tonight!"

Casey wrinkled her nose and accepted a dictate that would have incited all-out revolt a few months ago. Ross was right. She needed all her wits about her that night.

For a good hour while they relaxed over their drinks and the barbecued ribs, fried rice, and Polynesian fare that followed, Ross stuck strictly to business, drawing from her much that had transpired during his absence.

"I didn't have much luck trying to zero in on Miracle Bakeries," she told him somberly. "I threw out a wide net, calling in a lot of favors with contacts trying to get my foot in the door, but..." She shrugged philosophically, apologetically.

"Don't worry about it," Ross dismissed easily. "I told you it wasn't going to be easy. We'll join forces and work on it together, how's that?"

"I'd like that," she agreed softly.

"You're beautiful when you're acquiescent." Ross leaned forward and captured her hands, folding them warmly between his own. "These last two weeks have been hell, Casey. I don't want to leave you ever again. Day or night!"

"Well...the days should pose no problem," she intervened slyly. "But I don't think Tiny will approve if you try to smuggle me in to live in 'her home' at night."

"We'll live together for life!" Ross insisted fiercely. "I want you for my wife, Cassandra. Not as some kind of part-time lover."

"Your wife!" It was what she had feared all along. No matter how much she loved Ross, he was asking too much, and his next words sealed his doom.

"My wife, yes! And the mother of a little bundle from heaven by next Christmas. *Our* little bundle from heaven!"

Her heart breaking, Casey gazed at the man she adored and told him, in loving regret, "I—I can't promise to give you a child, Ross." There could be no deception, not when she loved so deeply.

Ross slammed back in his seat, stunned. The furious workings of his mind hardened his face into a brittle mask. "Explain that last statement," he demanded tersely.

"I—I—can't."

"You can't," he repeated cynically. There was a

long, tense silence. He was remembering now—recalling her discomfort every time the subject of children had come up in the past.

"Why don't you call a spade a spade," he gritted at last. "A child would clutter up your life, demand too much of you. Especially now that you're reestablishing your career."

He was fuming, while Casey was dying quietly inside, her head bent to conceal her despair. Miserably she sat through the angry tirade she had dreaded for weeks, never wavering from her steadfast resolve. Ross needed children, something she might never provide.

His scornful presumption that she was unwilling rather than incapable made everything easier. Five years of marriage had left her childless, and Quinn had been checked; the fault must have been hers. To fail Quinn had been one thing, but to fail a man like Ross, a man she loved with all her heart, would be agony.

Mired down in her own grief, her despondency screened out the pain, the utter defeat and disillusionment brewing in the dark-gray eyes nearby.

Bitterly, caustically, Ross accused, "My God, woman! No wonder your marriage was a farce. You emasculated Quinn, refusing to bear him a child!"

That brought her head up, and a merciless crop of hot tears to her eyes. "I don't want to discuss my marriage with you," she said shakily, swallowing a sob. "That was in the past. It has nothing to do with us."

"Doesn't it!" he thundered. "Why the hell didn't you level with me? You knew the direction I was heading. What kind of marriage did you think we were going to have, with no children?!"

"No marriage at all," she declared numbly, refusing to expand. Ross was an honorable man. Once he had proposed, if she disclosed the real reason she couldn't give him a child, he would insist they go through with the marriage...and a possible lifetime without children.

"No marriage at all," he reiterated harshly. "Surely you realized I'd come to care for you after that weekend up at the cabin? If you were just looking for a little dalliance, you came barking up the wrong tree!"

"Don't be crude," she cried. "It wasn't like that!"

"Wasn't it? What *were* you looking for, then? A one-night stand, a month, maybe even a year? Once I made you mine, it was forever!"

"I never agreed to that, Ross." It was a wrench, but she had to begin killing the feeling he had for her. Her own love would never die. In her heart Casey would be Ross Allen's woman until the day she died.

"Do you know," he began ominously, "in all my life I've never asked a woman to marry me. Until tonight. And what do I get? A narrow-minded feminist who wants to sit at the head of a company and warm her bed with thoughts of power and success. Well, I wish you luck." Cuttingly, he added, "I guess I ought to be thanking you—for having enough decency to let me in on your hang-ups before I got saddled with you for life."

"I'm sorry." People were beginning to stare, and Casey wanted nothing more than to retire to her little cottage and shrivel up in bed in a shroud of misery, but Ross wasn't through with her yet.

"Just for the record, why did you give yourself to me so sweetly up at the cabin?" he asked derisively.

She had an answer for that. Well thought out and wholly untrue. "It was just close proximity...and physical desire. I've never denied I was attracted to you physically."

Her voice was barely audible, but Ross's vicious string of oaths could be heard all over the restaurant. Their waiter hovered uncertainly, obviously hoping to

forestall an ugly scene developing in the high-class
night spot.

Thankfully Ross obliged, signaling for the check. His
angry, disillusioned eyes glared at Casey as they went
out to the car, but no more bitter words were ex-
changed.

For that much Casey was silently grateful. She
hunched into the corner of her seat. Never had she in-
tentionally hurt anyone, and little did Ross know, she
was hurting more than he was.

Eventually she began to shiver, the salmon-pink
crepe dress and matching stole that had lit a glow of
appreciation in Ross's eyes earlier offering scant protection from the chill pervading her entire being.

"Cold?" Ross queried curtly.

"Frozen," she agreed achingly.

"Pity," he drawled, leaning forward to switch on the
heater. "I can't offer to crawl in bed with you and warm
you up tonight."

Casey chewed on his words slowly, torturingly, the
rest of the way home. The magnitude of what she was
giving up—*who* she was giving up, laid on her like a
crushing weight. When they pulled up in front of her
cottage, she turned to Ross pleadingly, offering an alternative to his marriage proposal—an idea born out of
desperation, totally foreign to her nature.

"Ross?...I have a suggestion to make, if—if you're
willing to listen."

"Go on." His eyes fastened on her even white teeth
as she worried her lower lip.

The words seemed to stick in her throat, the idea
that had been forming in her mind for weeks spilling
forth unevenly. "Would you consider—I mean, could
we try—" Her voice broke and she drew in a deep draft
of air, determined to attempt this last-ditch effort.
"Could we just...live together, and see how things

work out? If we're happy together, or if a child comes along someday..." She spread her hands expressively, convinced of the beauty of the plan. If no child came along, Ross would not be tied to her. But if by some miracle they *did* make a baby...

"No!" His bitter rejection was immediate and final. "I wanted to marry you, Cassandra, not shack up with you. A sordid little affair sounds cheap and dirty after what we could have had."

"Please, Ross, I—"

"Don't humble yourself," he cut her off ruthlessly. "It doesn't suit your haughty demeanor. Let's just forget it; it would never work. No child of mine is going to come into the world backward, as an accident. And you'd make one hell of a mother, resenting the little nuisance that crowded in on you, unwanted."

Casey flinched as he drove each nail into the coffin of her love. Ross was the light of her life, the driving force that had prodded her back to vitality. She couldn't let it all end like this. "Couldn't we still be friends?" she managed weakly.

"Business acquaintances," he amended cruelly. "That's what you wanted in the beginning. It will just have to do now. I've seen through all of your inadequacies and I'm more choosy about my friends. You're an empty shell of a woman, Casey. Afraid to give even the tiniest corner of your frozen heart. God help the man who finally lands himself with you. And thank God it won't be me."

Casey could take no more of his abuse. Frantically she grabbed at the door handle, barely managing to tuck her purse under her arm and slam the door shut before Ross took off with a squeal of tire rubber.

Through a fog of tears she wrestled with her key and then threw herself on the bed in her darkened bedroom, finally giving way to a storm of helpless remorse.

In her blackest fantasies she had never imagined that
night turning out as badly as it had. Ross had exacted
such vengeance for her rejection of him, he had left her
empty of everything except tears...pillow-drenching
tears of hopelessness.

It was thus her mother found her, some time later.
Alarmed by the ominous squeal of tires, Muriel Thorpe
had made her way over to her daughter's cottage and
had let herself in with her own key.

"Honey?" The sight of her eldest child's prostrate,
sobbing form clutched at her heart. "Sweet baby,
what's happened?" She sat down on the edge of the
bed and pulled Casey's wet face into her lap.

Casey went unresistingly, wrapping her arms around
her mother's solid waist. Her shoulders continued to
shake with silent sobs.

"Can't you tell me about it?" Muriel prompted
gently. Casey was not given to emotionalism. She had
been remote and rudderless since her husband died,
but nothing like this. Instinctively she knew that Casey
loved Ross Allen. Whatever had happened tonight had
taken a devastating toll on her daughter.

"Just hold me, Mama," Casey managed forlornly.

"I'm here, honey." Muriel stroked the dark, shiny
head in her lap. "Just let it all out. I'll stay as long as
you need me." *And, please God, let this child open up to
me for once,* she added silently.

Her prayers were answered. For the first time in her
adult life Casey shared her private woes with her
mother when the barrage of tears finally stopped.

Leaning back against the headboard, she brushed her
limp hair out of her face and began raggedly, "Ross
asked me to marry him tonight, Mama."

"But, that's wonderful, honey! Your father and I
knew Ross was in love with you."

"I don't think so, Mama." Casey shook her head

sadly. "If Ross loved me, he wouldn't have said the things he said tonight."

"What do you mean?"

"I turned down his marriage proposal," she said flatly.

"Why? I've seen the way you look at Ross. I know you're in love with him."

"That's why, Mama." Casey sighed and reached for a Kleenex from the bedside table, blowing her nose long and noisily. Haltingly she set about explaining what she should have shared with her mother years ago.

"Didn't you ever wonder why Quinn and I had no children?"

At her mother's puzzled nod she went on quietly, "It wasn't by choice, you know. I wanted a child more than anything in the world. And I tried. Oh, how I tried! That last year, before Quinn died, it had become almost an obsession with me."

"Did you see a doctor about it?"

"Yes. And there didn't seem to be any physical problem. The gynecologist recommended that Quinn see a urologist." She smiled grimly. "Quinn wasn't too pleased about that, but he went, and...everything checked out."

"And?..."

"We tried for another year, and then I went back to the doctor. He suggested that I quit dwelling on wanting a baby so desperately and just take it easy; let nature take its course."

"And that didn't work either? Oh, darling, I'm sorry."

Casey sniffed unhappily. "The ironic thing is, I had finally worked up the courage to talk to Quinn about seeing a doctor who specialized in fertility problems. We discussed it the week before he died."

"I see." Muriel considered what she had heard

thoughtfully. "And this made a difference to Ross? That you might not be able to have a child?"

"I didn't tell him." Casey winced under her mother's disbelieving frown. "I couldn't, Mama. It wouldn't have been fair. Ross wants a family just as much as I do."

"You could have considered adoption, honey."

Wearily Casey shook her head. "I want to hold my *own* child in my arms. I did suggest an alternative," she admitted obliquely.

"What was that, dear?"

"Living together, rather than marriage. I thought, if by some miracle I became pregnant, then we could get married."

"I can just imagine what Ross said to that," Muriel assayed blandly. "I imagine he wanted to put a ring on your finger before he—"

"Took me to bed?" Casey inserted wryly. "Ross and I have already slept together once—that weekend up at the cabin. Or rather, we slept together every night, I was so cold! But he only made love to me once. Or one night, anyway." She flushed. "Several times. Have I shocked you, Mama?"

"No, darling, you haven't shocked me. I knew when you came back from Big Bear that you and Ross had become important to each other. A man isn't that possessive unless he believes a woman to be his own. The way Ross feels about you, though, I'm sure he wanted to put a ring on your finger before taking you to his bed on a *permanent* basis, and possibly conceiving a child."

Casey let out a difficult, shuddering sigh, and Muriel went on bracingly, "I think you should have told him about your problem and let Ross make the decision. If you're honest with yourself, holding back the truth wasn't very fair, either."

"You don't know what it's like, getting my hopes up

for a child every month, then being disappointed. Quinn wasn't particularly bothered about children. But Ross...Ross would be as disappointed as I was. Eventually he would begin to resent me."

"He wouldn't, dear. And you're wrong, I do know what it's like. It took me several years to have you, and ten years to get pregnant with Melissa. And through it all your father was right there at my side, never loving me any the less for my tardiness."

"But you finally came through, don't you see? I might *never* have a child."

"Discuss it with Ross, honey. Go together to that doctor who helps couples with fertility problems and see what he has to suggest."

"I couldn't face a doctor right now. And those gruelling tests!" She shuddered. "I don't even think I can face Ross Monday morning."

"Yes, you can. It will all work out in the end, you'll see. Love...love can conquer anything."

"You're a hopeless romantic," Casey chided, feeling perilously close to tears again. "Promise me one thing? Don't say anything in front of Melissa. She still believes in the old fairy tale 'First comes love, then comes marriage, here comes Casey with the baby carriage.'" She smiled, a brave little smile that in no way masked her despair.

The same brave, tremulous smile was fixed diligently to her lips Monday morning when Casey went in to work.

Ross merely shot her a cursory glance and went on with the pile of paperwork requiring his personal signature.

He seemed in a hurry. Tentatively Casey asked, "Do you have an early-morning appointment?"

"Not here," he said abruptly. "I'm trying to get

through this backlog of work so I can get over to Allen
Modeling. Carlotta Perini"—he glanced up briefly—
"you remember her? The director of my agency? She's
taking her vacation now that I'm back, and I'm going to
fill in for her for the next two weeks."

Casey's shoulders slumped in defeat. There was no
point trying to talk to Ross as her mother suggested. He
had already passed judgment and found her lacking. So
lacking, he was purposefully absenting himself from
her company for another two weeks.

Could she stand up under the strain? she wondered
dismally. The last two weeks in sole command had
taxed her heavily. A month at the helm of Spencer-
Allen seemed like an eternity.

As if sensing her misgivings, Ross rapped out crisply, "Don't sweat it. If you get in a bind, I'll come over
and help out."

"Thank you," she returned severely, "but I'm sure
I'll make out all right on my own."

"I'm sure you will," came the disinterested reply.
"Oh, and by the way . . . Cal McCoy has been clamoring
to meet you since our missed rendezvous up at the cabin.
I'll try to set something up for lunch next week."

"Fine." Casey was struggling to maintain her control
under his brisk, impersonal manner. "Do you—do you
want me to fill you in on any of that work on your
desk?"

"Bev came in an hour early this morning to do just
that." He declined brusquely, dropping his gaze back to
the proposal in front of him.

So cold and unfeeling! Casey rubbed her hands unthinkingly down the sleeves of her jacket, attracting his
attention involuntarily.

"It didn't take you long to revert to old habits, did
it?" He eyed her navy slacks and tweed blazer derisively. "Back to the austere businesswoman, is it?"

"I've been cold," she told him distantly.

"You can say that again! You're a veritable block of ice. Frozen solid, all the way through."

"Thank you! If you're through laying on insults, I'll retire to my own office." *Retreat* was more like it.

"Don't let the connecting door hit you in the backside on the way through," he sneered.

She didn't, but slammed it instead, deriving great satisfaction from the disgruntled growl in the next office.

It was the only sound she was to hear from Ross for the next few days as she immersed herself in the daily routine of shouldering two people's workloads. They were working incredibly short-staffed at Spencer-Allen. Secretarys on up to executives were dropping like flies, succumbing to the same influenza that had laid Casey low the previous month, and their best legal advisor had been out for days.

When Ross called to see how she was faring, Casey briskly told him everything was fine. Using his words: no fire drills, nothing she couldn't handle.

In fact, by Friday she was beginning to fear she might have a relapse and suffer a repeat bout of the contagious epidemic running rampant through the building. Tired to the point of exhaustion, she continued to plod on, carrying her own workload and Ross's, as well as the accounts of several important underlings out with the flu.

"Cassandra Spencer, you can't go on like this!" Bev stormed into her office late Friday afternoon and found Casey with her head on her arms at her desk, napping, for the second day in a row. "Ross is an absolute tyrant, leaving you alone like this! And I'm going to tell him so the next time he calls!"

"You promised, Bev." Casey sat up and rubbed the perpetual, of late, sleepy feeling out of her eyes. "I'll have a long rest this weekend. But don't mention anything to Ross." After the way he acted Monday morning, it was easier not having him around, she thought wearily.

"Under two conditions," Bev enjoined sternly. "One, you go home right now; you're out on your feet, anyway. And two, you let me call your mother and tell her I'm sending home a physical wreck so she can supervise your rest and recuperation."

"I'll go home," Casey consented. She was useless anyway, feeling this fagged. "But, no, you won't call my mother. She's aware of my ... er ... problem."

Bev glanced at her sharply, curiously, but let the matter drop, relieved that Casey had at least agreed to call it an early day. Taking in the younger woman's twill slacks and cardigan, she prodded reluctantly, "You ... uh ... won't forget your luncheon appointment Monday with Ross and Cal McCoy?"

"Don't worry, I'll dress the part," Casey bit out grimly, then repentently added, "Thanks for reminding me, Bev."

Her appearance Monday was faultless. Not even Ross could call her on the forest-green jersey shirtwaist dress that had been a mainstay of her new fall wardrobe. Her lustrous lioness mane gleamed darkly against the slender arms supporting her head, for Casey was asleep once again at her desk.

Strangely, after two days of intermittent naps and two full nights of sleep, she still felt exhausted, and missed entirely the flaring of tenderness in the dark eyes brooding down at her shiny head.

What finally woke her was the sound of someone clearing their throat, discreetly, but repeatedly.

"Ross?" She straightened, momentarily forgetting their estrangement, and sleepily warmed by the presence of the man she missed desperately.

A broad, mocking smile spread over his face. "Sleeping on the job?" Ross rebuked gently.

The sound of his deep, taunting voice snapped her back to reality. "Just resting my eyes," she countered tentatively, unsure of his mood. "I've been doing a lot of reading." The pile of papers to be gone through on her desk attested to that.

"Miss me?" he pressed sardonically. "It doesn't look as if you've been sleeping too well." His thumb brushed the faint, haunted darkening under her eyes, and she jerked back as if stung, morbidly afraid she would betray herself under his concerned touch.

"Are you ready to go?" she asked unsteadily, casting a surreptitious glance at her watch. With any luck Bev would be off on her own lunch hour, and unavailable to give Ross a piece of her mind on Casey's overworked condition.

Sure enough the outer office was empty, and a quick glance at Ross failed to reveal anything resembling anticipation or annoyance. Surmising that their secretary had already left for the cafeteria before he arrived, Casey was relieved that Ross had escaped the lash of Bev's tongue. This last week, the brief respite without his continual presence, had been a balm to her badly bruised heart. She did not relish having Ross back in the office prematurely out of some misguided sense of duty.

Calvin McCoy turned out to be a suave, blustery man in his late fifties. His lush, plant-decorated restaurant, one of many in a chain specializing in exotic variations of the American standby, the hamburger, was an unexpected delight. Even more unexpected was the fourth party joining them for lunch.

"I hope you don't mind." Cal McCoy apologized, inclining his head in the direction of the large, raw-boned man heading their way. "Since I directed Dallas to you initially, Ross, I took the liberty of inviting him to join us for lunch."

A muscle worked convulsively along Ross's jaw, twitching in annoyance, Casey realized, frowning in confusion. Who was this client she had never met? And why was Ross so tense?

The first question was answered in due course. Dallas Kendall was a client of Allen Modeling, a swimwear mogul from Texas. But the reason for Ross's anger was a little more difficult to discern—and equally perplexing.

Dallas Kendall was a flirt, with full-blooded Texas enthusiasm, and Ross didn't appreciate it one whit! He might not want Casey for himself, but the sight of another man courting her favor sent his temper soaring.

Casey played along with the game, ordering a hamburger smothered in mushrooms and Swiss cheese, and feigning deep flattery at the drawling southern appreciation.

"Ross, you've been holding out on me," Dallas accused, winking slyly. "You showed me them toothpicks at your modeling agency all week, when what I really wanted was some meat and potatoes." His eyes widened in frank admiration over Casey's curvaceous, womanly form.

"I showed you professional models," Ross pointed out tersely. "Some of the best in L.A."

"That don't mean diddley to me. What I wanted was a good-lookin' filly with some shape to her." The Texan's face split in a wide grin as he turned back to Casey. "This little gal's got the sweetest curves I've seen this side of Texas! And she's a *long* stick of candy as well." He rubbed his hands salaciously. "What she won't do for one of my bikinis!"

"Cassandra won't do a thing for your bikinis," Ross informed him grimly. "She's not for sale. At any price!"

"Little lady?" Dallas turned to her hopefully, a brilliant gleam in his eye.

"I don't model, Mr. Kendall," she told him quietly, trying not to flush as his eyes fastened on her rounded breasts once again.

A long, proprietary arm stretched out, jerking her along the vinyl seat and under a possessive shoulder. "Casey works with me, Dallas," Ross stated with harsh finality. The hand tightening around her upper arm said very clearly, "This is my property!"

"Whoa! I get your message, pardner. Don't go gettin' all riled up."

As if realizing his vehemence, Ross lessened his viselike grip, caressing away the marks Casey was sure she would find under the sleeves of her dress. Quivering nerves bunched spasmodically in the pit of her stomach, and the searing glance he slanted down at her did nothing to restore her equilibrium.

Ah, the agony of withdrawal! It was like coming down off some hypnotic drug, learning to do without Ross.

It was Cal who finally saved the day, entering the conversation with "I'm sorry the wife and I fouled up that little getaway at Big Bear. Martha was most distressed, seeing as how it was her fault—or so she felt. I hope the weekend wasn't a complete bust."

No, not a bust, Casey thought wistfully. More like a sunburst. For that was when she had begun to fall in love—hopelessly. "We made out all right, Mr. McCoy," she supplied quietly, eliciting a hard, meaningful stare from the man holding her so close.

Made out! Damn her witless double entendre! Would she never be able to put that weekend of closeness out of her mind?

She tried nobly to do just that for the remainder of the week. By Tuesday Spencer-Allen was moving on a more even keel, most of their ailing staff having rejoined the crew. And then disaster struck.

The head of the art department, a wiry wizard of a man who could work miracles single-handedly, went home with a raging fever, leaving Casey to carry on in his wake.

Briefly she considered summoning Ross, then dismissed the notion out of hand. Working with layouts and ad slicks was her real forte, and she reveled in the thought-diverting burden.

If she was tired, her appetite almost nonexistent, at least she was busy—exhaustingly, but productively. She was going to make it. Her work *would* be enough. Surely the last few weeks had proved as much! Life could go on without Ross.

When the fleeting little naps at her desk no longer proved sufficiently refreshing, she resorted to stretching out on her couch for a quick half hour each afternoon, sternly admonishing Bev to wake her after thirty minutes.

Bev went along with the dictate, grudgingly, until Friday afternoon. Casey had been asleep for long over her usual half hour, with Bev reluctant to rouse her, when Ross showed up unexpectedly and unwittingly ignited the fuse on the secretary's temper.

"You unfeeling monster!" she charged, thumping his chest, clearly holding no fear for her job. "You're working that poor girl inside down to a nub. A month!" Bev thundered. "You've been away for a month! Casey's gone downhill by the day, carrying such a load. *You* may be able to handle everything alone, but you're invincible. Casey doesn't have such broad shoulders, and Spencer-Allen is too much for her by herself. Especially with half the staff out."

"Half the staff?" Ross gave a start. His eyes narrowed in anger. "Why the hell wasn't I informed you were working shorthanded?"

"Because Casey wouldn't let me tell you," Bev shot back waspishly. "She can be just as stubborn as you when she sets her mind to something, and she was determined to prove she could stand up under the strain. But she's not. She's cracking, and she looks like death warmed over."

"Damn it to hell!" Ross was incensed. "Is that mule-headed idiot in her office?"

"Yes, and lower your voice! She's taking a nap."

"A nap! How long has this latest development been going on? She was asleep at her desk when I picked her up for lunch the other day." Concern overlaid his temper.

"Oh, Ross." Bev crumpled into her chair. "I don't think Casey ever completely recovered from that bout of flu up in the mountains. These last couple of weeks she's really been dragging. She says she's okay, but—"

Not waiting to hear any more, Ross stole quietly into Casey's office, staring down at her slumbering form as if mesmerized. She looked almost fragile, her lack of color all the more evident against the ivory turtleneck sweater rolled at her neck. His gaze traveled lower, and he noticed self-deprecatingly that she had acceded to his wishes and worn a skirt rather than pants. But her legs were curled up well under the voluminous folds, as if seeking sheltering warmth.

A wave of self-disgust and remorse washed over him. Shucking out of his suit coat, he spread it over her inert form and slipped soundlessly into his own office.

Swiftly he reached for the phone, his face grim as he placed a call to his brother's office. The receptionist put the call through immediately when she realized she had the doctor's brother on the line.

"Rich?" Ross wasted no time. His brother was the best doctor he knew, and he wanted Casey examined that afternoon. "I've got a droopy partner on my hands. Can you take a look at her today?"

Chapter Ten

"Just a few more minutes, Bev," Casey grumbled fractiously, shrugging away from the hand at her shoulder. Instinctively she burrowed deeper under the mysterious warmth, but the hand at her shoulder was not to be denied.

"Casey." The low voice close by was insistent. "Wake up. You have an appointment this afternoon."

"No, I don't," she negated with drowsy certainty, connecting voice with man. What was Ross doing here? She squeezed her eyes even more tightly shut. Maybe if she ignored him, he'd go away. Certainly she wasn't up to his barbed mockery, finding her napping like this.

"Up and at 'em!" The warm cocoon around her shoulders was removed and her recumbent form lifted into a sitting position.

Darn it! It seemed like she'd just drifted off to sleep, and now she was going to be put through an inquisition.

But the dark face above held an inscrutable expression—more moody than angry. "What have you been doing to yourself?" Ross queried dismally, keeping a tight rein on the fury Bev had witnessed earlier. "You look terrible!"

"There's nothing the matter with me." That a few years sleep wouldn't cure, she thought crossly. "Things have been a bit hectic this week, that's all."

"Hectic!" He shot her a hard, faintly contemptuous look. "With half your staff out! How many hats do you think you can wear on that marshmallow head of yours? You should have called me, damn it! If you didn't already look like you'd been dragged through a hedge backward, I'd—"

"What would you do?" Casey broke in hotly. "We're just partners, remember? At your choosing! You needn't act so offended. I was handling everything just fine. Now, if you'll just get out of here, I'll get back to work!"

"Not today, you won't," he stated decisively. "I told you, we've got an appointment this afternoon."

"This is the first I've heard of it!"

"Probably because I just finished making the call," he countered mildly, inclining his head in the direction of the bathroom. "Hustle on in there and make yourself beautiful. Or at least wash some of the sleep out of your eyes. You look like a disgruntled grizzly bear rousted out of its long winter nap."

"I'm not budging an inch until you tell me where we're going," Casey scowled.

"Manhattan Beach," he assayed blandly.

"To see?..."

"You'll find out when we get there."

"Oh, no!" She was suspicious of his mysterious air. "Who are we going to see in Manhattan Beach?"

"My brother, Rich." Ross shot back the cuff of his shirt impatiently, glancing at his wristwatch. "Get a move on. You have an appointment in a little over half an hour."

"*I* have an appointment?" Her mouth hung open in dismay. "*I* have an appointment," she repeated numbly. "Your brother is a—a doctor, isn't he?"

"A general practitioner." Ross named Rich Allen's field. "Rich handles everything from childbirth to lessening the ravages of old age. You fit nicely somewhere in between."

A militant light entered Casey's eyes, and Ross changed course abruptly. "Do you have a coat?"

"Immaterial! I'm not going anywhere. Certainly not to see a doctor. There's absolutely nothing the matter with me."

"Except that your shapely rear end is dragging."

"If and when I decide to consult with a doctor, I'll visit my own."

"And so you may—next week. Today we're going to see Rich."

"Wanna bet!"

Ross hunched down in front of her, his eyes dark with intent. "There are two ways you can make your departure this afternoon: walking, like a sophisticated female executive, or riding, high in my arms. The choice is yours."

And wouldn't you just love to carry me out of here, kicking and clawing? Casey thought mutinously. Her eyes flashed fire as she stomped into the bathroom, closing the door with forced solemnity lest she slam it right off the hinges. Of all the high-handed, domineering effrontery!

She dropped the lid on the commode and sank down grumpily, her eyes drawn to the scales standing to one side. Damn Ross Allen and his fitness fixation! There was nothing wrong with her, nothing a doctor could minister to, anyway. Unrequited love was incurable. Couldn't Ross see what was plaguing her? That she was shriveling, not just in her heart, but physically as well, without him? But no, she'd done her work well, denied the love she felt for him, killing any hope for the future.

And now he was stuck with a business associate in less than top physical form. If she were a man, Ross wouldn't be able to adopt this dictatorial attitude. But she wasn't a man, and they were right back where they started, supposedly as equals, but with Ross still calling the shots.

Well, she'd submit to a little chest thumping, let the learned doctor prescribe a few vitamins to build her up, but that was all. And she'd sleep the weekend twice around the clock. By Monday morning she'd be back in top form. No more naps at her desk, no more—

"The day isn't getting any younger!" came the growling admonishment outside the door.

"I'm coming." Casey jumped up hastily, grabbing a comb and lipstick out of the drawer beside the sink.

"Lift your nose any higher and you'll take off in orbit," Ross chided when she stepped out of the bathroom.

"Your day is coming," she hissed. If he marched her out like a child in front of Bev, she'd let him have it both barrels!

Thankfully Ross restrained himself, merely according an inconsequential "I trust you can handle things for the rest of the day" as they passed the secretary's desk.

Bev nodded, unfazed. *Surely she must be wondering where we're off to?* Casey thought bemusedly.

"What about my car?" she demanded of Ross when they reached the parking lot. "I'm going to need it if we're not coming back today." Inspiration struck like lightning. "I'll follow you in my own car." *And lose you at the first opportunity,* she thought gleefully. But Ross was shaking his head, an amused smile playing around his lips.

"And have you fall asleep in the fast lane of the freeway? Not a chance. I'll get your car back to you tomorrow."

And that was that! Unceremoniously he stuffed her into his Chrysler, and they were off. To her relief, his black temper of the last few weeks was nowhere in evidence, and they chatted amiably—and safely—about business on the way out to Manhattan Beach.

Who would have thought the high-handed tyrant would rise with Casey when her name was called in the waiting room? Angrily she spun around, hissing indignantly, "I don't need you to come in and hold my hand. I'm not a two-year-old!"

"If only you were; it would be so much easier that way." Ross turned solicitously to the young woman in white holding the door ajar. "We'll wait in Rich's office, if that's all right?"

"Certainly, Mr. Allen," came the smiling response. "Right this way."

Briefly Casey considered rebelling, but hard fingers encircled her wrist, and a quick glance around the half-full waiting room convinced her to move on. She'd give Ross a piece of her mind once they were alone, she decided judiciously.

The opportunity never came. No sooner had they taken seats in the wood-paneled, book-lined study when an older, disturbingly distinguished version of Ross joined them.

Ross jumped to his feet, but Casey remained seated, knowing herself to be outclassed. Amidst the back clapping and "What have you been doing?" she sized up the situation, feeling distinctly uneasy.

Not only did Rich Allen match his brother in physical magnitude, but there was the same glint of determined authority in the penetrating gaze he trained her way.

"Well, young lady," the doctor began, "for Ross to have brought you here today, you must be feeling badly under the weather."

Casey dismissed his concern with a shrug. "I'm just a little tired, that's all. I thought maybe some vitamins... If you could just write me out a prescription, we won't take up too much of your time. I'll see my own doctor next week."

"Now, just a minute," Ross began firmly, but Rich waved him off.

"Vitamins, hmm?" The doctor shook his head. "I never prescribe without an examination first." A dark brow rose, seeking her assent.

"She'll let you examine her, if I have to strip her down myself," Ross inserted tightly.

Casey grimaced at his implacable tone, eyeing both men dubiously. Her gaze settled on Ross. "Will you stay outside while I'm examined if I agree?" she posed wearily, suddenly feeling depressingly tired—too tired to protest.

Balanced tentatively on the end of the examining table, Casey let her feet dangle and shivered, infinitely grateful that Rich Allen hadn't succumbed to the trend of most doctors and opted for throw-away, tissue-paper-thin gowns that shredded at the first hint of nervous perspiration. The scratchy cotton covering, tied at three places in the back, left her feeling slightly less vulnerable and exposed.

Rich strode in, professionally impersonal now, and briskly lathered his hands at the sink. "How long has it been since your last physical?" he inquired conversationally.

A huge lump of discomfort rose in her throat and Casey swallowed painfully. "About a year and a half," she tendered. God, how she hated these things!

"That long, hmm?" Dark eyebrows lifted in surprise and a lean finger pressed the intercom, summoning the nurse. "Let's get this over with, then, shall we? You look as if you're about to fly away on me." Wrapping a blood pressure cuff around her upper arm, he went on soothingly, "Relax, I'm not going to hurt you. Ross would take me apart if I did—limb by limb."

He smiled gently, and Casey felt her heart lurch. How like Ross he was, except for the streaks of gray silvering his temples. The Allen men carried their age well. In five or six years time, when Ross reached his brother's age, he would still be achingly attractive.

"Hey, come back with the living," Rich chided, snapping his fingers in front of her glazed eyes. "What were you thinking, to send your blood pressure soaring like that?"

"I—uh—I've always hated physicals." A prevarication, but true nonetheless.

"We'll check her BP again when we're through," Rich directed his nurse's way. "It's a bit erratic right now."

Casey steeled herself not to tremble as another pair of Allen hands moved over her with methodical precision.

"How long since you've had a Pap smear?" Rich inquired, palpating deeply beneath her navel.

Oh, Lord! It took every ounce of perseverance she could muster not to fling the draping sheet up over her head as she submitted to the final indignity. Did all women hate these things as much as she did? she wondered dismally, fixing her gaze on the evenly spaced holes in the acoustical tile ceiling. The consoling squeeze at her shoulder told her they did. The young nurse smiled down in knowing understanding.

Casey scrambled gratefully into her clothes behind the screened enclosure a few minutes later, relaxing for the first time in the last half hour.

"Hey! Are you going to stay in there all day?"

She nearly toppled the portable dressing screen, startled out of her wits, thinking she'd been alone in the examining room.

"What are you still doing here?" she demanded shakily, brushing the curtain aside to confront the white-smocked doctor.

"Dracula!" Rich held a syringe aloft. "I want blood!"

Why not? She'd been poked and prodded already. What was a little jab? Meekly she sank down on the low stool, stretching her arm out across the examining table and turning her head away.

Her blood pressure, she was next to discover, had returned to near normal proportions—for the moment anyway. It fluctuated wildly when Rich pressed a small specimen vial in her hand and drawled, "I'll leave you to the privacy of the bathroom at the end of the hall to collect this. Just leave the bottle with my nurse. Ross and I will wait in my office."

The two men seemed a million miles away when Casey joined them, busily rehashing Ross's adventures on the ski slopes of Vermont.

"Ready to go?" Ross flicked an interrogating eyebrow her way and turned back to his brother. "We'll meet you back here at, say, five thirty?"

"Meet you back here?" Casey echoed dazedly.

"To get the results of your tests." Ross looked faintly harassed. "Rich is going to shoot things through before the lab downstairs closes."

"What do you think is wrong with me?" she asked of the older man.

"Nothing terminal," Rich dismissed easily. "We'll just have to wait and see. Now, scram, both of you. I've got a waiting room full of patients." His words were delivered lightly; it was obvious the brothers had shared years of camaraderie and affection.

"If we hurry, we can make it back to pick up my car," Casey suggested hopefully, watching as Ross strummed his fingers on the steering wheel in his car.

"Shut up, Cassandra." He turned to her, all inflexible male purpose. "One hundred and twenty-three pounds," he gritted. "You're down to one hundred and twenty-three pounds! What the hell have you been doing to yourself?"

"Working," she said succinctly. The devil take the man! Pigs would fly before she admitted how she'd been pining away for him.

"Working must be all you've been doing. You sure as hell haven't been eating!"

"Do you really care?" she challenged. "I thought you'd washed your hands of the empty shell of a woman you claim me to be."

"Well, we're going to fill up that empty shell right now. We've got a couple of hours to kill, and you're going to eat a banquet fit for a king, if I have to shove every bite down your throat!"

With my queasy stomach? she despaired. The thought of food had been anathema to her for the last few weeks, her usual disgustingly healthy appetite almost nonexistent.

Understandably the hearty green salad set in front of her filled her to the brim. Regardless of the fact that she'd gone without lunch earlier, she was certain she couldn't manage another bite.

"We should have skipped the rabbit food," Ross muttered, exasperated. "You need something substantial, not just greens." Signaling the waiter, he cajoled engagingly, "The little lady underestimated her capacity and filled up too much on salad." Displaying all the charm innate to his nature, he entreated, "And your lobster entree is unsurpassable; I know from firsthand experience. Do you think the chef would be offended if we took a brisk walk down the pier to stimulate my friend's full appreciation of his fare?"

"But, of course," the white-shirted waiter effused, just as if it weren't going to be a gross inconvenience. Ross reached for his wallet to pay for the meal in advance, and the little man waved him off. "No need of that, sir. I'll clear away the salad plates and hold your table for you. The lady does look a bit peaked. I'm sure a stroll in the beach air is just the thing."

Once outside the weathered seafood restaurant, Ross eschewed the invitation of the many varied shops studding the Redondo Beach Pier and led Casey down to the water.

The ocean always lulls, the sound of the waves so soothing, she had told him once, long ago. His instincts proved correct in returning her to the serenity she loved. Casey drank in the familiar beauty around her and quite visibly relaxed.

They walked in companionable silence, Ross pocketing her shoes when the fashionable heels proved an encumbrance along the hard-packed shoreline between ocean and sand.

The salt air worked wonders, invigorating Casey's flagging spirits and cooling the edge from Ross's earlier temper.

"Do you think you can do justice to a meal now?" he inquired softly, stopping to brush the sand from her feet before replacing her shoes.

They were the only words spoken during their brisk stroll, but they were delivered so warmly, with so much concern, Casey was sure she *could* handle a hearty meal. In fact, she felt ravenous, the rebirth of tenderness from Ross restoring her completely.

"What do you think your brother expects to turn up with his tests?" she posed a few minutes later, greedily popping a delicious chunk of lobster dripping butter into her mouth.

"I have no idea," Ross intoned briefly. "Infectious mononucleosis seems like a good bet, the way you've been pushing yourself."

"The kissing disease?" she mused. "You could be right. I've never been tired like this before."

"Or this run down," he opined shortly.

"What happened with your friend Dallas?" she interposed, hoping to lead him off before his anger reappeared.

"He went back to Texas," Ross allowed tersely.

"Did you find him a model with a shapely enough figure?" she pressed mischievously.

"I did." His gaze dropped suggestively. "Not that your spectacular bustline seems to have suffered with the weight you've lost."

Before his very eyes Casey's nipples seemed to harden, her whole body tingling under his warm, intimate regard. Frantically she dug at a morsel of lobster. A fork came into her line of vision, nudging the foil-wrapped baked potato forward.

"Eat your potato, as well," Ross directed sternly.

Her mouth flew open at his ordering tone—just in time to have a juicy cherry tomato popped inside. There was no way she could squawk without squirting tomato all over the table, but she glared back vexedly, her toes curling inside her damp stockings, her right foot itching to deliver a sharp, meaningful kick.

He was starting to sound like his old bossy self again. Mentally she readjusted some of her earlier fantasies. Sitting across the table from Ross Allen every night might not be the bed of roses she had once thought it could be. The man could be so damn managerial!

And never was it more in evidence than when they returned to Rich Allen's private office.

"What's the verdict?" Ross demanded peremptorily, holding a chair out for Casey and snagging one for himself. "Is she going to live?"

"To a ripe old age," Rich predicted, chuckling. "Now wait outside, little brother. I never discuss a patient's health with the benefit of an intrusive audience."

"Intrusive!" Ross could still be heard muttering when he was seated in the now deserted waiting room. To be shoved aside, his presence unwanted, was clearly an unprecedented experience. But the professional in his brother was not to be put off.

"You didn't have to send him out, you know," Casey imparted when the doctor returned from evicting his brother, shaking his head in amusement. "Ross and I are partners," she murmured softly. "We don't have any secrets from each other."

Rich merely smiled and said nothing. He tilted his spare frame back in his chair, a strange, unfathomable light in his hooded gray eyes.

"It's mono, isn't it?" Casey decided, feeling a sudden wash of defeat. If she *had* contracted mononucleosis, it was going to alter her daily routine—for the next few weeks, at least. She'd have to stay home and rest to build up her system. Rest in bed, most likely. An unpalatable thought.

"There are other diagnoses that suggest the symptoms you've been experiencing," Rich intimated. "The tiredness, the waning appetite, reflect a little. You said you couldn't recall the date of your last monthly cycle."

"I have it written down at home on my personal calendar," she allowed ruefully. "A leftover idiosyncrasy from months of temperature charts and regimentation during my marriage." Where was all this leading?

"You and your husband had fertility problems?" Rich interpreted thoughtfully.

She nodded absently, watching the lift of one shaggy eyebrow in a typically Allen gesture.

"Then I'd say you're a singularly fortunate young woman," Rich decreed.

"I—I don't understand."

"You're pregnant," came the gentle enlightenment.

He might as well have told her she'd grown a second head! Casey leaned forward across the desk, rigid, almost afraid to breathe in case she hadn't heard correctly. "I'm what?"

"You're pregnant," he repeated impassively.

"Are you sure?" Dear God! This couldn't be happening!

Rich broke into a slow, reassuring smile. "If I wasn't sure after examining you, my findings were confirmed when I got the results of your tests."

Tears swam before Casey's eyes, years worth of sorrow clogging her throat. There was silence for a long while, but no words were needed. The kaleidoscope of emotions playing over her mobile features were poignantly sufficient in expressing her overwhelmed delight.

"I—will you tell Ross?" she finally got out. "Of course—he's the father." She choked out the heedless afterthought.

"Of course," Rich echoed, just as if no other conclusion were feasible. "But I think it would be best if you discussed your news with my brother privately. It is a very personal, private situation, after all." His eyes crinkled warmly, compassionately. "I'll leave you for a few minutes to get yourself together and then deliver the impatient Ross, how's that? I imagine he's paced the finish off the tile in the waiting room by now."

With a tremulous smile Casey watched the doctor depart, her heart pounding wildly in her breast. A change in daily routine! she had pondered a few moments earlier. My God, how insignificant! Her entire existence had changed, enriched beyond her wildest dreams!

Ross entered alone, his brother, true to his word, busying himself elsewhere. A look of questioning concern creased his rugged features, and Casey, having no wish to dissemble, simply laid the truth at his feet.

"We're going to be parents," she relayed breathlessly.

"You're pregnant!" he deciphered with a rasp of undiluted joy and relief. His fingers trembled as he cradled her glowing face. "Why didn't you tell me you were suffering from—from morning sickness, instead of letting me wonder God knows what?"

"Because I didn't know," she insisted dreamily.

"Surely your feminine instincts must have suggested the possibility?" he pressed gently, but with no rancor.

She flushed, her breathlessness increasing under his possessive regard. "I've been...preoccupied" was the only explanation she could offer, and hopelessly inept for a grown woman who had missed several periods without reaching the obvious conclusion.

"You're thrilled about this," he perceived quizzically. "And still a little rocky from the news," he discerned when she quivered as he lifted her against the muscled wall of his chest.

For a long while he simply held her, each of them reveling in the shared closeness, until finally, reluctantly, Ross turned her toward the door. "Into the bathroom with you," he directed thickly. "I want you to splash some cold water on your hands and face and try to relax. Pregnant ladies have been known to swoon, and we can't be too careful."

His words were heavy with indulgent pride, and Rich was easily aware of his brother's exuberance when Ross returned, alone, after seeing Casey to the bathroom.

"You're a sly old devil," the doctor accused, his arm across the younger man's shoulders as they stepped into his office. "I knew you were crazy about your partner. Last weekend when Darcy and I had you to dinner, and you condescended to speak at all, in that black mood you brought with you, one name came up repeatedly: Cassandra Spencer. I figured you two were close. But I must say, this is a little outside your usual sphere of influence. You've never brought me a pregnant waif before."

"That's because I damn well took precautions against such a thing." Ross grinned. "What happened with Casey was unpremeditated—beautiful and spontaneous."

"And infinitely rewarding," Rich hazarded sagely. "She is the woman for you, isn't she? The one who's finally clipped your wings?"

"And tied me in knots," Ross agreed unevenly, his eyes riveted on the less shaky, but no less dreamy figure making her way down the hall. "And just for the record," he shot off in an undertone, "I've never brought *any* woman to this office, and you darn well know it!"

"Touché." Rich acknowledged the impassioned thrust, amused understanding lurking in his dark eyes as Ross slipped a protective arm around Casey's waist and nudged her into a chair.

"Tell me what I need to do, Rich," Casey implored, her expression rapt.

Get married first, he thought wryly. But, of course, Ross would settle for nothing less. "For starters, you need to begin eating better," Rich declared firmly. "Those little twinges of queasiness you've been experiencing are undoubtably the old nemesis morning sickness. I'll prescribe something if it gets too bad, but, naturally, I can't stand in as attending physician for this pregnancy. I deliver a lot of babies, but my own brother's child . . ." He shook his head. "You'll need to make arrangements within the next few weeks to get started on prenatal checkups."

"I will. But no medication," Casey said decisively. "I've heard it's best, for the baby's sake, not to take anything during pregnancy. I haven't been throwing up or anything." *And if I do, I'll do so gloriously,* she mused lightheartedly.

"And this fatigue you've been experiencing," Rich went on. "It's a typical manifestation of early pregnancy. Your body is hard at work nurturing a new life. Compensate for it and take a nap. Every afternoon." He sounded like Ross then, imperiously autocratic.

"I will," Casey promised vaguely. After she got home from work, she cogitated. There was too much to be done at the office.

"How long of a nap?" Ross broke in.

"An hour at the very least," Rich pronounced. "And I'm adamant about the eating, Casey. Nourishment is vitally essential during the early months of pregnancy."

"The little turkey will eat, if I have to stuff her myself," Ross avowed. His tone softened perceptively. "Can you recommend a good obstetrician?"

"Bob McMillan is a good man, but Casey may have her own preference."

"No!" The doctor she had consulted in the past was associated with failure. Casey wanted to start fresh. Oh, this seemed like a miracle! "I'll see whoever you suggest, Rich."

"Anything else?" Ross prompted patiently.

"The vitamins Casey suggested—they wouldn't be a bad idea. Bob will prescribe whatever he favors, but I'll get you some pharmaceutical samples of multiple vitamins with iron to see her through the next week or so."

Ross nodded. "Write out the OB's number while you're at it, will you? Then I think I'd better get the expectant mother home. She looks like she's about to fall asleep on us."

Her eyes were closed, her head tilted back against the soft leather chair, but Casey wasn't sleeping. She was dreaming of tiny little feet and hands.

Ross kept his arm firmly around her waist on the way out to the car, as if she were a helium balloon that might flit up to the heavens with her buoyancy if released. It was a warm, possessive clasp, and Casey made no demur when he pulled her next to his side for the drive home.

The blanket of ownership was unfurling again, enclosing her within its all-encompassing warmth. And it felt so right! How selfish she was being, thinking only of her own happiness today. Without Ross—without Ross she would still be unfulfilled. Achingly so. The empty shell was filled now, with the precious outgrowth of their passion.

Tomorrow, she decided unswervingly, tomorrow she would think about the future, let Ross bask in the glory of his impending fatherhood. Today was for her!

Ross seemed lost in his own thoughts. He cast her frequent sidelong glances but pressed no further on her ineptitude in diagnosing her own condition, seeming content just to hold her.

It was a short jaunt from Manhattan Beach to her cottage, but Casey fell into a light doze, lulled by the security of being in the arms of the man she loved.

Just as she had done once before when Ross brought her home, Casey clung to him, inebriated with happiness this time rather than wine.

"Come on, little mother," he chided, pulling her groggy form with him under the steering wheel and out the door. "Let's get you tucked up in bed. You're out on your feet."

When her incoherent efforts made a botch of undressing, Ross gave her a helping hand.

"Don't look," she pleaded sleepily.

"Honey, I'm familiar with every inch of you," he reminded her softly, slipping her pantyhose and half-slip down to her thighs. He sat her on the edge of the bed to expedite their removal.

"But you're always teasing," she complained non-sensically. "You'll probably say I look scrawny or something."

"You *do* look a bit undernourished," he agreed gruffly, unhooking her bra. "Such modesty," he clucked, prying her arms loose from their defensive crisscross over her bare breasts. "What am I going to do with you?"

"Sleep with me?" she suggested hopefully, but he shook his head.

"You need to rest, love. And if I held you ..." His expressive shrug spoke for itself. "Besides, I'm sure your parents will be along shortly. They'll be concerned when they see my car outside instead of your own, and I don't want to compromise their regard for me."

"My mother knows we've slept together," Casey relayed blandly. "She wouldn't be shocked to find us in the same bed."

"Your father sure as hell would! And I'm not going to rub salt in the wounds, curling up with his oldest, *pregnant* offspring."

"Why worry now?" she mused, punching the pillow and snuggling in drowsily. "That's sort of like closing the barn door after the cow's gotten out." She blinked open one heavy eyelid. "Are you going to tell them?"

"That's your province, honey," Ross allowed quietly. "What I am going to do is tell them I want you to get a good night's sleep and a little supper if you wake later." Warm lips brushed the shell of her ear. "Sleep well, my little protagonist. I'll see you in the morning."

"You're not staying?" she protested, on the edge of sleep.

"No. I want to tie up some loose ends and leave the slate clean for Carlotta. I need to be free to gather in the reins and take the load off a little idiot at Spencer-Allen who was too proud to call for help." His tone was tinged with reproach, and Casey turned her nose into the pillow, unwilling to acknowledge the gentle castigation.

"Tomorrow, then." She succumbed to his promise reluctantly and sleep gratefully, dreaming of the romantic marriage proposal she would receive in the morning, and happily wedded bliss ever after.

To say Ross caught her at an all-time low the next morning would be an understatement in the extreme. Bent over the toilet in the throes of her first full-blown bout of morning sickness, Casey was in no condition to receive the love of her life.

And he put his foot in his mouth with "Your face is about the same color as that apple-green bathrobe." Ross was not at all put off by her distress. "I knew you wouldn't be able to get along without me when it came down to the nitty-gritty," he taunted.

"Well, I can get along without you for this!" She shoved angrily at his chest, slamming the bathroom door in his face. Smug, supercilious father! How dare he be so condescending! Another wave of nausea washed over her and she hugged the bowl. The devil! The least Ross could do was appear solicitous!

There was no way she could see the stunned disbelief on Ross's face as he wandered aimlessly out of the cottage. It was inevitable he would meet up with Casey's parents; they walked along the shoreline every morning.

"The little snot!" he huffed, offended. "She's in the bathroom being sick—by herself. Claims she doesn't need me. She can't be sick without me!"

"Son," Blaine Thorpe advised laughingly, "Casey was flying in another orbit with her news last night." A conspiratorial gleam twinkled in his eyes. "If you're going to convince her she needs you, drastic measures are called for."

At precisely the same moment a daringly devious plan was forming in Casey's mind. A plan for subtle revenge.

No flowery marriage proposal had been forthcoming from Ross that morning. Just the arrogantly masculine "I knew you wouldn't be able to get along without me." And there had been no hearts-and-flowers offering a few weeks back, either. Just a quiet declaration of intent—to have her for his wife. And what Ross had put her through since then! That vicious character assassination when she turned down his proposal!

Well, she decided spiritedly, let him stew in his own juices for a while! Let him sweat out her promise to love, honor, and obey. She wanted the whole nine yards before she married this time; a little romantic wooing, a new bent avowal of undying love. And she was going to have them! Until then... She smiled wickedly. Until then things were going to be interesting. She was holding a winning hand. Four aces, the heir to the Spencer-Allen throne. Ross would have to play things her way!

But he didn't have to like it. In fact, he very nearly choked on the bitter pill she was determined to hand out.

Brashly, with his usual omnipotent decisiveness, he strode in, found Casey seated in the living room—considerably less green—and demanded, "Get dressed. We're going to Las Vegas to get married." There was a slight twinge of desperation in his tone, but Casey missed it altogether, intent on her own scheme.

If their eventual marriage was ever going to succeed, Ross was going to have to drop this domineering attitude. "Not today." Her words were a little breathless, underscored by the nervousness she was feeling, putting him off so boldly.

Interpreting her hesitancy to equate with her rocky stomach, Ross promised, "We'll wait until you're feeling settled, and I'll pull the car over at the first hint of queasiness. And hold your head,'' he added mockingly.

Beast! "No, thank you,'' she declined demurely.

At that Ross exploded, "No, thank you! You sound like you're turning down the dessert course after dinner. You'll marry me today and damn well like it!''

I'll marry you eventually and love it, she amended silently. "Not—not this weekend,'' she said determinedly. "I think we should...get to know each other better first.''

"Better!'' he roared. "We know each other as well as two people can, in the biblical sense. We're going to be parents!''

"Precisely,'' she averred sweetly. "And what kind of parents are we going to make if we're always at each other's throats?'' She smiled benignly. "After what we've been through these last few weeks, I think a little cooling-off period will do us both good, don't you?''

"I most certainly do not!'' he denounced savagely. "We've got a child coming in seven months. Every day we delay makes the circumstances of his conception that much more obvious!''

"Concerned about proprieties?'' Casey scoffed. "Sorry, I won't be hustled into a shotgun wedding.''

"I'd like to hustle you right over my knee!'' Ross thundered. "You've got to be the most obstinate female I've ever met. What is it you want?''

Three little words, none over one syllable. *I love you!* Casey knew them by heart; they had haunted her for weeks. Why hadn't Ross mentioned love when he asked her to marry him? Or today, when he demanded marriage? Short of her taking to her bed in illness again, how could they recapture the closeness they had shared up at the cabin?

"I just need a little more time,'' she finally put in.

"You've got one week! If you haven't come to your

senses by then, I'll hoist you over my shoulder and plunk you down in front of a preacher."

"He won't marry us without my consent," she pointed out reasonably.

"He'll have your consent," Ross stated with great certainty.

"What are you going to do? Drug me into submission?"

A malicious grin spread over his handsome features. "I have far more effective means at my disposal." Depositing his rangy frame beside her on the sofa, he lifted her chin and queried, "Did you brush your teeth, Miss Morning Sickness?"

"Mmm. What are you going to do?"

"Shut this quarrelsome mouth for a while!" His dark head descended, blocking out reality, and Casey succumbed to the taste and feel that was Ross. How long had it been since he kissed her that way? It seemed like an eternity.

"That's right," he coaxed, "curl up next to me where you belong."

She strained to get closer and allowed herself to be lifted into his lap. "Persuade me some more," she pleaded unashamedly. "I love the way you make me feel."

"I love the way you feel, too," Ross growled against her lips. "Open your mouth and let's see if this hot little tongue can do anything besides argue."

Her lips parted eagerly, hungry for more intimate invasion. She was moaning, deep in her throat, but it took a long time for her to assimilate the voice as her own. God! The power this man had over her!

As always, the sensuous glide of his lips over hers impelled her to respond in kind. Entranced, she offered no resistance when Ross lowered the zipper the length of her robe, parting the material widely.

A look of sheer reverence glittered in his dark, absorbed gaze. Could this be the same man who had undressed her so impersonally the night before?

"Enchanting," he breathed. Tenderly he cupped her burgeoning breasts, which swelled expectantly. "You're...exquisite!"

And you're irresistible, Casey attested, deeply disturbed. Only when his hands began to caress more insistently, kneading her breasts enticingly, did she demur, placing a shaky hand over his own. "I'm a little bit sore," she told him unsteadily. "A natural side effect of my condition, I expect."

"Undoubtably." Reluctantly Ross let his hand stray. His fingers moved seductively over her narrow rib cage and down to the flat planes of her stomach, tracing the sharp outline of her hipbones through her panties. "The soreness in your breasts didn't tip you off that you might be pregnant?" he queried indulgently.

"No." Casey was finding it increasingly difficult to breathe, her state of arousal highly evident. "I thought I was just overtired and achy, like I always get before my period."

"Are you achy right now?" He chuckled, brushing his clipped fingernails over the warm triangle of nylon protecting her vulnerable femininity.

"I want you, Ross!" There was no holding back her desire. Entreatingly she arched against his marauding hand.

"Are you going to marry me today?"

Sublime masculine victory radiated from the smiling face above as Casey threw back her head to agree. The words froze on her lips, danger looming like a furious black thundercloud. The man was seducing her, and making no bones about it as his fingers continued to foray persuasively.

"I—I thought you said I had a week?"

"So I did." The magical hand lifted, sifting through her hair to hold fast her head as Ross fastened his mouth on her lips with unerring precision. "And that's what you'll have. Exactly seven days," he promised roughly.

Then, vaulting to his feet, he faced Casey toward the kitchen, delivering a directional pat on the rear. "Let's go and see about getting the expectant mother some breakfast."

Casey seldom bothered with breakfast, and her kitchen boasted little in the way of culinary ingredients with which to accomplish an early-morning meal. Ross searched her refrigerator diligently and shook his head in disgust, finally producing a bowl of Cheerios, orange juice, and toast.

Casey wanted no more than the toast, but Ross was insistent. "Rich said you have to start eating better," he declared adamantly, and, remembering his promise to "stuff the little turkey himself," Casey cooperated, with chagrined poor grace.

Ross watched her, his gaze shrewd and unfathomable, as she ate and he did the dishes. "Just to show how magnanimous I can be," he inserted diffidently when he had dried the last dish, "I'm going to leave you in undistracted peace to make up your mind this weekend."

"Oh!" Perversely that was *not* what she wanted. "Why don't you come to dinner tomorrow? I'm sure Mama would be thrilled to have you."

Ross shot her a penetrating glance and shrugged. "If that's what you want. I thought you might like a little time alone—unpressured."

"Are you going to pressure me?" she teased.

"I said you had a week, and that's what you'll have. With no unwarranted forces brought to bear."

"I never knew you to be so accommodating," she

charged impishly. "You're getting mellow, Ross Allen."

"Not where you're concerned," he reflected enigmatically, and dropped a hard, hungry kiss on her bemused lips before taking his leave.

But, indeed, Ross was obligingly accommodating the next evening, politely steering clear of mentioning Casey's delicate condition.

Not so the bubbly Melissa. She had ferreted out the fact of Casey's pregnancy earlier and simmered with excitement the rest of the day. Missy resembled a Fourth of July firecracker about to go off in all directions at the dinner table, and it came as no surprise when she blurted, "When are you going to make an honest woman out of my sister, Ross?" Wide-eyed with teenage exuberance, she turned to their guest.

Unmindful of Casey's startled gasp, Ross raised two fingers on each hand in the V for victory salute, shook his head a la Richard Nixon, and loosely misquoted the ex-president: "Let me make this perfectly clear: It is not *I* who is dragging my feet."

"Casey!" Melissa turned to her sister, astounded. "How can you resist this gorgeous man?"

"Go soak your head!" Casey sputtered. Damn it! She'd marry Ross in her own good time, without any exhortations from her family!

"Casey doesn't like being led by the nose," Ross declared tolerantly.

"Led by the nose! You ought to hog-tie her!" Missy warmed to the subject. "I'm surprised at you, Ross. I never thought you'd let her manipulate you."

"Cassandra will come to the right decision," Ross declared unconcernedly.

"With a little help from the would-be father?" Blaine Thorpe suggested playfully.

Casey felt like an elusive football being nudged ever closer to the goal.

"Eat your dinner," came the implacable advice from Ross.

There were smiles all around the table. Except from Casey. She was seriously considering bolting from the room.

"Now, dear," her mother soothed, "Ross is talking sense, you know. You're eating for two now."

Thoroughly vexed, Casey concluded that inviting Ross to dinner had been imprudently shortsighted. Having Ross and her family all lined up on the side of the opposition was a formidable spectacle.

One-on-one she could handle the irascible tyrant. Four against one was impossible! Her plan to mold Ross into more manageable husband material had suffered a serious setback that night. She would have to be more careful in the future.

Despite her newly stiffened resolve, Casey was quiveringly *in*cautious when Ross folded her into a lusty embrace later before taking his leave.

"Take care, love," he husked into her hair, then dropped the bombshell. "I'll pick you up at eight tomorrow morning. Considering your early-morning delicacy, I think we'll start work an hour later for a while."

"You will not pick me up!" she declared wrathfully, dismissing his tender concern. Damn it, she wouldn't be here! she plotted furiously. There was no reason to alter her morning routine. She was perfectly capable of driving herself to work. She'd leave at seven, as usual, leaving Ross to eat her dust!

"Have a good night," Ross bid, smiling at some private amusement.

"Humph!"

Chapter Eleven

Casey was crafty, but not crafty enough. She hadn't allowed for the tenacity of Ross Allen. While she would have been ready to leave in her own car at seven, Ross arrived ten minutes before then, two unabashed conspirators in tow.

"Morning, son." Casey's father nodded cheerfully to the man he looked upon as his future son-in-law and began spooning coffee into her coffeepot.

"How's your stomach this morning?" her mother inquired breezily.

"What are you all doing in my kitchen?" Casey's gaping mouth formed the disgruntled words.

"Making breakfast," Ross advised imperturbably, shrugging out of his suit coat. "Run along and finish dressing so you can eat."

"You said you'd be here at eight," she muttered accusingly.

"And planned to be here before seven," he owned, "thwarting your attempt to take off without me."

"Who's making Missy's breakfast?" she demanded peevishly, turning to her bustling mother.

"Melissa isn't pregnant. I left her a packet of instant oatmeal. You're having the real thing, made from scratch."

"Yuck!" Gluey, rib-sticking oatmeal was the last thing she needed.

"Go and finish dressing," Ross repeated quietly. "Or sure as hell I'm going to give you a helping hand."

Fat chance I'll give you the opportunity! Casey thought rancorously. The nerve of the man, and her mother and father as well, barging in on her like this!

There was worse to come when they reached the office. Ross watched her every movement, infuriating Casey as he clucked around her with patronizing concern.

Bev commented on that very thing later as they sat around Ross's desk planning the weekly calendar. His stout determination to lighten Casey's workload produced a continuing round of sparks, and the secretary noted mischievously, "There seems to be some kind of pesty mosquito in here. Why don't you swat the darn thing and put it out of its misery?"

"Oh, I'd love to swat it." Amused, dancing eyes roamed over Casey's glowering face. "Unfortunately, the little devil won't light anywhere," Ross lamented. "And if it did, I'd probably get bitten."

"You can be sure of that!" Casey vowed stonily, still smarting at the way he had taken it upon himself to arrange an appointment for her with the obstetrician later in the afternoon. As she had no car, the smug beast would have to take her himself, and he darn well knew it!

Mercifully Ross was content to sit outside in the waiting room during her prenatal exam. But he had no such compunction about horning in on the discussion of her pregnancy that followed afterward in the OB's private office. His steel trap of a mind memorized all of the graying man's instructions, down to the finest detail.

By the next day Casey was chafing indignantly in the glass cage Ross had constructed around her. Damn it! she fumed, she wasn't made of cotton candy, and the sooner he accepted that fact, the better.

"What would you like for lunch?" the man in question quizzed, strolling into her office. He had that purposeful look in his eye, as if he expected her to claim her recent birdlike appetite.

She didn't. Tartly she reeled off, "A Big Mac, an order of fries, a vanilla shake, and a brownie!" That ought to keep him busy for a while. Casey was starved. A good sign. If she was going to nourish her cherished burden, she had to make hay while the sun—and her appetite—shined.

Whatever Ross thought of her ambitious order, he refrained from cynical comment. "McDonald's it is," he agreed, chuckling. "Just don't let Cal McCoy get wind of the fact that we've been frequenting the competition."

"*I* won't be." She indicated the stack of work papering her desk and wheedled, "Bring it back to me here, please?"

"Certainly," Ross assented genially. "Anything else for the expectant mama?"

"That'll do," she concluded sweetly.

The expectant father put away a hearty meal himself at Casey's hastily cleared desk, and was immensely pleased when she managed to eat three quarters of what she had ordered.

"Nap time now, I think," he intimated, extending a courteous hand to help her to her feet. When they got to her couch, he began methodically unfastening buttons and snaps.

"What do you think you're doing!" Casey flared, slapping his hands away.

"A nice rest every afternoon," he repeated the doctor's instructions verbatim. "Free of all restraining outer and undergarments."

Breathless, struggling futilely, she was reduced to her bra and half-slip. Her pantyhose were the next to go, despite her frantic grab to prevent their removal.

"Lie down on the couch, Cassandra," came the stern injunction.

Casey obeyed huffily, shivering with gooseflesh and fury. How could she love such a dictatorial swine? Not a day passed without their dissolving into some kind of tussle. How could they possibly make a go of marriage? Right now she had a good mind to flee the scene and reappear eight months hence, fait accompli—*un*pregnant! If Ross continued to watch over her like this until the baby was born, she'd go stark-raving bonkers!

"Here you go, honey." Ross returned bearing a blanket and a pillow. "Stretch out, and I'll cover you up."

She snatched the pillow, slammed her head down, and turned belligerently away from him, refusing to acknowledge her thanks. The blanket did feel deliciously cozy, snuggled up around her neck, but she maintained an affronted silence—for all of the three minutes it took her to drift off to sleep.

The sensation of something pressing finally roused her, and Casey frowned sleepily. Work! She had work to do. Her eyes flew to the neat pile of folders stacked on the corner of her desk. Could she afford to doze a few minutes more? The obstetrician had told her to give in to her sleepiness whenever possible.

No, not today, she decided. She had too much to do. Her eyes made a cursory sweep of the office, searching for the clothes Ross had removed.

They were nowhere in evidence, The bathroom seemed likely, but to Casey's dismay they weren't there either. Once again she checked her office, more carefully this time, but to no avail. Her eyes flew to her desk, her temper mounting explosively.

The rat! The dirty, rotten rat! Ross had taken her clothes *and* her telephone! Unplugged it at the desk connection, leaving her no means to beckon aid.

Like a whirlwind of fury she flew into his office, never considering he might not be alone. Thankfully only Bev was present, in addition to Ross, and Casey ignored her altogether.

Fists bunched on her hips, breasts heaving, she stood in her flesh-colored bra and half-slip and gritted, "What have you done with my clothes, you pervert!"

One dark brow rose in sardonic amusement. "Hung them up, of course."

"Where?"

"In the closet in the outer office," Ross advised implacably.

"Go get them, Bev. Right now!" Then, more politely, "Please?"

"Ross?" Bev was uncertain how to proceed.

"Oh, for heaven's sake!" Casey emoted, rounding on Ross. "When are you going to stop tormenting me?"

"When you agree to marry me," he responded evenly.

"Go to hell! Go directly to hell!" *No unwarranted forces brought to bear,* Ross had promised. This was insane!

"Feisty little thing, isn't she?" Ross was amused. "Are you through, Cassandra?"

At her contemptuous nod he directed, "Then go back and lie down. You've only rested for forty-five minutes, and you're supposed to nap for an hour every afternoon."

"I'll get you for this some day, Ross Allen!"

"Undoubtably." He nodded, unfazed. "And, Casey...don't slam the door, or I'll remove that, just as I did your clothes."

"I won't work here a day longer," she muttered, flopping down on her couch. But where would that leave her? Without professional stimulation, she'd be a basket case of frustration within days.

One thing was certain. She was not going to give Ross the answer he was looking for until the entire week was out! Not that he seemed concerned, but she was determined that he sweat out her answer until the last available minute. They still had a lot of things to work out before they married; chiefly, that two people couldn't climb into the same pair of pants. If Ross thought he was going to wear the only pants in the family, he was going to have to fight her for possession.

It would be so easy to lay down her arms in submission. She loved the man desperately. What had started as an innocuous scheme for revenge had mushroomed into full-scale war. But she had her principles to protect. Didn't she? a tiny voice prompted.

"I understand Ross is having a little get-together tonight," Bev mentioned chattily as Casey dictated a letter Friday morning.

"This is the first I've heard of it."

"Oh, dear. Did I let the cat out of the bag?"

"What's that supposed to mean?" Casey demanded suspiciously.

Bev squirmed in her chair. "Uh...well...I thought you might be making some kind of...of announcement tonight."

Casey bristled. She still had one more day! If Ross thought he was going to back her into a corner—announce the marriage she had yet to agree to—he had another think coming! "I really don't know what this is all about," she cooed, "but since I won't be coming—"

"You'll be there," a deeply timbered voice put in. Both women turned to find Ross lounging languidly in the doorway between connecting offices.

Ross had been out all morning. Now, Casey mused distractedly, his mysterious mission was explained. He'd been arranging a party.

Pantherlike strides carried him to stand beside her, and lean fingers bit into her shoulders. "My gathering tonight is a sort of thank-you for those who have worked tirelessly for me these last few months. You'll be there as my hostess, graciously, won't you love?" The fingers digging into the small bones of her shoulders warned Casey against claiming otherwise.

"Who's coming?" she asked dully.

"Bev and her husband, Carlotta and her latest flame, Sid Charles, and you—the star of the show and my biggest fan."

"Drop dead," she muttered under her breath.

"What was that, honey?"

"Anyone else?" Casey's voice came out in a croak. Ross was going to throttle her soon if he didn't let go! "Sounds like an awfully small party," she noted laconically.

"And, of course, your parents," he added negligently. "And my brother, Rich, and his wife."

"Of course," she echoed sarcastically. "All cornerstones of the Allen dynasty."

"Should make a well-rounded group, don't you agree?" he inserted cheerfully.

"That depends on what you have in mind," she countered cynically. The announcement of a merger, for instance. A three-way merger. Her hand went protectively to the third member of the trio nestled snugly in her womb.

"Really, Ross," the silent Bev chimed in. "Maybe Casey isn't up to this. I mean, all those naps this week..."

Casey glanced up sharply. Was it possible Bev didn't know the reason for her afternoon rest periods? Had she failed to grasp the fact of her impending motherhood?

The truth was only too evident; Bev's angelic features told all. Bev knew, and the secretive smile she directed at Ross raised hackles along Casey's spine. Conspiracy buffeted her at every turn. Even Bev was against her.

The voice of reason chided that Bev wanted nothing more than her happiness, but it was slim solace. She was lining up with Ross, all the same.

Simmering in her own thoughts, Casey listened inattentively as Bev inquired, "Is this evening to be casual, Ross, or can we ladies parade our new winter finery and spiff up?"

"Oh, dressy, I think," Ross decided affably. His hands settled on Casey's taut shoulders, lightly this time, turning her to face him. Kneading fingers soothed her rigidity, then wandered down the slope of her shoulders to traverse the length of each slender arm. "Your Chinese silk caftan should be perfect tonight," he decreed softly. "Sid will be flattered if you wear one of his gowns, and the loose, flowing style and vibrant red hues—"

"Are just right for a scarlet woman!" His bossiness inflamed! Rashly Casey put her own connotation on his words, never pausing to consider his motivation in dictating what she should wear. Goaded, she let her tongue run away with discretion and charged, "I don't need a billowing caftan to camouflage my condition; I'm not even showing yet. If you want my appearance to make an announcement, maybe I should just tape a big P on my chest for—"

"Enough!" Ross thundered, looming over her like a threatening god. "Leave us, please, Bev," he requested tersely. His eyes never strayed from Casey's angry, flushed face.

As soon as they were alone he barked out, "Don't you ever pull a tantrum like that in front of the staff! If you're ticked off at me, wait until we're alone to cut loose. I won't have our dirty laundry aired in public!"

Dirty laundry! Casey cringed at the metaphor. "I— I—"

"Furthermore," he roared on, "despite whatever your pea brain may have formulated, I was not looking for a means with which to announce our imminent parenthood. My sole consideration in suggesting the red caftan was in covering the ravages of the weight you've lost recently and offsetting your slight pallor. Do I make myself clear?"

She nodded mutinously, but her slumping posture betrayed her. The wind had left her sails as quickly as it had whipped up her spirits earlier. Even one-on-one, she was discovering, it was difficult to square off against such a formidable opponent. "I—what time tonight?"

"Eight o'clock," Ross assayed shortly. "And your parents will bring you. All you have to do is smile and look beautiful, two things you excel at."

"I'll be there," she granted tonelessly. Her eyes implored him to leave; she was drooping with fatigue.

"You'll have your nap now," he decided briskly, and for once Casey expressed no rebellion, allowing herself to be undressed and swaddled like a baby.

"Rest well, my tigress." Warm lips brushed her ear, accompanied by a surprisingly light chuckle. "I want you restored to one hundred percent for tonight."

"Casey? Are you ready, dear?" Muriel Thorpe's voice beckoned.

Oh, Lord! Her parents were here. Was it seven thirty already? Casey stood in front of the mirrored closet doors in her stockinged feet, most definitely *not* ready! Drat this unexpected weight loss, and Ross for being right, as usual. Nothing looked good on her except the red silk caftan he had decreed, and she had been determined to thwart him!

She shuddered. All her evening clothes made her look like a gaunt string bean, and Sid Charles was going to be at the party tonight. It would be sacrilege, dishonoring his creations. They hung on her. There was nothing else for it, she'd have to wear the caftan.

"Light a fire under that pretty little fanny," Blaine Thorpe admonished, observing her seething hesitation. "Ross won't appreciate it if we're late."

"Ask me if I care," Casey simmered, jerking the dress in contention over her head.

"You look very nice, dear," her father complimented brusquely. "Shoes now, and we'll be on our way."

Shoes...*shoes!* Casey sparked to life. It was brilliant—masterful! She shot her father a Cheshire cat grin and reached for the platform shoes Ross had hated from day one.

"No, ma'am!" Fatherly authority intervened. "I won't have you teetering around on those ankle twisters in your delicate condition!"

"Daddy..." Casey wheedled.

"No!" Distinctly.

"Damn!"

"Cassandra!" If there was one thing Blaine refused to tolerate, it was profanity from his daughters. "You need a keeper, young lady. This marriage can't come soon enough for my peace of mind."

"You sound just like Ross," she complained bitterly.

"A very sensible young man." He nodded. "He'll

make a fine son-in-law. Highly suited to your temperament.''

''Meaning I'm a brat?''

''Meaning Ross won't put up with any nonsense,'' he corrected smoothly.

''Are you two going to argue all night?''

''Argue!'' Casey choked on her mother's intervention. ''No one can argue with Daddy. He's always right.''

''You're heading for a set down, young lady!'' Blaine threatened darkly, whereupon Casey burst into tears.

Great hiccuping sobs racked her body as a week's worth of unhappiness spilled out and she crumpled into the cushioning support of her mother's shorter shoulder.

''Here, Muriel,'' Blaine exclaimed gruffly, brushing his wife aside. ''I started this, unwittingly. Let me have her.''

A warm bear hug enveloped Casey but in no way lessened her misery. Was she such a shrew that only outright taming by a stronger force could set things right? God, she'd made a mess of things! ''Ooohhh, Daaaddy!...''

''Hush, love,'' he soothed. ''It's my fault, all my fault. It's hard for any parent to accept that his little ones have grown up and away from his protective influence. I'm afraid, since I've had you so close this past year, I've reverted too much to my old fatherly ways. Don't cry, honey.'' He shook her gently. ''Everything will work out in the end.''

''I'll tell Ross I'm going to marry him. Tonight,'' she promised between sniffles. ''As soon as we're alone. Honestly, I will. I should have agreed last weekend. It's what I want with all my heart.''

The poignant conviction in her words was unmistakable. Blaine cast his wife an uneasy glance and pushed Casey away gently. "Go into the bathroom with your mama and see what you can do with your face. You've soaked my shirt," he teased. "I'll have to run home and change."

"I'm sorry," she hiccuped. "I must look a mess."

"A little red-eyed," her mother scoffed quietly, "but cold water will soon take care of that."

"I really blew it with Ross, didn't I?" Casey posed miserably.

"You made a tactical error in handling the man you love," her mother agreed, dabbing her daughter's eyes. "It's nothing insurmountable."

Meaning tonight. "I hope so." Casey drew a deep, shuddering breath. "I've been so unhappy." Briefly she set about explaining her intentions in holding Ross at bay this week—his omission in declaring his love at the outset.

"He does love you, dear," Muriel declared wistfully. "I think perhaps you've been too close...too involved to see it. Your father and I are delighted with the match."

"Aren't you just the tiniest bit embarrassed, having a twenty-seven-year-old daughter pregnant out of wedlock?" Casey teased. Some of her usual cheekiness was returning.

"Well...if I had my druthers, I'd rather have you married and then pregnant. But you always were an unpredictable child."

Casey hugged her mother impulsively. "I love you, Mama. And I love Ross. I'll give him my answer as soon as we get there."

"Wait until you're alone," came the glib suggestion. "Ross has been a bit...er...ruffled this week. I think he would rather accept your happy news in private."

"Ruffled?" That was putting it mildly! Casey's eyes

narrowed thoughtfully. "Have you been talking to Ross?"

Muriel flushed uncomfortably. "Several times. He's been worried whether you were eating and sleeping properly."

"Has he, now?" Casey drawled, tongue-in-cheek. "Is that why you've been over every night? To spy on me?"

"Now, dear…"

"Don't worry, Mama. I'll play it cool. I'm not going to lambaste the man."

It was just as well, too, for Ross, when they arrived, was in an exceptionally mellow mood, clamping Casey to his side instantly.

They were late. Not unforgivably so, but late all the same. Casey flashed a dazzling, apologetic smile around the already assembled social gathering, then froze when her gaze came to rest on Rich Allen.

The doctor returned her smile affably, but Casey felt a twinge of malaise, gooseflesh tingling down her spine. Never before had she interacted socially with a man who had examined her so intimately.

Keenly perceptive, Rich soothed her discomfort with a genial "Casey, nice to see you again." He thrust a plump blond woman forward. "Meet my wife, Darcy. Darcy… Cassandra Spencer."

A more unlikely doctor's wife Casey had never seen. Barely five feet tall, her blond curls obviously receiving help from Miss Clairol, Darcy Allen looked more the part of an effusive, if overweight cheerleader.

Smoothing what appeared to be size-twelve silver lamé lounging pajamas over size-fourteen hips, the husky voiced blond said, "Come sit with me, Casey. Everyone else seems to know you, and I haven't had the pleasure."

Very reluctantly Casey unstuck herself from the warmth supporting her around the waist. It felt so right, being held by the man she loved!

Ross brushed his lips across her forehead, studying her misty expression. "What would you like to drink, honey?"

"Whatever everyone else is having will be fine," she husked.

A fleeting smile curved his lips, the barely perceptible side-to-side movement of his head noticed by no one except Casey.

The drink he delivered could have passed for a screwdriver, or Darcy's tequila sunrise, except that it was a virgin mix—orange juice devoid of any alcohol.

"Tell me," Darcy began persuasively, "what is your secret?"

"Hmm?" Casey was only half listening. Her eyes were riveted on their host as he circulated, refilling highball glasses and passing pleasantries and hors d'oeuvres. God, Ross was an attractive devil, dressed in formal evening wear! Flat-hipped and broad-shouldered, his black dress suit accentuated his leanness, and the white evening shirt set off his deep, year-round tan. This man would be hers after tonight. If the child she was carrying was half as good-looking...

"Casey!" Darcy giggled. "Stop admiring my big hunk of a brother-in-law and pay attention!"

"Sorry." Casey turned to the woman, her cheeks flushed a dull red.

"Honestly," Darcy clucked. "I don't know why Ross planned a cocktail party with Tiny away. He'll be busy all night, looking after his guests. Strange," she mused. "Dinner parties are more his style, and planned farther in advance."

"Tiny's...away?"

"For the weekend." Darcy nodded. "Visiting her

sister in Alhambra." Before Casey could reflect on this
piece of information, Darcy went back to her earlier
theme. "Now, tell me your secret," she entreated. "I
heard Ross and my husband discussing your weight
loss, and I'm desperate. I'll try anything!"

Casey squirmed, unable to think of an off-putting
reply. Salvation appeared in the form of their hors-
d'oeuvres-bearing host.

"Casey's motivation in losing weight is a bit drastic,
even for you, Darcy." Ross threw Casey an audacious
wink and lectured, "Rich has been devising thousand-
calorie diet regimes for you for years. If you'd just stick
to one"—he brushed Darcy's hand away from the hors
d'oeuvres tray—"and leave the goodies alone..."

"Oh, you!" Darcy ignored his scolding advice and
popped a ham-and-cheese swirl into her mouth. "No
one starts a diet Friday night. That's what Mondays are
for."

"My darling dumpling, you're forever doomed,"
Ross pronounced, ruffling her hair affectionately.

"Don't *do* that! I spent a fortune at the hairdresser's
this afternoon!"

"Ah, I thought I detected a slight color variation."
His eyes roamed with amused speculation over Darcy's
blond curls.

"Condescending swine!" Darcy vaulted to her feet,
flashing Casey a sympathetic smile. "You're welcome
to the beast. I think I'll saunter on over and chat up my
favorite dress designer."

"Sid isn't a miracle worker," Ross chided. "Better
shed a few pounds before you lasso the poor man."

"He's designed for me before," Darcy reproached.

"Last summer, when you were a perfect size ten—
for all of six weeks," Ross chided.

Casey sat through the barbed interchange in won-
drous fascination. So! She wasn't the only woman to

fall victim to Ross's mockery. "You're crazy about your sister-in-law, aren't you?" she speculated, watching as Darcy flounced off in a shimmer of giggling silver lamé.

"Darcy's a breath of fluffy fresh air after dealing with female sharks in the business world every day. She's...enchanting."

"And Rich loves her dearly," Casey guessed, watching as the doctor removed two toothpicked tidbits from his wife's fingers, popped them in his own mouth, then swatted her briskly on the fanny when she started to protest.

"Rich is a lucky man" was all that Ross said. He set the serving tray on the coffee table and wrapped a proprietary arm around Casey's shoulders.

"Don't you like intellectual women?" she teased, pressing her face into the nubby fabric of his dinner jacket.

"Are you challenging me to prove otherwise?" When Casey could only stare, lost in the dark-gray glitter of his eyes, he husked, "So be it," and settled his mouth warmly over the covert invitation of her parted lips.

For a long moment they were lost in their own world, a world where nothing mattered except the intensity of their feelings. A tinkling female voice finally broke them apart.

"Hey," Carlotta Perini complained gaily, "what's this, a private party just for two?"

Her gentle reproach set the tone for the rest of the evening. Casey and Ross circulated repentantly, shelving their personal feelings temporarily to meld the widely divergent social gathering into a relaxed, enjoyable evening.

Casey was radiant, hoping Ross would announce their impending marriage at any time. But although he cast her frequent, enigmatic glances, no declarations of intent were forthcoming from Ross. As midnight drew near and the party began to break up, Casey sighed. Of course! She hadn't been alone with him long enough to give him her answer. And, being uncharacteristically gallant, Ross was sticking to his word, refusing to show his hand before she agreed to become his wife.

Her parents were the last to stir, deep in conversation with Ross. Secretly Casey was delighted with the friendship that had sprung up between the three people she loved. Quinn had never fit in. He was too formal and uncompromising for her family's relaxed ways. Ross...Ross was like one of the family already. The approval in her father's eyes as he gazed at the younger man warmed Casey's heart.

Loathe to interrupt, she excused herself unobtrusively to visit the powder room before the drive home.

Chapter Twelve

"Oh!" Casey returned to find Ross alone, studying the contents of his glass with deep absorption. "Mom and Dad have gone, then? Are—are you going to take me home, after we talk?" Suddenly inordinately shy, she trembled slightly as she stood before him.

"No." He shook his head slowly, watching her with disturbing intentness. "I'm not going to take you home."

"N-not going to take me home?" Her voice quivered huskily. "I can't stay here. I don't have any...any clothes. And my parents will be worried."

"They won't be worried." Ross dismissed her argument, indicating a brown paper bag on the coffee table. "It's all been taken care of."

"Taken care of?" Casey knew she was babbling, repeating his words like a robot. Hesitantly she reached for the bag, staring in startled dismay as she tipped out a pair of faded jeans, a red-checked shirt, her hairbrush, and her toothbrush.

"What does this..." Her words trailed off when she encountered the half pleading, half arrogantly quelling gleam in the big man's eyes. "You're—you're kidnapping me?"

"Hardly," Ross growled. "I have your parents' consent."

Traitors! Benedict Arnolds, both of them! No wonder her mother had carried that ridiculous diaper bag of a purse. She was smuggling contraband—her clothes! For a brief moment Casey debated the merits of indignant revolt and then dismissed the notion gleefully out of hand, hurtling herself into the arms of the man she loved.

"You're not going to kick up a fuss?"

"I'm not going to kick up a fuss," she repeated dutifully, wrapping her arms around his neck.

"You're under no illusions, hmm?" Ross chuckled, settling a large hand around her nape to position her head for his kiss. "You know what you're going to get tonight?"

"What am I going to get?" she whispered coquettishly.

"Seduced, out of your mind!" came the unequivocal avowal. "I'm going to take you up to my lair and enchant you with my prowess as a captor."

"Are you going to carry me up to this lair, my pirate?" She shivered with respectful impudence.

"No, more's the pity," Ross negated, spreading possessive fingers over her abdomen. "This little baggage you're carrying is too precious a cargo to risk bouncing down a flight of stairs."

"You've never dropped me before."

"I've never been an expectant daddy before," Ross rebuked gently, and Casey knew that her moment had come.

"Ross, I—"

"*No!*" His forcefulness, and the silencing fingers over her lips, cut off her response. "Tonight is for loving. And tomorrow we're going to spend a whole day together, without arguments or illness, just enjoying each other's company. Tomorrow night you may give me your answer."

"And if I don't agree?" She giggled. "You can't keep me quiet forever."

"Can't I?" Ross smiled, his lips hovering a mere inch away. "I can sure as hell keep this sassy mouth occupied for the duration!"

"Promises, promises!"

"By God, you're never at a loss for words, are you?"

Casey batted her eyelashes and smiled in placid serenity. A deep growl issued from nearby.

"You're asking for it!"

"I'm trying," she stated playfully, and was swept to her feet. "What about this mess, all these dirty dishes?" she posed just before Ross switched off the lights.

"Oh...the mess! Tiny won't be back until Sunday. We've got plenty of time to clean up before then. I've got more important things on my mind right now."

"Kidnapping and seduction." There was absolutely no fear in Casey's even tones, as Ross was quick to note.

"Show some respectful trepidation, woman! You're supposed to be terrified. I'm not sure I like this amenable pose."

"Sorry." She inched closer to his side. "A pregnant lady is hard pressed to feign virginal hysteria."

"Such willing prey," he clucked as they climbed the stairs. "And here I've been looking forward to a good fight. Been looking forward to it all week, in fact."

"Have you, now?"

"Yep." He nodded with no penitence whatsoever. "Ever since you gave me that prissy little speech about getting to know each other better."

"I didn't mean in bed!" came the embarrassed admonishment.

"Too bad. It's a damn good starting place."

Startled by his directness, Casey tried once again to tell him of her love, but his mouth cut her off when they reached the top of the stairs and he swept her into his arms and began a long soul-destroying kiss.

"Like the pirate's lair?" he husked, settling her down beside a massive satin-covered bed.

She stared, hypnotized. "Where—where did you get this monstrosity?" Of a certainty it was no period piece, no provincial antique.

"I had it custom-made, down to the last turning and carving, to match what was already here." Ross waved a directional hand around the authentic antiques dotting the rest of the bedroom. His voice tinged with offended pride, he asked, "Don't you like it?"

"Well, it's certainly . . . big." Twice as big as her own bed, Casey thought bemusedly.

"I'm a big man, honey!" And never had he looked bigger, linking his fingers behind his head, stretching dramatically.

"Are you going to lend me a T-shirt or something, to sleep in?" Dear Lord! Could that be her voice, squeaky with nervousness?"

"Nope. We'll sleep in the raw. I always do."

I'll bet, Casey thought agitatedly, and bit her lip in vexation. Darn her scatterbrained mother! The least she could have done was pack a robe for the morning.

"I'm not going to undress you, either," Ross continued. "I've had that privilege many times in the past. Tonight I want to watch you disrobe by yourself." He drew a fragile armchair up to the side of the bed and sank down to enjoy the spectacle.

"You want me to whet your appetite, is that it?" Casey sought to sound sexily reproachful, but her voice came out in a strangled whisper as dark eyes watched the flowing caftan rustle to her feet. Clad only in bikini briefs and a lacy bra, she felt as vulnerable as Eve, uncertain how to proceed.

"The bra first," Ross directed quietly. When Casey

complied, her fingers shyly cupping her tender breasts, he husked, "Are they still sore?"

"A little."

"I'll be very careful with you tonight," he promised softly, gesturing in a dismissing fashion to her one remaining garment. "The panties now."

The velvet softness of her thighs offered no resistance, but Casey's hands shook at the task, inching the briefs downward. Stripping before a man's absorbed gaze—even the man she loved—was achingly unnerving.

"Come here to me," Ross commanded throatily, spreading his knees to make room for her to stand within his reach.

God help me, Casey thought, *I do feel like a shy maiden going forth to the arms of her lover.* But the hands at the back of her thighs were warmly encouraging, and she offered no resistance when Ross pulled her into his lap.

"Exquisite," he murmured, burying his lips in the soft scented skin of her throat. "So beautiful, and tractable, and all mine! You'll never doubt that after tonight!"

I've never doubted it at all, not since I knew I was carrying your child, she longed to cry. But his hovering mouth brooked no more words, and Casey's lips parted under the persuasive onslaught. His hands coursed over the bare skin of her back, and he pulled her closer, crushing her tender breasts into the rough fabric of his jacket. She gave an instinctive moan of discomfort, easing away slightly.

"Sorry." Ross released her lips and cupped one pink-tipped globe tenderly. "I'll try to be more careful and remember your delicate condition." His fingers massaged with infinite gentleness, and a hard bud rose, probing his palm.

"That feels... wonderful!"

"I'm going to take good care of you." Ross stroked his hand soothingly over her other breast, and then down to the quivering muscles bunching spasmodically in her stomach. "I'll be so careful, my son here won't even know I'm taking pleasure with his mama."

"He'll know!" The stroking hand wandered lower, and Casey felt a loud roaring in her ears. "His heart-beat—if he has one yet—is connected to mine, and I'm—"

"Shameless," he teased, spreading her nakedness across the smooth satin sheets. "Shameless and yet so shy." Her wrists were captured high above her head when Casey would have covered her nakedness with a sheet. "No barriers tonight, love," he remonstrated with gentle firmness. "I've dreamed of having you bare beneath my hands like this for months."

"Turn off the light, then," she entreated.

"Uh-uh. Seeing is half the enjoyment, and I want to see, as well as feel, my treasure." Starting at her coral-tipped toes, Ross began a manual exploration of her curves, lingering for a long while to fathom the mysteries of her burgeoning breasts. "Marvelous," he worshipped. "I didn't think anything could improve your body, but, pregnant, you're breathtaking!"

"Lie down beside me, then," she pleaded softly. "You're not close enough."

"All in good time." Ross chuckled, gently disentangling her arms as she reached for his neck.

Seeing *was* a powerful stimulant, she was soon to discover. Her eyes darkened with passion as Ross shrugged leisurely out of his clothes. It was taking so long, and more than anything Casey wanted to help him speed up the task, but Ross held her body immobile with his dark, fathomless gaze as he casually draped each article of clothing over the chair.

"I never realized it was so erotic, watching your lover undress," she finally got out.

"Honey, the things you don't know about making love would probably fill a book. We're going to start on the first chapter of that book tonight."

"When?" she husked. "You seem intent on prolonging this male striptease forever!"

"Do I?" He grinned wolfishly, hooking his thumbs under the elastic band of his Jockey shorts. "Never let it be said I kept my lady waiting."

No shy schoolgirl, Casey gazed with undisguised adoration at the power of the man she was soon to know as her own. God! If Ross held her this spellbound in the bedroom forever, they'd never get on with the trivia of daily living.

"Enjoy, love," he groaned, pulling her into his arms, fusing their nakedness. "This night is long overdue."

Nothing, Casey's dazed mind formulated, was as long overdue as the finality of his possession when at long last Ross culminated their union.

Slowly, torturingly, he let his lips travel over every inch of skin his hands had worshipped earlier, until Casey was a writhing mass of unfulfilled longing.

Looming above her at the moment of completion, he coaxed, "Tell me what you want, love."

"You!" Her impassioned plea elicited even more tension as, slowly, dizzyingly, Ross led them to heights Casey had never before fathomed, seemingly above the heavens themselves.

"Why did you draw out the tempo of our lovemaking like that?" she asked bewilderedly, curling into his warmth long minutes later.

"Because...if I'd unleashed the full extent of my passion, you might have lost this little miracle." He spread a protective hand over the damp skin of her abdomen. "I told Rich what I had planned this weekend, and he warned me to take it slow and easy."

"You discussed my seduction with your brother?"

"Yes, Miss Prim, I did. Are you shocked?"

"No." She tweaked a curling hair on his chest distractedly. "I guessed you and your brother were close."

"Not as close as you and I will be," Ross promised, reaching for the bedside lamp.

One of the advantages of being a big man was having long arms, she mused wryly. Ross could reach almost anything when he snaked out one dexterous arm. The other arm held her firmly in place, right over his heart. And it was thus she fell asleep, locked securely in his possessive embrace.

Somehow during the course of the night their positions must have shifted, for Casey woke on her side with warm naked skin cradling her length from behind and a securing hand at her waist.

Gnawing her lower lip in concentration, she willed her usual morning queasiness to subside. But instead it accentuated as the hand at her middle tightened perceptively.

"Hey, lady," a husky voice growled in her ear. "How about an early-morning roll in the hay before we hit the deck?"

"I don't think so," she got out between tightly clenched teeth.

"No?" The arm beneath her head flexed spasmodically. "Move a little, then. I think my arm's gone to sleep."

Casey moved more than a little, hitting the metaphorical deck with the speed of light as she beat a frantic retreat to the bathroom.

"Ah, honey." Ross settled a soft velour robe over

her shoulders, as distressed as she was. "I didn't realize it was this bad. Is it like this every morning?"

She nodded through her misery, accusing irrationally, "Yes, and you did this to me, Ross Allen!"

"Are you complaining?"

"No, I'm ecstatic," she vowed shakily, easing away from her every-morning shrine to press a perspiration-laden brow against his chest. "I'll just be glad when this next month is over and I get my sea legs back."

"Such pretty legs, too," Ross drawled, sliding an arm under her thighs and hoisting her aloft. "Back to bed with you. For a while, anyway, until I get breakfast in order."

"Food," she wailed, "is the last thing I need!"

"You'll be all right in a few minutes," Ross decreed, looking for all the world like a ragged pirate as he stood, hands on hips, smiling down in a tattered terry cloth robe. Obviously Casey was wearing his company robe.

"Where did you get that relic?" she derided. "Out of the ragbag?"

"There's nothing wrong with this robe," Ross grumbled, pulling the gaping lapels over his brawny chest. "What would you like for breakfast?"

She named her lone choice: "Crackers."

"Nothing doing!"

"What are you offering, a frozen TV breakfast?" she asked impishly.

"Hold your tongue, woman! I wield a mean spatula. If you're not careful, you'll get two helpings of everything."

"Everything?" she mimicked enticingly.

"You're in no condition for a romp in bed," came the dry rejoinder.

Maybe not now, Casey plotted, but later?... Ross had been too much in control last night, too dedicated in his implacable determination to bind her to him. Just once she longed to render the man as wildly passionate as she had been last night.

But her amused little scheme was not in the cards. Ross simply refused to be drawn, treating her much as he had the helpless invalid he'd cared for up at the cabin.

By midafternoon Casey gave up her folly and allowed herself to bask in his possessive concern. A bird could have toted more than she was allowed to carry in, clearing the party litter from the living room, but she refrained from admonishing that pregnant women were not helpless.

Her strictly adhered-to afternoon nap was accomplished on a chaise lounge next to the pool as she and Ross both took advantage of the unusually warm December sunshine.

The tranquility, the sheer peace of spending a whole day in each other's company without dissension, had a mellowing effect on both of them.

"Have you enjoyed today?" Ross inquired later, surveying his pensive dinner companion.

"Yes." Candles flickered throughout the intimate family-style Italian restaurant, casting an enchanting glow over Casey's wistful features. "It was wonderful, being alone, just the two of us." She wrinkled her nose delicately, posing the obvious question. "How did you get rid of Tiny?"

"Shhh! Don't even suggest such a thing! I didn't *get rid of* the woman, I gave her a little well-deserved time off."

"She wouldn't have approved of what you had planned this weekend?" Casey deduced wryly, and he grinned.

"Bright gal!"

"While the cat's away, the mice will play?" she pursued.

"Would you like me to play with you?"

Their teasing interchange was exhilarating, and Casey couldn't help taunting, "You didn't seem interested in playing with me today."

Sexual tension was fairly crackling around them. Ross pitched his voice low and meaningful. "A man has to preserve his masculine resources. When I get you home tonight..." He let his voice trail off suggestively.

"Is that a warning or a promise?" she challenged wickedly.

Ross leaned forward and wrapped a caressing hand around the nape of her neck, murmuring against her lips, "Back off, Stretch. I have half a mind to whisk you out of this restaurant without any dinner."

"But you won't," she whispered, and with bold audacity circled the hard outline of his lips with the tip of her tongue. "Pregnant ladies have to keep up their strength, and I'm sure you plan on taxing mine tonight."

"Believe it!" Ross clipped out hardily, and settled a warm promissory kiss on her unresisting lips.

Casey scarcely distinguished what she ate, so great was the visual foreplay Ross danced on her throughout the meal.

There was no rancor in the silence that stretched between them during the short drive home, but rather a tightly leashed expectancy, each of them lost in their own thoughts.

Was it possible, Casey mused, that Ross was not as sure of her as his outward confidence bore out? Could he still harbor any doubts about the deep love encompassing her?

"Ready, love?" Holding the passenger door open for her, Ross looked ruggedly self-assured, and Casey dismissed her fanciful ruminations as absurd.

"Let's go for a little stroll and walk off our dinner," he suggested, and she nodded in misty assent.

Unsure of himself? A more self-possessed man than the indomitable Ross Allen had yet to be born!

The night was warm, almost balmy, and Casey allowed herself to be engulfed in the magic of the stars, mentally inscribing *Mrs. Ross Allen* in the heavens. Soon! Soon she would accept this man's name. And surely his love?

Deeply intuitive, Ross discerned her slight trembling instantly. "You're cold," he concluded. "Let's go inside."

She watched from the glass doors as, one by one, the outdoor lights that had served as beacons during their walk were extinguished. Then, certain her eyes mirrored her heart, she turned to Ross and held out her arms. "Let's go upstairs," she pleaded softly.

Did her haste seem indecent? At this moment Casey wanted nothing more than to be in the arms of the man she loved.

But once upstairs she faltered, her fingers stiff and uncooperative in baring her body and soul.

Ross chuckled, a rich, melodic sound that came from deep within his chest. "Not quite such a wanton now, hmm?" His hands went to work accomplishing what Casey could not. "Undressing you is so natural, I've done it a thousand times in my dreams."

Reverently he stroked what he had bared, then pulled her intimately into his length. This was not at all what Casey had planned, being naked in the arms of the fully dressed man she hoped to drive wild with passion. She struggled impotently, her fingers, busy with newfound nimbleness, working the buttons on his shirt.

"Get undressed," she coaxed, sounding for all the world like a husky seductress, and Ross complied, tossing the immaculate white shirt aside. His T-shirt followed, inched over the rippling muscles of his shoulders and up over his head. Unclasping his belt, his fingers shook slightly at the task, a barely perceptible trembling that Casey was quick to discern. Ross was eager, and aroused, she thought exultantly!

Shrewd, unfathomable eyes bore into her own. Ross seemed to stiffen momentarily. His fingers bit into her waist, lifting her aside as he drew back the covers. "Get into bed," he directed brusquely, and bent to remove his shoes and socks.

Darn it, he's checking himself, she thought in dismay. *Wilfully corralling his passion! But, why?*

Ross hesitated, his hands at the fastening of his pants, and then slid in beside her, still partially clothed.

"Your pants," she gasped, but he was shaking his head.

"Forget about me. You're the one who's important tonight."

She caught the hazy impression of the words "I've got to convince you" before his lips descended, blocking out all conscious thought.

Succumbing willingly, she parted her lips and allowed him to explore the deep cavern of her mouth. Who was seducing whom? she wondered dazedly as his lips traveled down to the warm hollow of her throat. *I won't respond,* she decided with conviction! The least Ross could do was struggle to breathe, as she was doing!

"Don't tense up on me," he commanded, palming her love-swollen breasts. "Just relax and enjoy and feel!"

His tongue encircled the dusky crown his fingers had aroused, and Casey gasped, tugging at the restriction of his pants. "It's not fair!" she berated. "You've got me at your mercy, naked, while you're still half dressed."

"Are you anxious, love?" His lips moved lower, nibbling at the sharp curve of her waist.

"Yes!" she wailed. Her fingers tried to work the catch of his waistband.

"Good!" Capturing her wrist, Ross slammed it up on the pillow. "Now get your other hand up here and be still. You're not calling the shots tonight."

"I'd like to shoot you!" she panted, struggling as he gained control of both hands.

"And deny yourself what you've been waiting for all day?" Clearly Ross was enjoying her agitation—and immobility. "Keep these greedy little hands to yourself while I reacquaint myself with your loveliness."

"I'll do no such thing. You'll have to tie me down first!"

"Not a bad idea." He glanced meaningfully at his belt.

"You wouldn't dare!" she flung desperately.

Ross neither denied nor conformed to the inclination. Patiently he uncurled her clenched fingers, smoothing her hands under her head. "Calm down," he soothed, brushing his thumb over her trembling lips. "And quit gritting your teeth. A most unprofitable enterprise."

"I want you, Ross!" It was a throaty little cry. Loathe as she was to admit it, it was devastatingly exciting, being subdued and caressed into mindlessness.

"Not badly enough, you don't," he vowed roughly. "Are you going to behave yourself while I build up the flames?"

"I'll try." And try she did—valiantly. But her restless hands often failed her, willed by some inner need to return the exquisite pleasure Ross afforded her with his practiced caresses.

Countless times he stilled her stroking and chided, "Patience, love. We'll get there in the end. The waiting will make it that much more pleasurable."

"I can't wait anymore," Casey mewed.

But she did, until Ross knew beyond a shadow of a doubt of her readiness to receive him. Only then did he rise, to gaze down with a fiery blaze of desire as he stepped out of his pants.

A pitiful sob of longing rose in her throat and Casey shoved her fist in her mouth, averting her gaze from the male beauty above.

Her torment was acute, blocking out all other sensations as Ross slid in beside her, parting her thighs with a hard, insistent knee. There was no holding back now, and neither of them tried, fusing their need in the explosive rhythm of love.

"Go with me, honey, not against me," Ross growled from a long way off, and when Casey failed to comprehend his meaning, he pinned her writhing hips to the mattress.

His pulse was racing as hotly as her own, of that much her dazed mind was certain. But the pace he set was sheer agony—slow and unalterable as he took firm command of their passion.

Dizziness was threatening to overwhelm her when they scaled the last peak, then lay spent and exhausted in each other's arms.

"Ross?..." Heavy with lethargy, Casey was compelled to pay heed to the uncomfortable weight resting across her midsection. "Could you...move your arm," she asked delicately. "I'm feeling a little—" A little what? *Nauseated* sounded maniacal after what they had just shared.

"It's not the baby, is it?" Ross asked, and she smiled in slumberous denial.

"Just queasiness," she assured him, lovingly brushing a fallen lock of hair out of his eyes.

"Queasiness!" The lines of anxiety disappeared from his face, to be replaced with indolent chagrin.

"Woman, you wouldn't dare get sick on me at this, my finest hour!"

"Not if I can help it," she teased.

"Unpredictable, impudent..." Ross muttered a string of long-familiar adjectives under his breath and vaulted out of bed, snatching his tattered robe out of the closet. "Sit tight," he directed, casting an instinctive glance in the direction of the bathroom. "I'll be back in the blink of an eye."

"I'm not going anywhere." Actually, the floating sensation was beginning to leave her, but Casey reveled in his anxious concern.

It was more like a dozen blinks of the eye before he returned, bearing a curative package of soda crackers.

Shamefaced, Casey studied the salt-encrusted offering and missed entirely the uncertainty in his dark-gray, smoldering eyes as Ross went down on one knee beside the bed.

"Casey?" His voice was husky, his hand unsteady as he framed her downturned face. "This is crazy," he began, swallowing deeply, "and not at all what I had planned, with you indisposed." His eyes narrowed in gentle reproach. "You were supposed to float back to earth in my arms tonight and beg me to—" He groaned. "Damn it! Help me, honey! I love you so much, I can't get the words out!"

The cracker snapped in her trembling fingers. It was all there, everything she had hoped for in her over-crowded heart. The bent-knee proposal, the heartfelt avowal of love! The tattered robe and wild disorder of his hair meant nothing to her, this was the man she loved! Weeks of unhappiness melted away as she opened her arms, pulling Ross next to her heart. "I'll marry you, with bells on, any day you like!"

A deep sigh of relief rustled through the cleft in her breasts. "It took you long enough to risk loving me."

"I took that risk long ago," she murmured. "The first time we made love—I think I knew then that I was lost."

"What!" Ross nearly choked on her breathless disclosure. "Then why did you turn down my offer of marriage?"

"It wasn't an offer," she dissembled. "More like an autocratic command. And an unromantic one, at that."

"The hell with romantic," Ross bit out grimly, gripping her shoulders. "If you knew that you love me—"

"I did," she broke in, and received a tiny shake.

"If you knew that you loved me, and that I loved you—"

"But I didn't know that." Her voice trailed off to a reluctant whisper as she glimpsed his disbelieving frown. "You never said you loved me when you proposed," she explained timidly.

About to shake her again, Ross gave pause at her last words and smiled self-deprecatingly. "I guess I made a botch of things, hmm?" His grin was pure charm now. "Reckon a man can be forgiven if he forgets a few poignant words in his first marriage proposal? You're the only woman I've ever coveted for my wife, and I *was* nervous."

"I love you so much." Casey was deliciously content now that his anger had evaporated, snuggling deeper into the warm cocoon of his arms. "Couldn't you hear the love in my regret when I turned you down?"

"No! All I heard was 'I can't promise to give you a child, Ross.'" He mimicked her stiff, uncompromising tone. "Why did you make such an asinine declaration?"

"Because I thought it was true," she explained unhappily. "Quinn and I—I never gave him a child."

"And you thought it was your fault?" he surmised gently, incredulously.

"Yes. And I couldn't marry you knowing I might never give you a child. I loved you too much."

"You thought this glorious womanhood was malfunctioning?" he chided, stroking her intimately.

Fresh waves of longing were consuming her, and with no reservation Casey returned the pleasurable caressing. "What about your virility? I didn't accomplish this pregnancy by myself, you know."

"Witch!" Ross nudged her flat on her back, his eyes narrowing with sudden insight. "Is that why you suggested we live together? To see if your ridiculous fear of not being able to conceive was unfounded?"

"Something like that," she admitted, wiggling enticingly under his stirring length.

"Insatiable wench!" He nibbled at her lips. "You want me again, don't you?"

"Umm." She pressed hot little kisses along his jutting jaw.

"Convince me, then." Ross collapsed in an uncooperative sprawl on his back, raising one sexy eyelid. "I did all the coaxing earlier," he pointed out fairly. "And soon...soon you'll be too cumbersome for bedroom athletics."

"Cumbersome! I'll give you cumbersome!" And she did, at long last thrilling in the victory of driving the carefully controlled Ross Allen to the brink of insanity.

It was late, dreadfully late, when they finally drifted off in the solace of each other's arms.

The uncomfortable sensation of being watched finally woke her. Casey marveled that she hadn't suffocated, so deeply had she burrowed under the arm of her lover, her nose pressed to the warmth of his chest.

"Young man!" The scandalized tones coming from nearby were gruff with shock and distaste. "You've got a woman in your bed—in *my* house!"

"What the hell!" Ross dragged himself up on one elbow, shielding Casey as best he could. "Tiny, get the hell out of here!" he cursed violently.

"Not until you get that harlot out of my house!"

"This is *my* house," he enunciated furiously, "and you're slandering my future wife."

"Your—your wife!"

"Cassandra Spencer," he enlightened with slightly less hostility, reaching for Casey's chin. "Get your face out in the open, you ridiculous mole. Attila the Hun won't be satisfied until she sees that I'm not pussy-futtin' her around. How many times," he directed his housekeeper's way, "have you berated me to quit fanning my feathers and marry this woman?"

"Not often enough," came the crisp rejoinder. Tiny took in Casey's green face. "It seems you got the cart before the horse, young man!"

"Because we've slept together?" Ross had seen to covering Casey decently but still hadn't grasped her early-morning distress. "Now see here, Tiny—"

"Quit struttin' like a banty rooster and cover yourself!" Tiny clucked with matronly disapproval. A bathrobe came sailing through the air, whisked up from the floor. "I've no doubt you're naked as a jaybird under that sheet, and your intended needs attention."

"Just quit rocking the boat," Casey whimpered, casting an embarrassed glance at the older woman as she hitched up the sheet. She stretched a shaky arm to the cellophane-wrapped crackers on the bedside table. "I'll be all right, as soon as the world quits spinning around."

"'Course you will, dear." Tiny began to unbristle. Truth to tell, she was downright delighted with this turn of events.

"You might at least step out and allow us to make ourselves decent," Ross prompted. There was no way he could move and shrug into his robe with the delicious bundle lying against him, munching crackers and sprinkling crumbs amidst the curling hairs on his chest.

"Nope." Tiny refused to budge. "I've waited a long time to see you take a wife to your bed."

"We're going to Vegas to get married today," Casey promised cajolingly.

"No big deal." Tiny grinned. "There's plenty of time, since you've done your plantin' before the main event." Her tone was still gruff but held no reproach. And then she winked, destroying her drill sergeant demeanor and endearing herself to Casey's heart for all time.

"I'll take good care of you, missy. Ain't nothin' gonna stand in the way of me and that godchild of mine. Except maybe his mama and papa." She gave credit to the father-to-be, grudgingly.

Chapter Thirteen

Incredibly the prospective mama very nearly blew the whole carefully orchestrated ball game.

The setting was breathtaking. They were entertaining at the tastefully elegant Odyssey Restaurant set high atop a hill overlooking the San Fernando Valley.

The purpose of the afternoon gathering was equally impressive—the result of months of careful planning, artful digging, and hard work on Casey's part. Like a platoon sergeant setting out to outflank the enemy, she had plotted her strategy in capturing Miracle Bakeries. Studying their low-key ad profile of the past had been child's play; getting them to sign with Spencer-Allen grueling and fraught with frustration.

But that day she was sitting on the throne of success, buffeted by the praise of the Brothers Grimm. *There are no cherubic grandfathers here,* she thought wistfully, listening to the high-powered sharks extol the merits of the slick, fast-moving campaign she had laid out for them.

Converting the angelic Calvin McCoy and his hamburger dynasty must have been a piece of cake for Ross, Casey reflected, compared to what she had gone through in cornering the family-owned conglomerate piloted by the tenacious predators sitting across from her.

How many smaller, shaky baking establishments had these brothers bought out in their voracious journey to the top? And why didn't they eat as greedily as they snapped at success? she wondered dismally.

"You're not eating much, honey," Ross chided from beside her.

Her husband's usual keen powers of observation were somewhat dulled today. Casey had not consumed one morsel from her plate—merely pushed the food around in agitated disarray. "The steak is delicious," she innovated, raising her fork to her lips and depositing the meat back on her plate as soon as Ross looked away.

Cripes! Would this meal never end? A fine mist of perspiration broke out on her brow, and she glanced unobtrusively at her watch, mentally ascribing a sequence to her discomfort.

Six minutes since her last contraction... fifteen since her last desperation trek to the bathroom. Damn all businessmen and the whole male species in general! Why did they have to size each other up over drinks, preening their talented feathers before getting down to the nitty-gritty?

The twinge of backache she had felt upon rising that morning had given her fair warning, but Casey had been sure she had plenty of time.

Lunch, followed by contract signing, and they'd be back in the beach area by early afternoon. *Hold on, little one,* she soothed her rigid abdomen. *We'll be home in plenty of time. Don't be so impatient!*

"Through, Miss... er... Mrs.?" The waiter hovered, correcting himself when Casey leaned back to display her swollen profile.

"Yeesss." She breathed an audible sigh of relief as the table was cleared. Papers were spread out, the lawyers for both sides sharpening their mental pencils.

Mercifully there were no hitches, save for the rhythmic every-six-minute hitch in Casey's distended abdomen, during the twenty-minute ordeal.

Despite their one-time pledge to work on this account together, Ross had been exceptionally busy lately, and this was a singular victory for Casey. The pride radiating from her husband's dark features kept her in her seat for as long as she could manage.

"Another round of drinks to seal our alliance?" A shark fin came out, followed by another, as the businessmen shook hands with husband and wife.

"Honey?" Ross turned to her inquiringly, and Casey shook her head, grimacing as another contraction washed over her.

"Nooo, thanks. My water is fine." And untouched. "If you'll all excuse me?" she said politely, and rose to her feet.

"Pregnant ladies." She caught the expansive snicker. "I remember when my wife was expecting..."

By then she was out of earshot, lumbering in the gait peculiar to all off-balance mothers-to-be as she made for the bathroom.

It was bliss, sheer bliss, splashing cool water on her overheated features, away from all prying eyes. She'd just weather out another contraction in there, or maybe two, and then tactfully suggest she and Ross take their leave.

She hadn't allowed for the fact that a fifteen-minute absence would attract her husband's concern.

"Casey?" There was a loud rap at the door, followed by another.

No answer.

Casey was gathering her composure to face her husband's censure. Of a certainty, she was in labor, one week early.

"Cassandra!" More insistently now. "I'm not above coming in there to fish you out!"

"Don't yell at me." She emerged in a hesitant waddle.

"How far apart are the contractions?" Ross bit out grimly.

"Five minutes!" she wailed, and hurtled herself into his arms, resting a weary, sweat-beaded brow on his shoulder. "Don't be angry with me, Ross."

"Angry?" Some of her fear must have transmitted itself to him. Ross stiffened, both in body and resolve. "I'm not angry, sweetheart. Just concerned. We've got a long drive ahead of us." He let out a deep sigh of self-reproach. "If I'd had any idea you would go into labor early..."

The awkward bundle in his arms squirmed uncomfortably, repentantly, and Ross caught his breath. "Did you have any inkling?" he began suspiciously.

"Just a little twinge of backache this morning," Casey said hurriedly.

"And after all our classes in natural childbirth, you let me start out today, knowing labor was probably imminent? Does this account mean that much to you?"

"I know how much it means to you!"

"Not this much!" Ross glanced around searchingly and located a seat for Casey in the lobby. "Sit tight," he remonstrated softly. "I'll make our apologies and put in a call to your obstetrician."

Casey relaxed through the next contraction, a contented smile on her lips as she awaited Ross's return. Everything was under control now that she had her husband's support.

"Holy Cross Hospital is just down the hill," Ross advised, hunching down in front of her. "Would you be more comfortable going straight to the nearest hospital?"

"No!" Casey clutched at his arm, suddenly panicky. "I want to go home to the hospital we've already visited. I want a doctor I'm familiar with!"

Ross smiled reassuringly, smoothing her knotted hands. "I figured as much, and Bob McMillan seems to feel we have plenty of time, first labors being what they are."

"Lengthy." She smiled in understanding, and allowed herself to be bundled upright.

The long dash through the L.A. freeway system was accomplished in one-handed concentration. Ross kept his right arm firmly around his wife, sensing her rising alarm. Much as he loved her, Casey was hopelessly inept at coping with any infirmity.

"If I could shoulder the pain for you, I would, honey," he comforted, slipping his hand under her voluminous sundress to stroke away the ravages of the latest contraction. Tugging at the elastic stretch panel, he lowered her maternity panties and caressed the shape of his child. "You've been fantastic throughout this whole pregnancy. I'm counting on you not to fall apart."

"I won't," she promised, but her words sounded weak, even to her own ears. To think, she'd prayed for the privilege of being laid low in womanly agony. "They lied, you know—in those classes," she panted. "Giving birth isn't all sugar and spice and everything—ahhhh!"

"Relax," came the uneven reminder. "Go with the contraction, not against it."

"I'm trying!" They were off the freeway now, and Casey was half lying in his lap, unmindful of the precision required by her husband in steering with one hand. The stroke of his warm hand over her bare skin and baby was hypnotically calming. God, how she loved this man! As soon as the contraction eased she couldn't help telling him so.

"I love you, too, sweetheart. More than life itself!" A hurried kiss brushed her damp forehead. "Ten more minutes and we'll be out of the woods."

"You won't desert me when we get to the hospital?"

"No, I won't desert you." Welcome a little professional expertise managing her distress, yes. But desert her, *never!*

True to his word, Ross lifted her into the obligatory wheelchair in which all laboring mothers were transported to maternity with all the possessiveness of a lioness protecting its only cub.

The nurse may have guided her transport, but Ross kept a supportive hand on her shoulder, the other toting the suitcase that had been packed and waiting in the car for weeks.

The labor room was comfortingly familiar, and Casey began to relax. She knew what to expect now. During a tour with their childbirth class she and Ross had visited the hospital's labor and delivery rooms, and she felt a warm cocoon of safety drawing around her—until Ross settled her in bed and began to draw back.

"Honey, the nurse wants to get you prepped," he chided, gently disentangling her stranglehold from his neck.

All her training in staying calm and relaxed, every vestige of womanly maturity, flew out the window as Casey clutched at his hand. "You'd better come right back!" she wailed. "I can't pull this off without you!"

Indeed, by the time Ross returned, clad in absurdly ill-fitting surgical garb, Casey was thoroughly overwrought, and only his low, patient coaxing and warm, soothing hands saw her through the trial of her labor.

"I never should have let you talk me into natural childbirth," she whimpered as they wheeled her into the delivery room.

"As I recall, it was your idea," Ross inserted, tongue-in-cheek. "It's almost over now," he soothed, helping her scoot onto the delivery table. "Just think of England, or the flag, or whatever diversion the ladies of old used to use."

"That was not during childbirth," she hissed.

"It was during lovemaking," came the cheerful advice from her doctor.

"Is that a fact?" Ross chuckled. "Terrible blighters, those husbands of yesteryear, leaving their wives so poorly prepared. Cassandra *loves* making—"

"Ross!" Nurses were twittering on both sides of her, heightening Casey's embarrassment.

"Don't pull at your gown, sweetheart." Ross captured her nerveless hands, folding them warmly in his own. "We all know what you look like."

"You're impossible!" Casey choked, missing entirely the sounds of preparation going on around her.

It was an age-old gambit. Ross had months of experience behind him, honing the effectiveness of his ploy. He could divert Casey's mind almost anywhere once he got her rolling with a few well-chosen, teasing barbs.

Then, miraculously, the moment of reward was upon them. Tears of joyful anticipation welled in Casey's eyes, and in the dark eyes above, as Ross held her hands and they gazed into the mirror. The black-haired, lividly squalling Allen heir joined his family with a howl of indignation.

"It's a boy!" the doctor announced jubilantly.

"Of course," Casey cried in exhausted ecstasy. "Anything that caused this much trouble had to be male!"

"You deserve to be punished for that, Mrs. Allen," Ross growled, and lowered his dark head, capturing her mouth in a long, congratulatory kiss that would fuel hospital gossip for days.

Much later, after Casey had been settled in a private room by the briskly efficient Nurse Pram, the man of the hour reappeared, fresh from a lengthy sojourn at the nursery room window.

"I've been visiting our son," Ross informed his glowing wife. "You did a fantastic job, love. Your son has the lustiest set of lungs in the nursery."

"Do you think Ross Junior is going to have your temper?" Casey asked pertly, basking in the glow of her husband's love.

"I think Joshua Allen is going to have his mama's temper," Ross amended wryly. "I may love you to distraction, but you're not going to hang *junior* on any son of mine!"

Casey shivered at his poignant words. Her mouth curved into a mischievous, reminiscent smile. "I think I feel a case of the chills coming on. The last time that happened..." She trailed off invitingly.

The guardrail on her hospital bed was lowered, followed by the heavy thud of shoes hitting the bare floor, and then Ross was beside her. "For you, love, anything. It's a good thing you have a private room. I shudder to think what Nurse Prim is going to say if she catches us like this."

"Nurse Pram," she corrected, giggling. "And I don't care what she thinks. I need you tonight." *And I'll love you forever,* she added silently.

"I called all the interested parties and gave them our happy news," Ross informed her huskily.

"My parents?..."

"Were ecstatic. They'll be here tomorrow. And Tiny, as well. You'd think *she* was the new grandma, the way she was carrying on."

Hesitantly Casey began, "Ross, I was thinking...Since your parents are gone, maybe we could indulge Tiny? Let her fill the unofficial role of Grandmother Allen?"

"You love Tiny that much?" Ross was delighted with the suggestion.

"Almost as much as I love you," she affirmed. Her hand lifted to caress his smiling face, then wandered down to her almost flat tummy.

"I feel so strange . . . so empty." Her eyes darkened with emotion. An aching question just *had* to be asked. "Ross? What if this is the only child we ever have?"

"Then we'll love him all that much more for his singularity. I put a lot of store in Tiny's requests, though and she made a big one tonight."

"Which was? . . ."

"'You've done well today, young man,'" Ross parroted his housekeeper's gruff voice. "'But might I remind you, there are still three empty bedrooms upstairs!'"

"What did you say to that?"

"God willing, we'll fill them all."

God was willing.

Get this book FREE!

Mail to:

Harlequin Reader Service

In the U.S.
2504 West Southern Avenue
Tempe, AZ 85282

In Canada
649 Ontario Street
Stratford, Ontario N5A 6W2

YES! I want to be one of the first to discover **Harlequin American Romance.** Send me FREE and without obligation *Twice in a Lifetime.* If you do not hear from me after I have examined my FREE book, please send me the 4 new **Harlequin American Romances** each month as soon as they come off the presses. I understand that I will be billed only $2.25 for each book (total $9.00). There are no shipping or handling charges. There is no minimum number of books that I have to purchase. In fact, I may cancel this arrangement at any time. *Twice in a Lifetime* is mine to keep as a FREE gift, even if I do not buy any additional books.

Name _____ (please print)

Address _____ Apt. no. _____

City _____ State/Prov. _____ Zip/Postal Code _____

Signature (If under 18, parent or guardian must sign.)

CHARLOTTE LAMB

The outstanding author of more than 50 bestselling romances with her exciting new blockbuster...

A dramatic contemporary novel for every woman who has feared to love!

Clare Forrester had everything life had to offer. Then fate intervened with a nightmare – a violent rape that changed traumatically Clare's existence and that of everyone close to her. And now, the question was, would the power of love heal the deepest wound a woman can know....

In November wherever paperback books are sold, or send your name, address and zip or postal code, along with a check or money order for $4.25 (includes 75¢ for postage and handling) payable to Harlequin Reader Service, to:

Harlequin Reader Service

In the U.S.
Box 52040
Phoenix, AZ 85072-9988

In Canada
649 Ontario Street
Stratford, Ontario N5A 6W2

VIOL-5